It Happened Once Up

After a moment, the High Priestess began to sing the Maypole chant. The dance started slowly as the participants worked out a rhythm. The dancers' speed increased as the ribbons were woven into a multi-colored braid around the pole. The circle became tighter. When the ribbons reached their ends, the accompanying dancers tied them to the pole. They stepped outside the circle to watch those who remained and aid them in the dance by clapping along to the beat of the chant. Those who knew the words sang along with the High Priestess.

With the removal of some of the dancers, the over/under pattern lost its rhythm. Laughter erupted inside the circle and the dance became a chaotic jumble of confusion. Julian tried to maintain a steady pattern, while Fiona allowed her dance to disintegrate into a free-form frolic. Julian's ribbon reached its end before Fiona's. He stepped away to wait for her. With a determination he admired, she continued weaving her ribbon down to its last inch. When her ribbon ran out, she left the circle, panting, and went to stand next to Julian to catch her breath. The dance was down to two last merrymakers. When they could wrap no more, they tied the ribbons together to lock in the desires of all the dancers.

Overwhelmed by the joy permeating the celebration, Julian grabbed Fiona, then swung her around in an impulsive hug. She looked into his laughing eyes and tilted her head down, her lips meeting his with the fleeting touch of a hummingbird, then again with more pressure. Their lips had never met before in this lifetime, but they knew the geography of each other in an instant, recognizing each other from the kisses of lifetimes past.

Once Upon a Beltane Eve

by
Selene Silverwind

Spilled Candy Books
Niceville, Florida USA

Once Upon a Beltane Eve
Copyright 2001

By Aryn Kennedy

Published by: Spilled Candy's Novel Teaching Tools for Wiccans
Spilled Candy Publications
Post Office Box 5202
Niceville, FL 32578-5202
Staff@spilledcandy.com
http://www.spilledcandy.com

This book is a work of fiction to illustrate spiritual themes. Any resemblance to persons living or dead is coincidental.

Spilled Candy Books is committed to its authors and their work. For this reason, we do not permit our covers to be "stripped" for returns, but instead, we require that the whole book be returned in saleable condition, allowing us to resell it. Resaleable is defined as no markings, stamps, scuffs, bent covers, or any condition in which you yourself would not wish to buy the book.

ISBN:1-892718-37-5 (disk and download version)
ISBN: 1-892718-34-0 (trade paperback)

Library of Congress Card Number: 2001087322
First edition

Cover Art copyright 2000 by Ravon of WitchWay

Spilled Candy Books is grateful to Ravon of WitchWay for the cover art and continuing support of Spilled Candy Books. We encourage you to visit Ravon's web site at http://www.users.drak.net/ravon/. Ravon's art truly is a form a worship.

Dedication

To Mom, Dad, Heather, and Rachel for your eternal support.

To all those too numerous to name
who offered love and encouragement.

And to Brian for being my Julian.

About the Author

Selene Silverwind is the author of *Once Upon a Beltane Eve*. She is also a screenwriter and activist out of Los Angeles, California. She sees it as her duty to educate the public about Paganism through her writing. Her columns on Pagan Family Values have appeared in *Cauldrons & Broomsticks, The Blessed Bee,* and *Triple Spiral.*

She is a Celtic Shaman. A graduate of Loyola Marymount University, she is President of Pagan Pride Los Angeles and works to further religious tolerance and understanding of Pagan faiths. She also serves as a representative for the Alternative Religions Education Network.

Visit www.SeleneSilverwind.com to see Selene's terrific list of pagan resources and advice.

ONCE UPON A BELTANE EVE

Chapter 1

Beltane Wishes

Fiona paced in front of the entrance gate of the New Denver Beltane Festival. She skimmed her hands down the length of her hair to make sure none of the artfully placed purple petunias had fallen from her dark hair. Was she doing the right thing, agreeing to meet Julian here? Even though she liked to think of herself as a wild child, free from worries about mundane matters, she was nervous about meeting someone like him. Not only was he two years older, much less than the five year gap she normally preferred, but she'd always dated fellow artists, men she thought would understand her artistic drive. Perhaps it was time to give up on that ideal. In her experience, no two artists saw anything the same way.

She flicked her gaze up to the platform of the Personal Rapid Transit Station, but from this distance she couldn't make out whether the person stepping out of one of the trapezoidal white cars was male or female. And having no idea what Julian looked like, she wouldn't know if it was him anyway. Why hadn't he let her send him a photo of herself? How would they find each other? She recalled their weeks of online conversations and smiled. The fluttering in her stomach settled. Intuition told her that she and Julian would have no problem finding each other, today or any other day. This was it. . . .

Julian fidgeted aboard a Personal Rapid Transit Vehicle, or PRTV, as it zipped over New Denver. He was still amazed at himself for agreeing to meet Fiona in the first place. He wasn't the spontaneous type. He had spent much of the last week hoping he would be what she expected and vice versa. He'd never known a woman like her before, let alone dated one. He didn't date that often and the few women he had taken out recently were fellow computer programmers. They were nice women, safe women, but none of them got his blood boiling the way one online conversation with Fiona could. His nervousness rose again. Would he be what she expected? To distract himself from his anxious thoughts, he concentrated on the view of the City passing by his window. It was a maze of high and low buildings with fiber-optic cables strung between them. The wires formed a web over the tightly constructed City, but there was an order to the chaos, an order Julian had a hand in maintaining. The tangle of wires unsnarled and came to an end as the car approached the festival site just outside the City borders.

Julian looked down at the fairgrounds, a grassy field edged by dense groves of evergreen trees at the sides and rear. Curious, he peered into the woods at the far end. He had heard rumors that they became sexual playgrounds once dusk fell on Beltane, but for now all he could see was a mass of thick foliage preventing anyone from spying the secrets of the shrouded forest.

As the PRTV detached from the main track and slowed into the station, Julian surveyed the festival site below. City-dwellers dressed in an assortment of ceremonial robes, jeans, bright skirts and tops, dresses, shorts, and short-sleeved shirts milled about the flower-bedecked gate. Inside, a large tent had been erected on one side of the meadow. Festival attendees flowed between it, a group of smaller tents, and the stage. Revelers danced around tall poles with riots of brightly hued ribbons suspended from the tops, the ribbons undulating over their heads, mimicking the ancient Beltane rhythm of man and woman. The poles were arranged in a large circle around a huge stack of wood, which would become a bonfire come nightfall.

The door of the PRTV swung open in front of Julian. He stepped out of the car and onto the platform that led down to the fairgrounds. As he rode the escalator down to ground level, he checked his waist to make sure his polo shirt was properly tucked into his shorts, then smoothed a hand over his perfectly clipped hair. Satisfied with his neat appearance, he followed the well-worn path out to the gate. As he neared the entrance, he noticed a small group of protesters waving placards. A thin blonde—his ex-girlfriend, Sarah--was among them. He altered his course slightly to avoid her and scanned the crowd for someone he thought might be Fiona.

His attempt at averting a confrontation failed. Sarah saw him coming down the trampled path. She pranced over to welcome him into her group. "I'm glad you finally saw our truth," Sarah said. "I'll get you a sign." She started to move back toward the other protestors, calling out for a sign. When she realized Julian wasn't following her, she stopped and turned back to him. "What are you waiting for?"

"I'm not here to join you. I didn't even know you would be here. I'm meeting someone for the festival."

Sarah stared at him, incredulous. "How can you join the heathens in this mayhem? They make a mockery of all our leader says is right and good."

Julian tried his best not to wince at her pronouncement. He shook his head, disappointed she had not escaped the cult before their zealotry had become so intense, then pointed toward the merry festivities taking place inside the flowered gate. "I'm going in there, and I'm going to enjoy myself. I wish you could see the good that comes from this."

Stricken but not ready to give up, Sarah tried another tactic. "I can see there's no stopping you, so I'll pray for you."

Exasperated by her attitude, Julian lost his cool. "Go right ahead!" he snapped, then walked past her toward the gate. Once clear of Sarah's throng, he slowed his pace to give himself time to regain his composure before he found Fiona. He couldn't believe how quickly Sarah had gotten his hackles up.

When he spotted a curvy young woman in a flowing, dark green skirt and top standing just a few feet ahead of him, he stopped short. A tumult of purple flowers cascaded down the back of her waist-length, wavy hair. A shock of recognition shot through him. That was Fiona. *He was going to spend the rest of his life with her.* He ran up behind her.

Sensing his approach, Fiona whirled around. A strong, fit man—a twenty-eight-year-old blond—swept her into his arms. She cried out in surprise at the jolt of connection that ran through her. She smiled into his pale green eye, and he twirled her around once more, sending a blossom tumbling from her hair.

He caught the petunia in his hand, then set her back on her feet and handed the flower to her. "I sure hope you're Fiona, or I've just made a huge fool of myself."

She tilted her face up to him and smiled. She tucked the blossom back into her hair. "I guess you're Julian then!" She stepped back into a playful curtsy and motioned toward the gate. "Shall we?"

Julian's wide grin softened his angular jaw. He reached out for her hand. His fingers joined with hers as if they had been holding hands for years. "I had no idea there would be so many people here," he told her as they passed through the entrance.

"This is a day devoted solely to pleasure. Who wouldn't want to be here?" She winked at him. He turned a pleasant shade of pink. "What do you want to do first?" she asked.

He scanned the grounds. "I've never done that before." He pointed toward a Maypole.

"Then we'll do that. There's one starting in a minute."

As they walked to the pole where several revelers were already gathered, he asked her how long she had been Wiccan. She glanced over at him. "Oh, I'm not."

"But you seem to know so much about this . . . ."

She laughed. "I guess I do have a lot of Wiccan tendencies. My parents had several Wiccan friends in Old San Francisco. That's where I'm from. We adopted a lot of their practices, but my family never formally studied the faith. I am Pagan, though."

"There's a difference?"

Fiona nodded and launched into the explanation she had heard some of her Wiccan friends give. "Paganism encompasses many earth-based faiths. Wicca is just one of them. Kind of like being Lutheran or Catholic. They're both Christian religions, but they're not the same."

They arrived at the pole and joined the circle. Fiona walked to the middle and carried the ends of the two remaining ribbons back to the edge of the circle. She handed Julian a blue ribbon. He turned away from her to face the same direction she faced. She gently placed her hand on his shoulder, turning him toward her. "The men go widdershins, the women go deosil." Seeing the confusion in his eyes, she clarified. "Counterclockwise and clockwise. You go under the first woman's ribbon and then over the next, or at least you try. We keep dancing until the ribbons run out."

The High Priestess called the circle to order and they turned to face the center of the circle. She explained that the pole was a symbol of fertility, then asked the participants to make a wish for something they wanted to manifest in the coming year, then send it into their ribbons. The revelers went around the circle stating their wishes aloud. Fiona wished for success in new friendships, blushing and casting a sidelong glance at Julian. He grinned and wished for the same thing. After the last man had stated his wish, the High Priestess wished that all the attendees would see their desires granted during the next year. The participants bowed their heads in silence, empowering the ribbons with their desires.

After a moment, the High Priestess began to sing the Maypole chant. The dance started slowly as the participants worked out a rhythm. The dancers' speed increased as the ribbons were woven into a multi-colored braid around the pole. The circle became tighter. When the ribbons reached their ends, the accompanying dancers tied them to the pole. They stepped outside the circle to watch those who remained and aided them in the dance by clapping along to the beat of the chant. Those who knew the words sang along with the High Priestess. With the removal of some of the dancers, the over/under pattern lost its rhythm. Laughter erupted inside the circle. The dance became a chaotic jumble of confusion. Julian tried to maintain a steady pattern, while Fiona allowed her dance to disintegrate into a free-form frolic. Julian's ribbon reached its end before Fiona's. He stepped away to wait for her. With a determination he admired, she continued weaving her ribbon down to its last inch. When her ribbon ran out, she left the circle, panting, and went to stand next to Julian to catch her breath. The dance was down to two last merrymakers. When they could wrap no more, they tied the ribbons together to lock in the desires of all the dancers.

Overwhelmed by the joy permeating the celebration,

Julian grabbed Fiona, then swung her around in an impulsive hug. She looked into his laughing eyes and tilted her head down, her lips meeting his with the fleeting touch of a hummingbird, then again with more pressure. Their lips had never met before in this lifetime, but they knew the geography of each other in an instant, recognizing each other from the kisses of lifetimes past. Memories of experiences they had never shared washed over them. They continued their embrace until their lips were parched and they had to part.

Fiona slid down Julian's body to her feet. Unsure how to explain what had just happened, she searched for something innocuous to fill the silence. "Are you thirsty?"

He was torn between his desire to renew their kiss and his confusion over what he had just experienced. He needed time to process the new information. "Yeah, I could use a drink."

Fiona took his hand in her own, trying to become accustomed to the sparks that shot between them at the slightest touch. They walked toward the refreshment tent. "They have ale, lemonade, water, wine, and mead. What are you in the mood for?"

One answer to that question sent Julian's pulse racing, and he flushed a deep red. Knowing that wasn't what she had meant, he gave a different answer. "Ale sounds good. I'm getting hungry, too. Is there any food?"

"Why, of course! What's a Pagan celebration without a feast?" They entered the tent and served themselves. Julian chose a New Denver brewed ale, and Fiona selected from an assortment of homemade mead. They wandered to the dessert table and chose a few brownies and cookies to go with their drinks. All the seats inside the tent were taken, so Fiona and Julian walked back outside.

"Where do we pay?" he asked.

"We don't. The City Corporation paid for this festival. They see it as one more way to bring joy to the people who live here."

"You sound like one of your propaganda posters," Julian teased.

"I prefer educational advertisements, thank you very much!"

"What other kinds of art do you do besides that?" he asked.

"Mostly paintings. I mean, they're all computer generated, but I do abstracts and life scenes. The City stuff just pays the bills."

"Are you in one of the network galleries?"

"Actually, I have a few on display here, if you'd like to see them." The butterflies in her stomach took flight again at the thought of showing him her work. She led him through Merchant Row to a booth near the end.

The booth host greeted Fiona warmly and told her several admirers of her work had popped by. Some were interested in purchasing her pieces if Fiona would agree to sell them. Fiona said she'd think about it. She introduced Julian to her friend, then pointed to one wall of the booth where several pieces were prominently featured. Julian was drawn to two paintings. One was a watercolor depicting a young woman standing in a flowered meadow. She was draped in a robe of silken spider webs, raising her arms to the full moon. A spider crawled across the moon. The other painting was edged by an abstract jumble of colors and shapes that bled inward and fused together into order at the center. It was Fiona's idea of chaos and entropy played out on canvas.

"What do you think?"

"They're breathtaking," Julian said, not taking his eyes off her work. He pointed to the spider web clad woman. "I feel like I know this woman." He turned his attention to the abstract. "And this, this is the perfect depiction of a network."

Fiona laughed. "Spoken like someone who is truly meant to be a network administrator."

Julian chuckled at his own single-mindedness. "Yeah, I guess it is." He smiled. "You're work really is good though, and not just because you can paint the spirit of a network."

"Well, we'd better move on before you start planning how to organize my next painting." Fiona reached again for Julian's hand. They left the booth and wandered back up Merchant Row, stopping at several booths to browse through the homemade goods brought by City-dwellers to barter or sell.

Julian noticed that Fiona was particularly impressed by

an amber and jet necklace. After they had wandered away from the booth and she was in deep conversation with another vendor, Julian found an excuse to double back to the first booth where he bought the delicately beaded piece for her. He tucked the tissue-paper package into his pocket for later, then hurried back to the booth. He met up with Fiona just as she was about to go in search of him.

They went to the stage to listen to the folksingers perform old favorites and new songs of their own creation, then walked back to the poles to watch other Maypole dances. The day passed quickly. Just as the sun had started to dip behind the trees, they sat down near the stack of wood to wait for the ritual that would start in a few minutes. Julian turned to Fiona. "I don't remember having this much fun in a long time. I'm glad my ex didn't ruin it for me."

Fiona's stomach knotted. "The one that's in the cult?"

Julian swallowed and nodded.

"Where did you see her?"

"She's here. She's one of the protesters outside," he said, looking down.

"What did she say?"

Julian hesitated. How would Fiona react to the details of his past? Probably not well. "Oh the usual. I kind of snapped at her. I feel bad about that, but she's more intolerant than she was when we dated. She practically called me a heathen."

"I'm sorry," Fiona said in sympathy. Her anxiety eased, and she sought to lighten the mood by skimming her hand down Julian's arm. "You know, one has to earn the title of heathen," she murmured. She leaned forward and kissed him again.

Stifling a laugh, Julian returned the kiss. Their lips remained connected until the sun had sunk the rest of the way beyond the horizon and a circle was forming on either side of them. Embarrassed by the public embrace, although no one else appeared to care, Julian scrambled to his feet, pulling Fiona up with him.

The wood was lit. After the flame took hold, several members of the Pagan Coalition formed an inner circle around the blazing fire. The High Priestess, a middle-aged woman with long blonde hair and a tall, lean body, stepped forward into the glow cast by the flames. "Welcome everyone to the Beltane Festival. Please join us as we recognize the Lord and Lady on this, the eve of the consummation of their union."

She moved back into the small circle as a priest turned and faced east. The outer circle followed suit. He lifted a conch shell to his lips and blew three loud blasts through it. Another priestess turned and faced south, as did the inner and outer circles. She raised two pieces of flint into the night in front of her and struck them together until they created sparks, which she used to light a candle. The circle turned in unison to face west, where another priest used a large pitcher of water and a funnel to fill a large balloon with water. Finally, the revelers turned to face north, where a third priestess bent over and picked up a handful of soft dirt, allowing it to sift back to the ground through her fingers. She kissed a clump and deposited it back on the earth at her feet. Everyone turned to face into the circle once more. They joined hands and shared a moment of silence to ground and center.

The High Priestess stepped forward again. The gathering looked toward her. She raised her arms as she said, "Lady, watcher of lovers, Goddess of passion, dancing in the moonlight, uniting us in love, come join us in our celebration this Beltane eve." She stepped back to her place in the circle.

The High Priest, a strong man, taller than the priestess and with dark, thick hair, stepped forward from beside her. He stretched his arms overhead as he said, "Lord, protector of mates, God of sensuality, running under the sun, uniting us in love, come join us in our celebration this Beltane eve. "

At the edge of the larger circle, a drum began to beat through the shadows. The inner circle spread out into the outer circle. The High Priestess and Priest turned to face each other. In unison, they began the dance, hooking elbows and swinging around each other, then moving through the outer circle, bringing all the revelers into the dance. The dancers twirled in perfect rhythm, weaving in and out, exchanging arms and laughing merrily as they went round and round the circle. The dance sped up until the drumming stopped with a loud beat. The dancers collapsed on the ground.

The High Priest remained standing to lead the participants through a guided meditation. "Close your eyes and feel the cool air as it rushes through your lungs. Feel your breath moving within you, nourishing you, filling you with life. Feel the ground beneath you, supporting you, filling you with strength. Feel the heat from the fire, warming you, filling you with passion. As we pass this cup around, feel the coolness of the water on your tongue and the smooth flow of the liquid down your throat. Before you drink, imagine your desires for the year and as you let the water of life pass over your lips, visualize your desires in fulfillment.

A chalice was passed around the circle. Each person took the chalice in both hands and meditated for a moment before taking a sip and passing the cup on, bidding the person to the right, "May you never thirst." When the chalice reached Fiona, she held it while she pictured her desire, a growing relationship with Julian, then drank from the cup. She handed it to Julian, who caught the romantic gleam in her eye and unknowingly made the same wish.

Once the chalice had returned to where it started, the High Priestess stood and the circle followed suit. She raised her arms over her head once again and said, "Lady, watcher of mates, Goddess of sensuality, we thank you for your presence here tonight and for the love with which you have blessed us. Stay if you will, go if you must. Farewell and blessed be!"

"Blessed be!" those in the circle cried in reply.

The High Priest stretched his arms skyward and said, "Lord, protector of lovers, God of passion, we thank you for your presence here tonight and for the joy with which you have blessed us. Stay if you will, go if you must. Farewell and blessed be!"

The revelers again called out, "Blessed be!" in answer.

The caller of the north led the circle to face her position and drew a banishing pentagram in the dirt. The caller of the west turned with the circle to face his position and drew a banishing pentagram on the balloon that he then popped overhead. The circle turned to the south and the caller of her position extinguished the candle, then drew a banishing pentagram in the smoke. The caller of the east led the circle in turning to face his position where he drew one last banishing pentagram in the air before blowing a long blast through his conch shell.

The High Priestess stepped forward once more. "The circle is open, but unbroken. Go in love and celebrate this merry eve."

After the circle was released, some of the revelers gathered to sing folksongs while others formed a large chain and danced around the fire to a sensual drumbeat. Every so often couples or threesomes would leave the circle and walk toward the woods, pausing at a small booth before disappearing into the trees.

Fiona and Julian sat on the grass by the fire to listen to the songs and watch the dancers. Julian marveled at the exciting yet comforting sensation of Fiona's delicate body nestled in his arms. This was the perfect time to present her with the gift. He reached into his pocket and retrieved the tissue-wrapped gift, which he placed in her hands.

Surprised, she glanced down at the small package, then turned to look up into Julian's warm eyes. "What's this?"

"Open it and find out," he urged.

Fiona looked back down at the package and carefully opened the delicate tissue. When she saw the string of amber and jet beads tucked inside, she cried out in shocked glee. "I can't believe you did this!" She threw herself around him. "Thank you!"

"The look on your face is thanks enough," he said, laughing.

With a lewd tone, Fiona said, "You've earned more than just a look on my face."

Taking her up on the suggestion, Julian brought his lips to Fiona's again. When their kiss parted, he nodded toward the woods. "Are the rumors about those woods true?"

Fiona smiled widely and nodded. "It is a fertility festival, after all. No rules apply tonight."

Julian raised his eyebrows. "Interesting. And why are they stopping at that booth?"

"To get condoms and a blanket. It can get chilly back there and not everyone here is interested in testing their physical fertility right now." She smiled at him, her eyes twinkling.

He grinned, catching her meaning. "So, you've been in there before?"

Fiona elbowed Julian in the ribs. "I've been coming here a long time. Care to join me in a little merrymaking?" When Julian hesitated, Fiona held up her hand to make a pledge. "I promise to respect you in the morning."

He laughed and shook his head. "Can we just stay here and kiss a little longer?"

In answer, Fiona pressed her lips against his. He ran his hands through her silken hair as he deepened the kiss. As their passion grew and their lips began to wander to other areas, Julian's arousal reached an undeniable level. He pulled away from her, gazing into her inviting face. "I think I want to go into the woods now."

"I think I want to go into the woods, too."

Fiona rose. Julian followed. Arm in arm, they walked over to the booth. They retrieved a soft cotton blanket and condoms, then headed into the woods. Fiona took him to a cozy spot in the middle of a redwood cluster where she spread the blanket on the ground. She lay down on the blanket, then pulled him down to lie beside her. He brushed her soft hair away from her face, knocking a few blossoms from her hair. Moving closer to him, she crushed the purple petals beneath her shoulder. As Fiona and Julian became engrossed only in each other, the sounds of the festival faded away.

***

Dawn broke on the morning after Beltane. The revelers emerged from the forest, still flushed from their night of passion. Fiona and Julian dropped their blanket off at the booth, then meandered back to the PRT station where several PRTVs waited. They decided to share a car and sat silently lost in thought as the PRTV zipped back toward the center of the City.

After they passed the first tall, gleaming, white building, Julian turned to face Fiona. "Thank you for inviting me."

"Thank you for coming. It wouldn't have been as fun without you."

Julian leaned in. His lips met with Fiona's once again in a kiss that lasted until they felt the PRTV unhook from the main track. "Will I see you again?" Julian whispered.

Fiona rewarded him with a bright smile. "I certainly hope so."

Julian sighed, relieved, and they moved back together for another kiss.

The PRTV came to a stop at Fiona's building. Fiona stood, then stepped out of the car. She turned back to face him again. "E-mail me when you get home."

Julian laughed as the door closed and called out, "You bet I will."

Chapter 2

A Midsummer Day's Hike

Julian kept his word and e-mailed Fiona as soon as he reached his apartment. She fired back a response, and they made plans to get together the next day. That next day turned into one more, and another after that. They spent every night wrapped in each other's arms, overwhelmed by the incredible feeling of right-ness that blessed their relationship.

The alarm went off just before dawn, and Julian rolled over to look at his beloved. She slid across the bed toward him, moaning at the beeping intrusion into their time together. "Don't go," she said.

Julian kissed her forehead, then slipped out from under the covers. "I have to. I've got to finish the network update plans by ten this morning. Go back to sleep." Julian reached down to caress Fiona's soft hair. She drifted back to sleep. He smiled, then turned with a sigh to gather his clothes. He dressed quietly, then left the apartment.

Fiona awoke to early morning light streaming through the window and stretched her naked body beneath her soft sheets. For a moment, she relished in the joy of having the whole bed to herself but quickly started to miss their morning ritual of cud-dling and telling each other how happy they were to be together.

The six short weeks since they had met in person seemed much longer. She felt as if they had spent their entire lives together. She couldn't remember what her days had been like before him.

She rolled into a sitting position and pushed herself onto her feet, crossing over to the window. She pulled open her sheer drapes. It was a bright, clear day, and the sun had begun its ascent to the top of the sky. Fiona turned back around and surveyed her bedroom, mentally sorting through everything that would have to change if this day went as planned. It was time to put her plan into motion. She went into her office, where she sat down at her terminal and brought it back from sleep mode. She called up her e-mail program, then sent a quick message to Julian, as she did every morning after he had returned to his own apartment to start his workday.

TO: Julian@aptf.ndc

FROM: Fiona@aptz.ndc

SUBJECT: A hike

MESSAGE: Hi, my love

I miss you terribly this morning. I must be head over heels for you. What do you say we go for a hike today? There's a place I've wanted to show you since we met. E me back and let me know.

Your love, F.

Fiona went out to the living room and looked it over. It could do with a little cleaning, especially if she was going to be making room. She crossed over to her over-stuffed couch and fluffed the sage velvet cushions. The couch was staying and she was keeping her faux walnut and iron coffee table and end tables. Julian's glass tables were too streamlined for her artistic temperament. Julian's brown pseudo-leather armchairs would go well with her décor though.

A chime from her office terminal alerted Fiona that she had an incoming message. She scurried back to her workstation, hoping it was from Julian and not a publicity assignment the City Corporation had neglected to send over earlier. She leaned toward the terminal and instructed it to bring the message box up on her screen.

TO: Fiona@aptz.ndc
FROM: Julian@aptf.cdn.
SUBJECT: A hike
MESSAGE: Hi, my temptress
      A hike is just what I need to celebrate the end of this project. By the time you read this
message, I will be aboard a PRTV zipping over to your apartment. See you soon.
Till then, J.

      Fiona closed the message, then looked down at her naked body. He was on his way over, and she still had to shower and dress. She dashed into the bathroom where she stood under the warm stream to wake herself up the rest of the way. She stepped out of the water and in front the air dryer, then darted into the bedroom to pull on her hiking clothes. She was foraging in the closet for her good hiking boots when she heard the outer door and then the inner door open. Before she'd had a chance to come out of the closet, Julian's arms slipped around her waist. He swung her into a warm hug just as he had the first time they had met in person and every day since then. She bent her head from her position aloft, granting him a greeting kiss.

      "So where are we going on this hike?" Julian murmured as he brushed his lips against her chin. He set her down on her feet.

      "It's a surprise," she said.

      "A far surprise? I didn't have lunch yet."

      "We'll stop and get some provisions before we go."

      Julian bowed low before her. "I will do as you command, fair maiden." Fiona laughed. She turned back to grab her backpack, then moved into the bedroom to tug on her shoes.

      As Julian stood before her waiting for her to finish slipping on her shoes, she noticed his satellite phone clipped to his belt. She reached over, unhooked it, then set it on the bed.

      "Why did you do that?" he asked, reaching for it.

      "We're not bringing our phones."

      Fiona grinned and stopped his hand.

      "What if there's an emergency?"

Fiona held up her wrist, bringing the emergency beeper attached to her wrist to his attention. "I can signal for help with this, or it can signal for us if there's serious trouble, but there won't be."

After a long pause, Julian sighed. "Okay. I'll trust you on this."

Fiona stood and took his hand, leading him out of the bedroom. He cast a long glance back at his phone as she pulled him away from it, still unsure about leaving his constant communication device behind. He'd never been without a phone.

They stopped at the building convenience mart on their way down to the PRT platform to get snacks. Like all convenience marts, it was stocked with everything a City-dweller might need, and then some. Julian grabbed two one-liter water bottles with carry straps while Fiona poured trail mix into a recycled plastic bag. Once they had loaded their basket with junk food, they proceeded to the sandwich shop at the back and studied the options listed on the overhead panel. They both selected ham and cheese. Individual portions of fresh sandwich fixings slid out of the refrigerator, ready to be assembled. Fiona made their sandwiches while Julian retrieved their order voucher. Once the sandwiches were ready, they went to the scanner and slid their basket under it along with the voucher. The computer rang up their purchases, then it scanned the iris of Fiona's eye to verify her identity before deducting the proper amount from her account.

"You didn't have to pay for everything, sweetie," Julian said.

"It's okay. It'll all come out even in the end."

Julian smiled at her certainty as he smothered his own fear over the deep-seated knowledge that this was *it*. There wasn't going to be an end to this relationship. He didn't know why that scared him, but he supposed it was a male thing. Fiona didn't appear to have any doubts.

They linked hands as they left the store and continued over to the PRT loading platform. A few residents of Fiona's building were already waiting for cars, so Fiona and Julian settled on a bench to wait. Fiona draped herself around Julian. He nuzzled her neck, eliciting a giggle from her. That giggle drew the attention of the other City-dwellers on the platform who were embarrassed by the public show of affection. One of the women on the platform shot a conciliatory smile Fiona's way, however, and reached out to take her husband's hand in her own. He glanced at his wife with a surprised look, then let a wide grin spread across his face.

Several PRTVs pulled into the station. When it was their turn, Fiona and Julian boarded one of the two-seated vehicles. To extend the surprise a moment longer, Fiona shielded the command panel from Julian as she selected their destination

"Where are we getting off?" he asked as she sat back down beside him. The PRTV zipped away from the platform and joined the main tracks. As their confirmed destination appeared on the panel, Fiona pointed to the screen. Julian looked at the panel. "Mount Komo? I've never taken the PRT past the fairgrounds, and I did that only once."

"You need to get out more." Fiona leaned in to drop a kiss on his lips.

"Then it's a good thing you came along to help me with that," he whispered, his eyes turning soft.

Fiona's cheeks grew warm. He was always saying things to make her blush. She suspected he did it on purpose.

As the PRT track passed out of the City, Fiona directed Julian's attention out the side window to the startling sight of the mountains climbing out of the horizon before them, the view unobstructed by even a single manmade structure. He turned to look the other way. The City disappeared into the background. Julian faced forward again to watch the mountain approach. "That's where we're going?" he asked, awestruck. Wrapped in a cloak of rich evergreens, the mountain was topped by a rocky peak that reached majestically into the heavens to brush against the clean blue sky.

Fiona nodded. "Beautiful, isn't it?"

"Yeah." He looked to her. "Can I just tell you how happy I am that I met you? You've introduced me to a whole new world."

"I love you," Fiona said. Julian responded with a look that said as much and more.

The PRTV detached from the main track and pulled to a

stop at the Mount Komo station. Fiona and Julian stepped onto the platform. Moments later, the door closed and the car accelerated back onto the track, heading back to the City. Julian watched it depart with apprehension. "How do we get back?"

"Same as in the City, silly. A car comes when we call it." Fiona took his hand again and gave it a reassuring squeeze to soothe Julian's obvious discomfort at being this far from the City.

As much as he'd liked the idea of going for a hike, he hadn't really been prepared for what that meant. When Fiona turned Julian away from the track and pointed out the faint path leading into the green mountain, his concern turned to excitement at the chance to explore new territory.

They rode the escalator down to the exit and emerged from the station at an overgrown footpath leading to the lightly trodden Mount Komo hiking trail. Out of the corner of her eye, Fiona watched Julian's amazement at the beauty of the place and took pleasure in the knowledge that she was the one to introduce him to it.

A few feet down the path, Julian stopped and turned to face her. "Fiona Rowan, I love you as I have never loved anyone." He chuckled at his own seriousness. "I just wanted you to know that."

Fiona smiled as another warm blush colored her cheeks and brightened her eyes. She threw her arms around his neck. "Julian Edward, you need to learn to be less serious." She pulled away, then placed her hands on her hips, in mock seriousness. "Now come on, we have hiking to do."

Hand in hand, they meandered up the path. Fiona cited the names of the plants they passed on the way. Yarrow, known for healing wounds and fighting fevers, grew beside four-foot stalks of purple foxglove, poisonous, but still useful in treating heart failure. She never ceased to amaze Julian with her knowledge of nature. He had spent most of his life in cities, even before the Cities had come to be. He was sorry he hadn't paid more attention on the few trips he had taken out of Old Chicago with his aunt when he was a child. "You remind me a lot of my Aunt Mariah," he said as they walked.

Fiona glanced at him. "How's that?

"She loves places like this, and she knows all the names and uses of the plants, too. I know she'll love you when she meets you."

Anticipation, excitement, and reassurance fluttered through her stomach. She couldn't keep the smile out of her voice. "Guess that means you're keeping me, huh?"

Julian stopped walking and tugged her back into his arms. "If you'll let me."

Fiona giggled and kissed his nose. "Hmmm. Yeah. I think I'll let you."

She slipped out of his arms. They continued up the path in silence. As they walked, Julian admired the lush beauty of the place. Why didn't the City Corporation promote it more since the PRT came out here anyway? The reason came to him with another glance around. Too many City-dwellers still didn't respect nature. They hadn't learned their lesson after the disasters. They would just ruin it as they had the old cities and bring on new disasters. The City Corp spent a fortune rebuilding New Denver and wouldn't risk the destruction of one of its natural landmarks. Better to keep the mountains a safe haven for those who did respect it until the City Corp's educational campaign had succeeded.

Julian's meditative pondering was interrupted by the sound of rushing water in the distance. "What is that?"

"That's the waterfall. It's just around that bend up there." Fiona pointed about 300 feet up the trail.

"I've never seen a real waterfall."

Once again aware of how different their upbringings had been, Fiona remembered her first visit to a waterfall. The intense power of the water had been stunning. Eager to share that experience with Julian, Fiona tugged his hand, pulling him along until they were running up the path toward the waterfall.

The majesty of the cascade of water as it roared over the cliff and pounded into the roiling lake at the bottom with a loud crash stopped Julian on his path. "Wow," he said. He felt Fiona leading him toward the bank of the lake but couldn't pull his eyes off the water. When he was able to tear his gaze from the magnificent sight, he turned around to see Fiona stripping off her white tank top. He watched as she slid her khaki shorts off her slender hips, then stood naked before him.

"C'mon, take your clothes off," she commanded. "I want to show you something."

Never one to disobey his love, Julian made quick work of his shorts and T-shirt, although he wasn't sure he would be comfortable being naked outside. He glanced around for signs of other hikers, then inched down his boxer shorts until he also was naked.

Fiona stepped closer and pulled him against her for a passionate kiss. She happily noted the speed with which his body responded to her bare flesh, but she stopped him when he started to lower her to the soft sand. "I want to show you something first." She stepped away and took his hand, leading him over to the rocks near the edge of the waterfall.

When they reached the rocks, she let go of his hand, then scampered across the rocks with familiarity. She disappeared behind the awesome sheet of water while Julian carefully picked his way over them and around to the backside of the falls. He found Fiona waist deep in a calm cove. He slid into the chilly water, then swam toward her. With a giggle, she splashed him as he approached. He dove underwater, tugging on her feet and pulling her under.

Moments later, they tumbled to the surface wrapped around each other. Julian pulled Fiona in for another deep kiss. "Thank you so much for this," he murmured against her lips. Still held in Julian's arms, Fiona led him over to the moss-covered bank inside the cove created by the wall of water behind them. He lifted her onto the bank and moved over her, their bodies melting together atop the soft moss. His lips sought out hers. Their passion intensified as he ran his hands down her firm breasts, causing her to quiver with anticipation. She parted her legs for him. The welcoming flesh beneath him urged him to seek out more. He shifted his weight so as not to crush his love and then pressed into her. They were at one with nature and each other.

After their lovemaking, they lay together on the velvety moss-covered ground, their limbs entwined. Julian took her hand in his. "Am I to expect outdoor lovemaking every six weeks?"

Fiona pretended to contemplate the idea. "Nah, it gets too cold in the winter. I wouldn't want you getting frostbite anywhere," she teased, tracing a hand down between his legs.

Julian chuckled. "I'm happy to hear that." He nuzzled her neck. "But I could get used to this." He lifted his head and gazed into Fiona's eyes. "I've never felt closer to you than I do right now. I want to make you mine forever."

Fiona caressed his cheek and returned his serious gaze. "I'd like that." Overwhelmed by the depth of their love for each other, Fiona grew quiet. The moment had come. "Let's go back to the other side," she said.

Sensing that Fiona was planning something, Julian followed her lead without question. They separated and slid off the bank into the cold water. They swam around to the front of the waterfall and then toward a patch of wildflowers growing just across the small pool. They climbed out of the water. Julian lay back on the grass while Fiona picked several stems of moonlight cosmos, thanking each one as she did so.

"What are you doing?" Julian asked.

"I'm thanking the flower faeries for letting us have these."

"We have to thank the faeries?"

"Of course," she said. "They take care of these, and maybe they'll bless us if we thank them."

Julian leaned over, grazing his lips over her neck. "I think they already have," he whispered against her skin, his voice husky, his desire for her growing stronger by the moment.

Fiona moaned and moved to return the gesture. The heat swelled inside her until she remembered why she had brought him to the waterfall in the first place. She stopped herself, then sat up and faced Julian. "Do you know what day it is?"

"June 21st. Why?"

"Because I suggested we go for a hike today for a special reason. It's the summer solstice, a day when we Pagans believe our desires and wishes come to pass."

Julian reached over and slid his fingers across her flesh, making her sensitive skin rise at his touch. He pulled her back down to him. "I already have what I desire."

"I love you." She sat back up. "Do you know what handfasting is?"

Julian leaned up onto his elbows and gave Fiona's words his full attention. "That's the Pagan marriage ceremony, right?"

She was glad he was at least familiar with the idea. She took a deep breath before posing her next question, steeling her nerves against the possibility that he might say no or might not be ready for what she was about to suggest. "Yeah, but it doesn't have to be a big legal thing. It can be symbolic. Just between a couple."

"Like here and now between you and me?"

Fiona let go of the breath she hadn't realized she was holding. "Yeah."

Julian sat up and turned to face Fiona. He looked into the eyes of the woman he knew he would spend the rest of his life with. Why he was afraid to make a formal commitment to her? He didn't want to be with anyone else, couldn't imagine being with anyone else. And then he knew. What if Fiona was disappointed by her choice in him once the blush of new love wore off and she learned more about his past involvement with the cult?

Fiona tried to read the emotions in Julian's eyes as she waited for his answer. She battled back her fear that he would say no. What would she do if he did? What would they do? She took a deep breath and released it, and then another, and another, to soothe her jangled nerves, but nothing worked. Only one thing could soothe her.

Julian saw the nervousness, hope, and love in Fiona's eyes and knew that she would never be disappointed by her choice. "So how do we do this?"

With an elated smile, Fiona hugged Julian. They could feel each other's hearts pounding and used the moment to slow their breathing and unknot their stomachs. Fiona settled back into a sitting position. She explained the basics of the ceremony they would perform while she wove the cosmos stems into a head-wreath for herself and slender branches of oak leaves into a crown for him. He helped her weave the cosmos and oak leaves together into a cord that they would use to bind their hands.

When Fiona finished the cord, she set it between them.

They moved to sit facing each other, knee to knee. Julian took her hands in his. "I never want to lose this feeling."

Fiona leaned forward and kissed him gently, then leaned back and picked up the oak crown from beside her. He tipped his head forward, and she placed the crown on top. She set her hands in his and waited for the words to come to her. When they did, she looked into his eyes and said, "I promise before all the universe to love and respect you for as long as the elements shall blow with the wind, flow with the water, burn with the flame, and support us on this earth."

Julian picked up the wreath from his side and set it on her head before taking her hands in his again. "I swear before all the powers that be, this waterfall, the sun overhead, the wind in the trees, and the earth beneath my feet, that my love for you will grow as we grow together."

They stayed lost in each other's gaze, hand in hand, until their promises came to rest in each other's hearts. Fiona picked up the cord. She wrapped it around their joined hands, then slipped her free hand inside, saying, "We are bound to each other for as long as our love shall last."

They leaned in and exchanged a long, deep kiss to seal their bond, then parted and slipped their hands out of the cord without untying it. The tied cord would serve as a symbol of their promises. Julian pulled Fiona into the cradle of his arms. He tipped his head down to kiss her before the gentle call of sleep lulled them into its embrace.

Several hours later they awoke to see the sun beginning to slide behind the falls. Fiona lay enfolded in Julian's arms as they watched the last of the sun's face slip beneath the cliff above. They basked in their own joy until the sun had disappeared, then quickly packed up their belongings. They were careful not to leave anything behind, especially not the crowns or cord. After taking a last look at the magical place, they set off down the mountain trail toward the PRT station.

They reached the station after what seemed like a much shorter hike down. Fiona went to the pad to call a return PRTV. As they waited for its arrival, they took a last look down at the earth below. Fiona had never been happier. This day had come to her in a dream, but it had been more perfect than even the dream had been. It was just the beginning for them.

Their PRTV arrived, and Julian helped Fiona aboard. He selected their destination and settled back for the ride home. As the car zipped toward the City, Julian reflected on the events of the day. He had been completely drawn in by the peace of the mountain, something he had never experienced before. Fiona had already changed his life in so many ways. He was eager to see what new changes their handfasting would bring to his life.

As the PRTV made its descent into the City, the glint of sunset on the mirrored windows of the stark white skyscrapers of New Denver jarred Julian from his peaceful ruminations. Other cars carrying single passengers slipped past them on the tracks. They passed over the squat white meeting house where evening socials often took place. The sharp contrast of the technological silence against the breathtaking calls of the birds in the forest and the wind blowing through the trees slammed him back into the reality of the City. Would anything that had happened at the waterfall carry over to their everyday lives? He turned to Fiona. "So are we still handfasted?" he asked.

Fiona started in shock. "Uh…unless you don't want to be."

"I do. I do want to be," he said. "Do you?"

"Oh, yes." Tears of relief and happiness slipped out of her eyes.

"I love you," Julian said. He took her face in his hands, wiping the tears from her cheeks with a gentle caress. "Now let's get home and celebrate."

The PRTV rolled to a stop at Fiona's building and the couple tumbled from the car, dropping their water bottles down the nearby recycling chute as they left the platform. They reached her apartment. Julian dropped the backpack by the door, then scooped Fiona up and carried her to her inviting bed. He eased her down onto the soft pillows and plush comforter, then pulled away and stood back to gaze at her. Desire rushed through him.

Fiona reached out with her mind to connect with Julian's. His lust washed over her. Overcome, she pulled him down to her, wanting him to melt into her, needing him to become one with her. They moved together in abandon, led by an instinctive drive to join together in every way possible.

After their desire had been sated, they lay in bed discussing the more mundane matters that accompanied handfasting. "Who's moving where?" Fiona asked.

"I'll move here, since we spend most of our time here anyway."

Fiona agreed that it was probably the best way to do things. She would submit a new housing application for a larger apartment in the morning. Now that they were living together, they were going to need a bigger place, somewhere to merge their stuff. At the thought of merging, an idea came to Fiona. Ignoring the questioning look from Julian as she slid out of bed, she padded out to the living room. She retrieved her backpack, then removed the handfasting cord and crowns from it. She carried them back into the bedroom.

Julian watched with curiosity as Fiona climbed back on the bed and stood up. She reached over his head and took down the poster hung above the headboard. Behind the poster were two hooks. She suspended one crown from each hook, hers on the left, Julian's on the right. As a final touch, she draped the cord around and between the two crowns until all three were intertwined and looked as if they were one.

"What do you think?" she asked, looking down at Julian to get his approval. His smile was all she needed. "Well, that settles it. You're mine now! And you know what else?"

Julian grabbed hold of her legs, tugging her down to him. "What?"

"We have more celebrating to do," she giggled. His lips devoured hers, and her chest melted against his.

"I can do that," he said, rolling her onto her back. He traced his lips down her neck. "I'm all for that."

Chapter 3

Under the Spell

A few days after their Midsummer hike, Julian puttered in the kitchen, fixing their lunch of peanut butter and boysenberry jelly sandwiches. Julian had first found Fiona's penchant for child's food amusing and a little odd, but he had grown to like her choices.

Fiona sat at her terminal reading her e-mail. She flipped to a message from the Pagan Coalition. When she got to the part about their plans to host another Lammas camping trip on Mount Komo, her feet did an excited jig. She called out to Julian, "Have you ever been camping?"

The question was met by silence. Julian popped his head into the office and shot her one of his *I'm a city boy* looks.

"Sorry, silly question. Would you like to?"

Julian mulled over his answer. He'd never given the idea much thought. He hadn't even considered joining the boys' clubs that had been in existence during his childhood. "What does it entail?"

Fiona paused, trying to figure out how best to word this. Camping may have been a part of her upbringing, but she had learned long ago that die hard City-dwellers, like Julian had been when they'd first met, didn't see the point of sleeping in tents and not showering for two days. It would be best to skip that part and just include the enticing bits. Her explanation tumbled out in a rush of nervousness and anticipation. "The Pagan Coalition, the group that put on the Beltane Fest, has a campout on Mount Komo every year. They just sent me the info. I'd really like us to go. It's a lot of fun. I'll do all the packing, and I have all the gear. It's only from Friday to Sunday," she said, pleading with him with her *please if you do this I'll love you forever* look. The one that Julian was unable to resist.

Julian dashed across the room and snatched her into a hug. "You know you're not playing fair. But okay, we'll go."

He looked at her with a wicked gleam in his eyes. "But you owe me . . . ."

"Yes, master. Whatever you want."

Julian pressed his lips into hers. His breath grew ragged as their kiss deepened. "Lunch can wait . . . ."

Their lovemaking was quick and boisterous, yet comfortable and easy. They had both become accustomed to each other's quirks and knew exactly what to do to elicit the most heated response from the other.

Much later, they went into the kitchen to finish the lunch Julian had prepared. As they sat at the table munching on corn chips and sandwiches, Fiona told him she had sent the apartment application in. They would know soon when they could move.

"What should I do with my stuff until then?" Julian asked.

"Some of it you can bring here. You can get rid of the rest," Fiona said.

"I'm not quite ready for that yet. I'll put whatever we don't have room for in storage."

"Works for me. I'll make a list of what I want you to bring."

Julian glanced at Fiona, amused that she had already taken charge of their living arrangements. No matter, he could handle that.

***

Julian moved his belongings over the course of the next few weeks, squeezing some time into each day to visit his old apartment and pack a few things for storage and a few others to bring back to his new home. Fiona sent some of his choices back with him the next day but found room for the items he really wanted to keep. During those weeks, Fiona made a list of everything they would need for the camping trip and checked her supplies. She then had Julian pull the gear down from the high closets as he put away his own stuff.

By the date of the Lammas Fair, Fiona had all their gear packed and piled at the door, and Julian had his belongings unpacked and put away. Julian helped Fiona carry the gear down to the PRT platform where they hopped aboard a waiting car. Fiona was eager to get the trip underway; Julian was apprehensive about what he was getting into.

As they approached the Mount Komo station, Julian surveyed the mountain, seeking out the path they had taken to the waterfall. It had been a long hike. The trail was very narrow at certain points. He glanced down at their bags, then turned to Fiona with concern. "How are we going to carry all this stuff up there?"

Fiona laughed. "We don't. They have a bus to take us up there. We're going a lot farther than the waterfall." Fiona looked at him closer, noticing that he was eyeing the mountain with more concern than a difficult hike warranted. "Are you okay?"

"Yeah. This is only my second Pagan event, remember." A more foreboding thought flickered by, but he couldn't quite catch it before it was gone. He shook his head to banish the hint of trouble further from his mind and looked out the window.

As the PRTV slowed to a stop and docked at the platform, Fiona squeezed Julian's hand and flashed him a reassuring smile. She popped open the door and started unloading their gear. Julian looked at mountain once more, then at the other campers carrying their stuff to the escalator. They looked just like him. He had nothing to fear. He stood and helped Fiona transfer the rest of their gear to the platform. Then they followed their fellow participants down the escalator to the solar-powered bus waiting at the bottom.

While Fiona checked them in with Lady Celesta, Julian went to stow their gear in the undercarriage. Julian counted the bags as he loaded them to be sure he hadn't left anything on the platform. Satisfied that he hadn't, he walked around the bus to find Fiona. He saw her standing with a striking woman he recognized as the attractive High Priestess who had presided over Beltane. She was now dressed in shorts and a t-shirt. In this setting she looked much less mystical and much more like the regular City-dweller she was.

Fiona introduced them, then Lady Celesta excused herself to check in a few more new arrivals. "Ready?" Fiona asked when Lady Celesta was gone.

Julian looked once more at the mountain. His anxiety flared again, but he nodded slowly. They boarded the bus and found a seat in the back. Not ten minutes later, Lady Celesta boarded. The door closed behind her and as she took a seat, the bus powered up. Then it began to traverse the bumpy dirt road that led to the campground. Julian quashed his anxiety as the bus lumbered up the mountain. Fiona took the opportunity to clear her mind of the City and transport herself to the peace of her surroundings.

Julian jumped at her side, snapping her back to her present location. Fiona reached one hand out for him, then turned to give him her full attention. "What's wrong?"

"Sarah e-mailed me last week. I forgot all about it until just now."

"I'm sorry, sweetie. What did she want?"

"Her group is having a camping trip up here this week-end too. She wanted me to go."

"What did you tell her?"

"I didn't answer. I want her out of my life, but she won't go."

Fiona leaned over and put her arms around him, resting her chin on his shoulder. She placed a soft kiss on his cheek. "It's over now. You're with me. She can't do anything to you."

As those words left Fiona's lips, Sarah came down to the gate of her campground to inspect the bus passing by. Julian saw her before she had a chance to peer inside the bus and buried his face in Fiona's waiting shoulder. It was more than fear about Sarah seeing him that made him hide. It was fear of the power the cult had once held over him.

Once he was sure they had passed Sarah's camp, Julian popped his head up and rested it against the seatback. He watched out the window, concentrating on the scenery to help him forget Sarah and the cult. The bus passed through a stand of thick evergreen trees. They were in their own world now, free from everyday demands. The trees seemed to shine with a green aura and to Julian it looked as though the rocks glistened more brightly under the sun overhead. The bus emerged from the trees and entered the Pagan campground. "It's incredible," he said

Fiona was happy he thought so. She nodded, eager for the bus to stop at their site and let them off so they could start exploring the surrounding forest. The bus stopped every five sites to deposit the passengers close to their campsites. Fiona and Julian disembarked at the third stop, directly in front of their campsite. It was the perfect site. It had a large tree to shade their picnic table during the hottest part of the day, two smaller trees just the right distance apart to support a hammock, and a pine-needle-covered flat area for the tent. Julian helped Fiona string up the hammock, then they set up their tent in the flat area and arranged their ground pads and sleeping bags inside.

The work stirred their hunger, so they fixed a quick lunch of peanut butter and jelly sandwiches, chips, and water. Lots of water. Fiona had probably overpacked—she always did—but it was better to have too much water than too little. As they ate, pieces of pinecone rained down on them from the tree overhead. Fiona looked up into the tree and pointed out the noisy squirrel tearing at the cone to get to the seeds tucked inside. Julian watched with rapt attention, having never seen a live squirrel. The plant shower continued until the squirrel had finished its lunch, then it left them to theirs.

Once peace had returned, Fiona looked over the event schedule she had downloaded into her page-viewer before they had left that morning. "The opening ritual starts at sunset and it's noon now. What do you say we go for a hike after lunch?"

"Sounds good to me." Julian swallowed the last bite of sandwich and rose from the bench to clean up their meal. He grabbed two more bottles of water from their cooler and slipped them into carry straps. Fiona took one of the bottles from him. They turned to survey the surrounding hills, searching for the right path. Julian spied a rocky outcropping resting 500 feet up the mountain. He pointed towards it. "That one."

Fiona looked in the direction of Julian's finger. He had chosen the rock she had wanted to hike to since she had first come to the Lammas campout a few years earlier. With a hearty swig of water to start them off, they set off across the overgrown meadow of weeds toward the rocky path left by spring run-off. They passed a mess of pinecone husks scattered under a tall pine tree. "I guess our squirrel's been busy," Fiona said with a laugh

Julian backtracked a few feet to inspect the pile. "Looks

like it. Let's hope that he's found a new spot and won't be bathing us in debris again."

Fiona grinned. She hadn't really minded the plant shower. "Julian, you're so citified." She shook her head in mock confusion. "Why do I love you?"

"I don't know. Why do you?" He wrapped Fiona in his arms and grazed his lips over her neck, eliciting a moan.

"That's why," she said.

Julian's smile widened. He pulled away and moved back onto the path. Putting on his best show of manliness, and despite Fiona's greater experience as a hiker, he led her though the prickly bushes and hardy mountain growths that reached out to scratch their delicate City flesh. When they came to a clearing in the brush they looked ahead for some sign of their goal. Julian insisted it was to the left, and Fiona was sure it was to the right.

After they spotted the rock, in the opposite direction Julian said they should go, Fiona took over as leader of the expedition. They emerged from a shrub to find themselves facing the boulder they had sought. Julian climbed on top of it, then reached down for Fiona, pulling her up to meet him. They settled on the rock and gazed down at the campsite below. They could just make out the tents of the other campers and hear their laughter drifting up from the valley floor. Overhead, a hawk soared on the wind. Its cry echoed through the rocks. Julian turned to look at his beloved, admiring her beauty as the soft breeze brushed her hair off her face.

Fiona felt his gaze on her and turned to face him. Something about the desire in his eyes made her blood clamor through her veins. The awe of lust rolled through her. She moved in to kiss him, pressing her firm lips against his, letting them part just enough to share a breath with him. He twined his arms around her and pulled her closer. From the valley below, the tribal beat of a drum drifted up to them. The beat matched the beats of their hearts. Julian rose, pulling Fiona up with him. He slid off the rock and motioned for Fiona to slide into his waiting arms. As her body met his, he began to move his feet to the hypnotic rhythm, guiding her into a dance.

"Julian!"

The sudden call of his name startled Fiona and Julian out of their trance-like dance. They turned to face the direction from which it had come. Sarah and another member of the cult stood in front of them. As all four stared at each other, the sound of the drum faded.

Julian fumbled for words to fill the uncomfortable silence. "Um…what are you doing here…Sarah?"

At the utterance of Sarah's name, Fiona's hands clenched, her back tightened, her breath quickened. Struggling to remain calm, she unclenched her hands. She leaned in to whisper in Julian's ear. "That's Sarah?"

The whisper wasn't very soft. "Yes, I'm Sarah," she said, with a chill in her voice. "And who might you be?"

Fiona's desire to flee warred against her desire to deck the woman who had made Julian so miserable for so long. She reached out for Julian's hand to keep herself from lashing out. The barely contained rage in Sarah's eyes registered with Fiona. No long explanation would improve the situation. "Fiona," she said, surprised to hear herself squeak as she said her name. What was this woman doing to her?

Sarah eyed Julian. "I gather that you're with her," she snarled. "What happened to our beliefs?"

Julian sighed, more frustrated than angry. He wasn't in the mood to fight with Sarah. All he wanted was to enjoy his first camping trip. "We've been over this. Those were *your* beliefs."

"I thought you understood the cause. What has she done to you?"

"I love Fiona, so I'm with her. That's all there is to it." He turned from Sarah and hugged Fiona, holding her against him. He wished she hadn't witnessed the confrontation.

"Come back to my camp," Sarah pleaded. "We'll talk this out. You don't belong with her. She's one of those Pagans." She tried to take his hand and pull him away from Fiona. "You're under some kind of spell."

Julian angrily snatched his hand from Sarah's grasp. "Sarah, it's over. Try to get that. It's over. I want you out of my life. For good."

Taking Fiona's hand in his, Julian turned his back on Sarah. He stalked away from her, leading Fiona back down the mountain the way they had come. Fiona looked back once to see Sarah staring after her, hatred glowing in her eyes. Dread rolled through Fiona. She sought to soothe herself by making a pointed effort to take in the beauty of the trees they were passing. She allowed the serenity of the place to fill her once again. Their pace slowed. Fiona could tell by Julian's loosening grasp that he was relaxing again. By the time they reached their camp, they both felt much better about the confrontation and agreed not to discuss it.

Fiona glanced at her watch. They had just enough time for a quick dinner before the opening ritual. They devoured their chili, then raced down to the center of the campground to participate in the simple rite.

The ritual was short, lasting only fifteen minutes. Lady Celesta greeted everyone and then invited the spirits of the place to come forward and meet their guests. She promised the guardians of the land that the participants would not harm the place. Then she guided those gathered through a brief meditation to bring them into sacred space for the duration of the weekend.

Lady Celesta concluded the ritual with a joyous call for the drumming to begin. As the post-ritual festivities got underway, flashlight beams from a side path bounced across the merrymakers. Four people appeared at the edge of the clearing. It was apparent at first glance that they were not participants in the celebration.

Lady Celesta set her bodhran down on a wooden bench by the fire. She approached the small band of interlopers. Julian could see from his vantage point on the far side of the fire that Sarah was one of the uninvited visitors. He and Fiona couldn't hear what was being said, so they crept closer to the conversation.

Sarah's cult leader directed his attention to Lady Celesta. "I understand you are holding a Pagan ritual here tonight. We are here to ask you to stop this debauchery and join us on the true path."

Lady Celesta had dealt with zealots many times before. With a calm voice she said, "We are in a private campground.

You don't have the right to be here. We do have a right to practice as we choose. Please leave now."

The leader puffed out his chest with self-righteous pomposity. "We have a right to be wherever people are being misled into following the darkness."

"We are all here by choice. No one is being misled. I would welcome the opportunity to explain our beliefs to you, but this is not the appropriate time," Lady Celesta said. Fiona was impressed by her ability to maintain her composure.

Sarah stepped forward and whispered in the leader's ear. He nodded and peered into the faces of the Lammas celebrants, all of whom had silenced their drums and were watching the exchange. The leader raised his voice so all could hear his next words. "There is one who is not here by choice. Give Julian back to us, and we will go away."

Still without a trace of anger, but with a tone that said she was not to be challenged, Lady Celesta responded. "I will not *give* you anyone. As I said, anyone here is here by choice. Leave our celebration immediately, or I will report you to the ranger."

Her threat worked. The leader backed off from his stance, stepping a few paces back on the path. "We'll go now, but we'll return in the morning to lead you in prayer."

"You will not come back unless you wish to listen to our chants and songs. Should you interrupt us again, you will be reported. I know the rangers won't take kindly to your disregard for City ordinances," Lady Celesta said.

The leader glowered at Lady Celesta before turning and motioning for his group to follow him away from the celebrants. As she turned, Sarah spotted Julian standing by a thicket of trees. She approached him for one last try. "Julian, please come with me. You belong with us."

Julian stepped back and reached for Fiona. He placed his arm around his waist. The leader called Sarah to him with a stern order. She skittered away, head down. Julian moved to a bench and sat down hard. He buried his head in his hands.

Lady Celesta took a seat beside him. "Don't worry. They won't come back."

Julian looked up at her, dubious. "How can you be sure?"

"I've tussled with him before. His cult's beliefs have become increasingly fanatical, and New Denver law enforcement has been investigating him for quite some time. His church is in danger of being disbanded at any moment. He knows that one more report is all they need to shut him down," she said. "I'm sorry for your friend, though."

Julian glanced at Fiona. She sat down next to him and put a supportive arm around his shoulders. Looking back to Lady Celesta, he said, "Don't be. She had some of those beliefs before. He only intensified them."

"I'm sorry for you then. May you find peace from her." Lady Celesta looked to the celebration that had resumed around the fire. "I'd better get back there. We have hours of merriment left. Try to enjoy it."

Lady Celesta left the bench and joined a chain of dancers snaking sinuously around the rising flames. Fiona and Julian watched for a moment before Fiona lightly kissed Julian's shoulder. "Let's go to bed now. I think we need some time alone."

"Are you sure?" Julian asked. "I don't want to ruin your fun."

"It won't be any fun for me if you're miserable. Let's go." Fiona stood, tugging Julian to his feet. They walked away from the fire and toward their campsite. They crawled inside their tent, then nestled into their joined sleeping bags.

"I'm sorry you had to see that," Julian whispered.

Fiona snuggled deeper into Julian's arms. "It's okay. It's not your fault." As they fell quiet, the exchange replayed in her mind. "What did the leader mean by 'Give Julian *back* to us'?"

Julian slid his arm out from under Fiona. He rolled away from her. He had hoped they would be together longer before it came out, if it ever did. "I didn't just date a member. I was a member."

"What?" Fiona sat upright, shocked and confused.

"I'm sorry," Julian said, his voice muffled by his pillow. "I didn't want you to know. I'm so ashamed that I was drawn in by them."

Fiona struggled for words. "You don't seem like the type."

"I'm not. Any more. But I was. And they weren't like

this back then. I was looking for something to believe in. I was gullible. I was lonely. I met Sarah, and she led me to it."

Fiona shivered. "Like I'm leading you toward Paganism."

Julian hadn't intended it to sound that way. He sat up and turned to Fiona, folding her against his chest. "No, never. You haven't led me to anything I haven't wanted to do. I'm not as weak as I used to be."

"And you won't go back?" Fiona asked, nervous that the cult might still hold some sway over him.

"No. I know better now." He hoped it was true.

"How did you get out?"

"I wasn't completely brainwashed when they first became more extreme. They started planning protests and talking about necessary violence, and I started to have my doubts. They sent me on an errand one day, and I went to my parents instead. They took me for deprogramming."

"When did all this happen?"

"Last fall."

"Oh, my Goddess. I had no idea. Are you…are you sure you're okay being here?"

Julian lifted Fiona's head and kissed her cheeks. "Yes. I love being here with you. That part of my life is over. Trust me."

Fiona nodded and lay back down, resting her head on the pillow. She wanted to trust him. He certainly hadn't shown an indication he still felt some tie to the cult. He had never mentioned any fanatical beliefs. He'd never mentioned any beliefs at all. She hoped he was telling the truth when he said she wasn't pushing her beliefs on him. Could she have done it unintentionally? No, he'd said he wanted to be there, and she believed him. She pushed all other doubts from her mind and focused on the meditative rhythm of the distant drumming to lull her to sleep.

Julian leaned over her and grazed his lips across her forehead, then lay down beside her. He closed his eyes and tried to banish his self-doubt. He wouldn't fall prey to the cult again. He wouldn't, would he? Could he ever really get them out of his life? He didn't want anything to ruin what he had with Fiona. He hoped she wouldn't let his past taint their relationship. He needed to know she understood. He slipped one hand between them and pinched Fiona's bottom with a kitten's soft touch, as he did every night. She responded with her customary yelp and the gentle tap of her heel on his shin. Reassured by their nightly ritual, Julian quelled any further anxiety and allowed sleep to pass over him.

***

The bright rays of sunlight illuminating the tent walls woke them early the next morning. They emerged from their shelter, and Fiona dug a couple of nutrition bars out of their food pack for breakfast. After they ate, they made a futile attempt to wash off some of the layers of dirt, insect repellant, and sunscreen that had accumulated the previous day before applying fresh coats of the latter two.

Once they were re-protected from the harsh mountain sunlight and biting insects, they sat down to review the day's schedule of activities. Fiona suggested that Julian might like to go to the drum class at eleven while she went to the Goddess making workshop.

"I don't have a drum," Julian said.

With a mischievous grin, Fiona went to the duffel bag. She pulled out a wrapped object a shaped like a large goblet, which she presented to Julian with a flourish. "Surprise!"

He took the object from her with a smile and unwrapped the fabric to reveal an ornate metal drum. "Where did this come from?"

"I bought it when you said you'd come with me. I hope you like it."

Julian stood and kissed her. "I love it. Thank you." He picked up the doumbek, then pulled the strap over his shoulder. "And now I'd best be off to learn the manly art of drumming." He turned on his heel and marched toward the class, banging loudly and without any rhythm. Fiona smiled with satisfaction as she watched him leave. Then she made her way down to the clay Goddess molding class.

A couple hours later Fiona was resting in the hammock reading an art book on her page-viewer when she heard Julian returning, still banging away on the drum, but now with more skill and a discernible rhythm. She leaned up and kissed him hello. "How was it?"

"It was great. Thanks. Where's your goddess?"

Fiona pointed to the picnic table where she had propped up the miniature model of the Willendorf Venus she had learned to sculpt in the workshop. "She's still drying," she said.

Julian set his drum on the table next to the small figurine and bent to peer at it, admiring the fine artistic features Fiona had etched on the face and head. "She's beautiful." He turned back to Fiona. "So what's next?" he asked, eager for another new experience.

She swung herself off the hammock, then hugged him. "I'm so happy you're enjoying yourself. I was worried it would be too much for you."

Julian leaned back and looked her in the eye. "I always enjoy myself when I'm with you. I can handle whatever you throw at me."

Recognizing the challenge in his eyes, she responded with one of her own. "Then I suggest we play a little Pagan trivia."

"What exactly is Pagan trivia?"

"You'll see." Fiona tugged Julian's hand and started toward the center camp. Julian followed, filled with curiosity about what she was getting him into this time.

Several other campers were already waiting when Fiona and Julian arrived. Lady Celesta chatted with a man standing beside a game board. He wore loose cotton pants and a tunic. The board held several cards bearing questions about such topics as Celtic mythological animals, Norse Gods, and tree lore. Fiona and Julian sat on a large rock to watch the proceedings. "There's no way I'm playing this," Julian said.

"Don't worry. There are plenty of contestants already. I couldn't begin to compete with most of these people."

After a few more players had arrived, Lady Celesta called everyone to order, and the raucous game began. The contestants listened to each question, trying to discern any clues or tricks from the wording, and competed to be the first to answer. They collected points for each correct answer and turned to the audience for help when they couldn't figure it out. Most often the audience would yell out the answer with a tone that said any idiot should know the answer, but even the audience was stumped on occasion. Julian was proud to note he knew a few of the answers and Fiona knew more. After five rounds, he prodded her until she agreed to take her turn as a contestant.

She was thrilled when she won her round. After the game, Fiona collected her prize, a miniature deck of tarot cards. They returned to their camp for dinner. While Julian helped her prepare the tacos, she explained what he could expect from the main ritual.

"What exactly does Lammas mean?" he asked.

"It's the first harvest celebration. Better bring your drum to circle. There's going to be another drum jam after the ritual."

Following dinner, Fiona changed into a sweater and long green skirt that swirled about her legs. Julian put on jeans and a sweatshirt. Two loud conch shell blasts alerted them that the ritual was about to begin. Fiona went back to their pack to get two cups and the loaf of braided bread she had baked as offering for the Lammas alter. Julian grabbed his drum, then the two left their campsite, heading for the center camp.

One hundred other campers, some in robes and ritual garb like Fiona, others in jeans and sweatshirts like Julian, milled around the edge of the fire pit and exchanged greetings. Fiona pointed out the altar set up at one end of the site, already piled high with offerings of fresh loaves of bread, corn dollies, corn muffins, and home-brewed mead. Fiona added her gift to the table, and they went to a bench to wait for Lady Celesta to begin the ritual.

As they waited, Julian's tension mounted. What if Sarah and her cult returned? He didn't want any more trouble from her.

Feeling his hand tighten on hers, Fiona leaned over and kissed him on the cheek. "Don't worry. They won't come back," she said.

Julian looked to her, surprised she had read his mind exactly. Then again, he often did the same thing with her. His thoughts were interrupted as Lady Celesta, assuming her role as High Priestess, clanged a bell at the center of the circle to signal that the ritual was beginning.

Starting in the east, Lady Celesta and the High Priest

walked around the outer edge of the gathered participants, beating out a heartbeat rhythm on their drums to mark the boundary of the circle. They returned to the east, and the circle was cast. The High Priest began a whispery rhythm. Lady Celesta began to dance. The participants followed her lead, drawing down the element of air through the movement. Julian watched, mesmerized by the union of the Priestess, the participants, and the elements. The fire changed its dance with each change of the beat and mimicked the movements of the Priestess.

To his right, Fiona allowed the drum to bring her into its music, to guide her body into the same dance as the Priestess'. In the east, they danced the flight of the eagle soaring on the winds; in the south, the High Priest charmed out of them the sinuous movements of the snake. In the west, they became whales breaching the surface of the ocean, and in the north, they recreated the walk of the bear to a slow, ponderous beat. One by one, the elements of air, fire, water, and earth joined the ritual.

When all had come, the Priestess and Priest stepped once again to the center to invoke the Lady and Lord. They joined hands and lifted them skyward, arching their arms up to the full moon and inviting the Goddess and God to come down into them. The Priestess spoke with a booming voice. "Come, Great Lady, come join us on this full lit night as we celebrate the bounty that comes from your earth. Watch over us as we give thanks for the sustenance that is your gift."

The High Priest waited a moment for the Goddess to join them in circle, then called out to the Lord in his powerful timbre. "Come, Great Lord, come join us on this joyous night as we celebrate the harvest of your grain. Watch over us as we give thanks for the life that is your gift."

The ritual leaders approached the altar at the north to bless the offerings placed there by the participants. In unison, they said, "We charge these herbs, fruits, and grains. Blessed are they, blessed are the grounds from which they grow, and blessed are those who consume them."

Lady Celesta turned to the women and called out, "We bless this food with the gifts of the Mother!" The women repeated her words three times.

The High Priest turned to the men and called out, "We bless this food with the gifts of the Father!" The men repeated his words three times.

The High Priestess and Priest retreated to the outer circle and joined hands with the participants, forming a long chain. Lady Celesta guided them into a spiral dance. The dust swirled high up into the night air as the dancers moved with increasing speed, hands locked together, their line twisting into a tight coil, the force of the dance holding them up and driving them on as they spiraled in and out of the center. When all thought they could not move one more step, nor stop if they chose to, the Priestess led them back into a large circle and the dance ended. The buzzing participants released the energy they had just raised with a thunderous shout, sending it up into the ether to mix with the energy of the Universe and carry their blessings and thanks back to the Lord and Lady.

From one side of the circle came the beat of a single drum. A woman moved out to the center to dance around the fire as the High Priest added more logs to it. Lady Celesta joined the dance and another drum joined the first. As more dancers stepped into the circle moving around the fire and more drummers added their beats to the song, other participants went to the altar to uncork the mead, offering some to the earth before pouring it into their own cups.

Fiona went to get a cup of mead for her and Julian. He picked up the drum, using his new skills to participate in the drum jam. Fiona took a sip of the smooth honey wine as she returned to Julian. She set the cup at his side, then joined the circle of women dancing seductively around the fire, moving to the rhythm of the drums. Their bodies united with the spirit of the flame as it danced to the beat, pulling them into its spellbinding embrace.

The drumming continued. The mead served as cool elixir to goad the merrymakers on. When the mead ran out, it was replaced by ale, and the dancing and drumming continued. Julian watched Fiona, in awe of the grace of his beloved. She twirled and pranced around the fire, entranced by the rhythm of the music. He was seeing a side of her he had not seen before. It was a side he ached to make love to.

As she continued around the circle, Fiona's eyes met Julian's. His heated gaze was enough to break the spell cast on her by the drums. She stepped out of the dance and collapsed on the bench next to him, pulling a long draught of mead from the cup. Her thirst quenched, she leaned over and placed her lips on his, igniting a fire between them. Julian rose, pulling Fiona up with him. Moving as one, they raced back to their tent. They tumbled inside, lips locked together, tearing at each other's clothes. The drumbeat in the distance guided their fevered passion. They moved over each other with heady abandon, melting into the flames of desire.

When the beat of the drums slowed and their ardor had subsided, they lay wrapped in each other's arms. "I'm glad you agreed to come with me," Fiona whispered.

"I wouldn't have missed it for the world. It was...amazing."

They reached for each other and moved together to make love again, their passion rising and falling over and over throughout the night. An hour before daybreak, they drifted to sleep.

***

The echoing call of a wolf pack greeting the morning sun awakened. Bleary-eyed and exhausted, Julian and Fiona stumbled out of their tent and devoured a breakfast of nutrition bars before cleaning up their camp. The bus would arrive immediately after the closing ritual to carry the campers back down the mountain.

The day had already grown hot by the time of the early morning ritual. Lady Celesta promised to keep things brief as she thanked everyone for attending the Lammas gathering. She thanked the Goddess and God for gracing them with Their presence, released the quarters, then drew the circle in. The gathered participants exchanged hugs all around and made promises to see each other again soon, even those who had just met.

The center camp emptied out as the participants moved back to their own sites to drag their bags to the nearest bus stop. The slow-moving vehicle to trundled around to each stop, then carried them down the mountain to the PRT station.

As Fiona and Julian stepped off the PRTV at their apartment building, a few fellow building residents shot them disgusted looks. They noticed how filthy they really were. "I'll race you to the shower!" Fiona cried as she took off at a run, dragging some of their bags behind her. Julian caught up to her and passed her, moving into the elevator ahead of her, despite the burden of carrying more bags. She reached it just as the doors would have closed, had Julian not been pressing the open button. He released it. As the car ascended to their floor, they wrestled to be closer to the door when it opened. They spilled out of the car and into the hallway, then ran toward the apartment doors. Dropping their gear inside the inner door, they rushed to the shower where they helped each other remove the dirt and sunscreen that had been ground into their flesh.

"This weekend was wonderful," Julian murmured under the steaming spray.

"Yeah, it was." Fiona remembered the passion that had overtaken them the night before. She grazed a sponge over her belly and was stunned by the jolt that ran through her. It was followed by a premonition that something truly magical had happened while they were under the spell of the Lammas drums.

Chapter 4

Reaping More than Grain

As soon as he stepped off the City Corporation's elevator, Julian spotted Sarah lurking on the PRT platform. He was not in the mood to deal with her. Fiona had been agitated that morning but had pushed him out the door when he'd tried to back out of his meeting. He wanted to get home and find out what had her so upset. He tightened his hand on his bag and fixed his gaze on the PRTV locator kiosk at the edge of the platform. Sarah stepped into his path, making it impossible for him to ignore her. "You're following me now?" he snapped.

Sarah pasted a serene smile on her face. "No. I knew you had a meeting today, so I came to talk to you."

"How would you know I had a meeting?"

"The leader knows everything, Julian."

"Then he knows I don't want to see you again," he said, continuing past her.

"That's not why I'm here. He needs your help," Sarah called after him.

"If he knows everything, why would he need my help?" Julian turned to look Sarah square in the face. Was this just another ploy to win him back or something more?

"He needs a separate network for our organization. You're the best designer in the City. Everyone knows that." She knew she was stretching the truth. Julian was the best, but the leader's network was set up already. Still, it would need to be maintained. Julian could do that. Then he would be with her and away from the evils of that Pagan woman, she thought. That's what mattered the most.

"I'm not interested."

"But Julian, you could be a part of something new. *We* could be a part of something new."

Shaking his head, Julian moved to the panel and called a PRTV. He stepped to the docking station and waited, his back to Sarah, willing her to leave. When she didn't walk away, he spoke again without turning around. "I'm going home now. I'll trust you not to follow me."

Indignation shot through Sarah. His home was with her and their church, she thought. Not with that evil woman. "I don't have to. I know where you live, and I know you're living with her," Sarah said. She saw Julian stiffen. She backed off. It wouldn't do to alienate him from her church. He would find his way back to them soon. She continued, softening her voice. "But I want you to know that when you see through her tricks, there will always be a place for you with me and the leader."

The PRTV arrived. Ignoring Sarah's pleas, Julian stepped inside the car. The door swung closed behind him, sealing him off from her. As the PRTV accelerated out of the station, he peeked out the window to see if Sarah was still standing on the platform. She was, watching the car carry him away from her. Her eyes had gone cold and empty.

***

Fiona waited for Julian's return, anxiety lurching through her stomach. She checked the clock for the tenth time that hour and glanced down at the pair of white plastic circles staring back at her. The word *positive* was etched across the face of each in bright red letters, silently confirming Fiona's suspicions. She was pregnant. After another glance at the door, she grabbed her page-viewer and flipped it on, bringing up the calendar function. She located the first day of her previous cycle, then counted forward. There it was. Exactly fourteen days after the beginning of her cycle, she and Julian had been carried away by the drums of Lammas. She had been so driven by animal lust that she hadn't given a single thought to protection. And they were usually so careful.

She sighed again. There was nothing she could do to change that now. Hopefully they would agree about what to do. To distract herself from the turmoil of her mind, she called up a list of books on her page-viewer, scanning them for something uncomplicated to read. None of the titles registered in her memory. She finally chose one at random. She looked up at the clock once more. It was still 11:30. She directed her attention to the small screen in front of her, but the letters refused to form into words that would distract her from her confused thoughts. Frustrated, she tossed the page-viewer aside.

The sound of the outer door opening called up a fresh swell of panic. Fiona swept the plastic circles under a throw blanket as Julian entered.

He dropped his bag next to the door. Fiona stood to greet him, her face blank, her back stiff. Julian could see the tension in her posture as he approached. "What's wrong?" he asked, placing a gentle hand on her upper arm.

Fiona bent her head and sat down again. Julian perched on the edge of the couch, afraid she was about to tell him it was over. Instead, Fiona lifted the blanket up to reveal the pair of pregnancy tests. He looked down at them, his eyes shifting from one *positive* to the other. "Are those…?" He trailed off, not sure he wanted to know the answer.

"Yes."

"Oh." Fear, happiness, and pride rushed through him. He

sat still for a moment, struggling to get his emotions under control, then reached out for Fiona, pulling her into his arms. He leaned back against the soft velvet cushions for support. They held each other until Julian broke the long silence with, "How do you feel about this?"

From his chest, Fiona uttered a muffled, "I don't know."

Julian moved his hand up to Fiona's hair. He toyed absentmindedly with the silky strands as he pondered their options. He wasn't ready for a child, but he didn't think Fiona would be willing to give it up. To be honest, he wouldn't be that comfortable knowing he had a child out there somewhere either. There was no easy answer. "We *have* only been together a few months," he said, as if that would make the decision easier somehow.

Fiona had no solution to offer. They sat together for a longer spell until Fiona managed to wade out of the mire long enough to notice it had grown dark. She was hungry and suggested they eat. Over dinner they debated the pros and cons of having the baby. The discussion continued long into the night, but by 3:00 a.m. they were no closer to a decision.

Too exhausted to talk anymore, they fell into fitful sleep and awoke at sunrise, feeling no more rested than they had at 3:00 a.m. Julian reached for Fiona, and she nestled into his arms. He placed a gentle kiss on her forehead.

In a flash, she saw herself holding a newborn baby and Julian grinning proudly. She had her answer. "Let's have the baby," she said. "We knew we wanted to have children eventually. This is just sooner than we planned."

Julian didn't share Fiona's certainty. After a long pause, he said, "I . . . I'm not sure I'm ready."

Fiona rose up on her hands and looked him in the eye. "Julian, this baby is a result of our love. We can do this together. I know we can."

The resolve and strength in her eyes overcame his reservations. "Okay."

Relief flooded through Fiona. She pressed her lips to his. "I love you."

"I love you," Julian said. He pulled her down to his chest, and she lay in his arms as they let the magnitude of their decision settle in. As they drifted back to sleep, he began to like the thought of having a child with Fiona. He only hoped he would be the father Fiona expected him to be.

***

As morning approached afternoon, they awoke and realized they had slept through half the day. They went into the office. Fiona checked her e-mail to warm up her brain before starting her assignment. The discussions of the previous night had left her emotionally and mentally spent. The first message was from her mother. "My mom wants to meet your parents," she said to Julian.

"We knew that would happen eventually. When?" Julian sat at his terminal, reviewing information on the first trimester of pregnancy. He should have started on the changes to the network the City Corp had requested at the meeting, but preparing for this new change in his life seemed more important.

"On the fall equinox. She wants to have us all over for dinner," Fiona said.

Julian continued to scan the facts and figures as he answered. "I'll check with my mom." He flipped to a page listing early miscarriage statistics. With a pang of about the many dangers of pregnancy, he made another request. "Could you not tell them about the pregnancy yet?"

"Why?" She saw the flash of nervousness on his face and peeked at his terminal. "What makes you say that?"

"Nothing. I'm just not ready for people to know yet." He changed the screen, then got up from his chair, hoping he was just being overly cautious. Why did he have to look instantly for the downside of every situation? He needed to clear his mind of such negative thoughts, and he had the perfect idea for how to do that. He got up from his chair and walked toward the door.

"Honey, where are you going?" Fiona asked.

"We should celebrate. I'll be right back."

Before Fiona could respond, he was out the door. As she waited for Julian to return, Fiona sent her mother a message saying she and Julian would indeed attend and he would check with his parents. She went along with Julian's wishes and left out any mention of her pregnancy.

Julian returned with a bag from the convenience mart, which he brought into the office. With his free hand, he grabbed one of Fiona hands and pulled her out of her chair. She tried to angle for a view of the bag's contents, but Julian kept it away from her as he led her into the bedroom.

He sat her down on the bed, then handed her the parcel. She unpacked everything onto the bed with a delighted grin. He had bought her favorite sinful snack: a loaf of thick-crusted French bread, a round of brie cheese, and—to top it off— a bottle of ginger ale.

As Fiona went into the kitchen to get two glasses, Julian prepared for the post-feast merriment. He reached over to the bedside table and pulled out a box of condoms to have at the ready. As he set the box on top of the nightstand, he realized they didn't need condoms this time. He picked the box back up, then turned to Fiona as she returned. "We always used these," he said. "How did this happen?"

Fiona set the glasses on the table. "Don't you remember? At Lammas. The night of the bonfire. We didn't use anything." She sat down and grabbed the loaf of bread, tearing off a chunk. She slathered it with the soft cheese as she waited for the lightbulb of recognition to go on.

"Ohhhh." Julian tossed the box aside and took Fiona into his arms. She giggled, stuffing the brie smothered hunk of bread into his mouth as he came towards her. He swallowed it quickly, then moved his mouth over hers, devouring her lips and making her his celebratory feast.

Later that evening, Julian e-mailed his mom to invite her to the fall equinox dinner. Jensa answered that she loved the idea and couldn't wait to meet Fiona's parents. Julian gave Jensa Fiona's mother's e-mail address so she could write personally to thank her for the invitation and find out what she could bring.

***

In the weeks between the invitation and the date of the dinner, Fiona began to struggle with morning sickness. The morning of the dinner, Julian was in the bathroom with Fiona, helping her deal with her nausea. He handed her a glass of water and wiped the perspiration from her brow. "Are you sure you want to go tonight?" he asked.

Miserable, Fiona rested her head against the wall behind her and looked up at him. "Yeah, I'll be okay by then. And if I'm not, we'll tell them I have a little flu or something. I hope they won't be able to tell."

"How could they? You're not showing yet."

"Women, especially moms, know these things. We'll have to tell them soon." As another wave of nausea surged forth, she lurched forward. When she had finished dealing with that bout, she leaned back again.

Julian placed a gentle hand on her flat belly over the place where their child was growing. "You know they'll be thrilled when we do tell them." He kissed her belly and then her nose. "Do you need anything else?"

Her stomach began to settle, and Fiona tilted her head off the wall. She pushed herself up to her feet. "I think it's over for now. I'll get some crackers and juice." Julian followed Fiona into the kitchen. As soon as she opened the refrigerator door, her nausea reared up again. "Julian, I think you're going to have to make the dessert."

Julian moved behind her and wrapped his arms around her waist to support her. She leaned into him. "Okay, you can supervise from the couch. Tell me what to do, and I'll do it."

"Thank you, sweetie. You are too kind. I'll go download the recipe so you can assemble the ingredients." With an amused chuckle, Fiona left the kitchen. This was going to be entertaining.

The rest of the day was filled with mirth. Fiona guided Julian through his first attempt at baking a caramel pumpkin pie from scratch. Her spirits had lifted, and her nausea had subsided by the time they dressed for dinner. "I think I'll be okay tonight," she said.

"We'll leave whenever you need."

Fiona smiled tenderly at Julian's nurturing. In the weeks since she had told him she was pregnant, he had grown more comfortable with the idea of bringing their child into the world. He now doted on her, fussed over her, and satisfied her every whim, all of which she enjoyed very much.

They left the apartment. Silence reigned in the PRTV as they rode to Fiona's parents' station. Neither could think of anything to say to dispel the nervous energy fluttering through them. This was a big day. The grandparents of their child were meeting for the first time. They wanted them to like each other. The PRTV pulled into the station where Julian's parents had just stepped from another car. Julian called out for them to wait. They stopped to greet their son and the woman they hoped would be their daughter-in-law.

Jensa, Julian's mother, moved to give Fiona an affectionate hug. She felt the maternal arms move around her, and some of Fiona's tension released. She returned the gesture. "It's so wonderful to see you again," Jensa said.

Eion, Julian's father, was next in line to hug Fiona. He gave her one of his renowned bear hugs. She pretended to grunt with discomfort. He smiled. "I'm so glad to see my son is taking good care of you," he said as he released her.

"The best!" Fiona and Julian said in unison.

Talking excitedly, the merry band rode the elevator to Fiona's parents' apartment and caught each other up on the news of the last week. Fiona and Julian neglected to mention the most important new development. The elevator doors slid open. The apartment door loomed ahead, and the couple's anxiety returned.

Fiona pushed the button. The outer door opened. A moment later, the inner door slid open with Vyviane, Fiona's mother, standing on the other side. Jensa and Vyviane greeted each other with hugs and delighted squeals, as if they were old college roommates at a reunion. Eion and Gregory, Fiona's father, exchanged a firm handshake.

Vyviane ushered her guests into her comfortable and welcoming apartment. Julian wasn't surprised that it was quite similar to Fiona's in layout and design, although the furniture choices were different. Rather than velvet, Vyviane's couches were upholstered in light red and off-white striped twill and her coffee table was synthetic oak. Vyviane took the dish of potatoes from Jensa and the pie from Julian, then asked Fiona to show them into the sitting room while she took the food into the kitchen. Gregory took their drink orders.

Gregory and Vyviane soon joined their guests in the living room with the drinks and a plate of Fiona's favorite cheese puffs and stuffed kalamata olives. Fiona waited for her mother to set the plate down, then hungrily devoured three cheese puffs. She noticed Vyviane's raised eyebrow and made an excuse about not having had them in awhile.

Jensa saved her from having to make further excuses by resuming the e-mail conversation she and Vyviane had been having all week. They each recalled with fondness the harvest traditions of their youths, which most City-dwellers didn't bother with any more. It had been years since a hay ride had been organized down any Main Street, probably long before Denver had been rehabilitated by the City Corporation.

Jensa's tale from Julian's toddlerhood was met with gales of laughter from Vyviane and Gregory. Eion had taken him down to a park in Old Chicago to see the leaves change color. Julian had been so excited by the three-foot piles of leaves in the park that before Eion could stop him, he had ripped off all his clothes and jumped into the nearest pile so he could "feel the colors." Julian blushed a deep fuschia and shrank down into the sofa.

Vyviane responded with a similar tale of a time when she and Fiona had gone down to the lake in Old San Francisco's Golden Gate Park for a late summer picnic. Four-year-old Fiona had sat on the banks watching the paddleboaters glide across the smooth surface while Vyviane set out their basket. Vyviane had turned her back for just a moment when she heard a splash and turned around to see Fiona floating in the water wearing all her clothes. Fortunately, Fiona had been taught to swim at birth, but Vyviane had still overreacted and yanked her daughter out of the cool water. That was the end of that picnic.

Jensa wiped tears of laughter from her eyes. "I can just see Fiona doing that!

Mortified, Fiona turned a lovely shade of crimson and tried to join Julian under the sofa cushions. She and Julian were rescued from further embarrassment by the chime of the kitchen timer. Dinner was ready. They adjourned to the living room where the table was set with Vyviane's finest china and linens. The guests oohed and aahed as she and Gregory brought the feast out from the kitchen, filling the table with roasted chicken basted with thyme, butternut squash, apple bread, Jensa's basil mashed potatoes, sweet yellow corn, and blackberry wine. Vyviane took a seat at the head of the table and asked Fiona to lead them in a brief blessing of the food.

Fiona thought for a moment, then said, "Lady and Lord, we ask you to bless the abundance we share, on this, the Witches' Thanksgiving. We thank you for the meats, fruits, and grains you have provided us with this season. We promise to continue to honor you, your creatures, and the land through the cycle of the seasons."

The others echoed "Thank you." The dishes were passed around the table. Fiona avoided any she thought might make her gorge rise, until all she had on her plate was skinless chicken, bread and mashed potatoes. She turned down Vyviane's offer of wine, explaining that she had woken up feeling slightly fluish. She didn't want to take alcohol until she felt completely well.

Julian noticed that Fiona's face had grown pale and reached under the table. He squeezed her knee in support, hoping the sumptuous aroma of the meal wasn't nauseating her.

"Are you all right, dear?" Vyviane asked.

"You should have said something. We could have re-scheduled," Jensa said. Vyviane and Jensa exchanged a look that said they weren't buying Fiona's story.

She willed the color to return to her cheeks. "No, no. I'm feeling much better." Vyviane and Jensa dropped the issue without further questioning, but something in Fiona told her they didn't believe her.

The evening continued smoothly after that. The table was filled with lively reminiscences of the days before the disasters. "You know, I don't think I ever asked you when you came here," Vyviane said to Eion and Jensa.

"We came here after the tornadoes. We hated to leave our home, but frankly, after the twister came through town, there wasn't much left of it," Eion said.

Jensa continued the explanation. "When we heard that the reconstruction project would take years, we decided to move here and make a fresh start." Jensa smiled at Eion. "We're very happy we made the decision. I'm going to have to visit New Chicago when they're done, though. I can't wait to see what they did with it." She turned the conversation back to Vyviane. "What about you?"

Vyviane sighed. "We lost almost everything in the quakes." She caressed the Irish lace tablecloth. "My mother's china and this tablecloth were up in the attic. It was the only room with anything salvageable. We moved here as soon as slots opened up for non-construction residents."

"You were here in the stark days, then?" Eion asked.

"Stark is one word for it," Gregory said. "The technology was here, and we lacked nothing material, but there was no sense of community. Vyviane was a key player in changing that." His eyes glowed with pride at his wife's achievements.

Jensa and Eion offered a toast in thanks to Vyviane for making the new city a community. It was Vyviane's turn to blush. She excused herself to get dessert.

"No, we'll get it, Mom," Fiona said. Thwarted, Vyviane had no choice but to sit down and accept the gratitude.

Julian followed Fiona into the kitchen and twirled her into his arms. "This is going well."

"Yeah, better than I'd hoped." She nuzzled his chin with her forehead.

"I think we should tell them."

Fiona pulled back and looked him in the eye. "I think our moms already know."

Julian's eyes widened with surprise. "Really? Then we might as well confirm it." He turned and picked up the caramel pumpkin pie as Fiona retrieved another bottle from the wine cabinet. They steeled themselves with deep breaths, then went back out to the dining table. They were greeted with delighted cries from their parents.

"That looks delicious!" Eion said.

"Well, that's enough for me. What will the rest of you have?" Gregory joked.

Peals of laughter filled the room. Fiona sliced the pie and passed the plates around the table while Julian refilled their glasses. Once everyone had a full plate and glass in front of them, Fiona and Julian stood together and linked hands.

"We have an announcement to make," Julian said, glancing at Fiona one more time. Their parents turned to look at them. Julian took one more deep breath before saying, "I know this will be unexpected, but Fiona is pregnant. We'll be having a baby in about seven and a half months."

Their parents sat in stunned silence for a brief moment before Vyviane slid back her chair and moved to hug Fiona. "Honey, if you're happy, then I'm happy for you." Gregory and Eion ribbed each other with calls of "Gramps" while congratulatory hugs were exchanged between the parents and their two delighted children.

When the families came back to order and settled down at the table, Gregory proposed a toast to the newest member of the family. "May the child in waiting be blessed with intelligence, wit, strength of character, and kindness. May it bind our two families together in peace and love."

Baby chatter dominated the dessert conversation. The discussion continued as they moved back to the living room for after dinner herbal tea. Vyviane and Jensa took turns regaling Fiona and Julian with stories of their own pregnancies. They also gave Fiona advice about what she could expect and how to deal with the nausea and back pain. Vyviane promised to bring a special chamomile tea blend she had concocted during her own pregnancy. Jensa recommended ginger cookies.

As the evening hours drifted by, Fiona grew tired and more than a little nervous about the coming months, thanks in part to Jensa and Vyviane's war stories. She slid down on the couch and rested her head on Julian's shoulder.

He looked down at her and recognized the fatigue in her face. He nudged her to her feet. "I think we should be going," he said to their parents.

Eion glanced at the clock for the first time. The lateness of the hour startled him. "Yes, we should be leaving, too."

The six of them went into the kitchen to divvy up the leftovers. Fiona and Jensa retrieved the dishes they had brought with them. Once everything had been divided and bagged, they moved out to the entryway and hugs were once again passed around the families. Jensa and Vyviane insisted Fiona call them if she needed any advice or just wanted to talk to a woman who'd been through it. Fiona felt tears welling, but wiped them away before anyone noticed. She promised to call if she was ever in need of anything.

Fiona, Julian, and Julian's parents left together and went down to the PRT station. Eion insisted Fiona and Julian take the first car that arrived. Fiona complied without argument. They sank down into their seats. Relief flooding through her, Fiona collapsed against Julian. "We did the right thing telling them. I feel like I have more support now," she said.

"Me, too," Julian said. "This baby is coming into a wonderful family." He dropped a kiss on her forehead and looked down at his beloved a moment longer, then turned to gaze out the window at the Cityscape zipping by. He thought about what it really all meant and reassured himself once more that they were doing the right thing. Fiona winced beside him. He flipped around. "What's wrong?"

Fiona released a slow breath. "Just a twinge. I have them sometimes. The doctor said it's okay." She looked up at him. "I love you."

"I love you." He reached out a hand to stroke her belly. "And I love our baby."

Fiona nodded, a small smile spreading across her lips, and nestled her head back against his shoulder. All was right in her world. Of that, she was positive.

Chapter 5

Goodbye Too Soon

Heart pounding with fear, Julian raced down the long corridor in search of a phone. He had left his satellite phone at home in the rush to get Fiona out of the apartment. Snatching up the receiver of the first phone he found, he pounded out his mother's number.

The shrill ring startled Jensa awake. She glanced at the

clock. It was the middle of the night. She scrambled for her phone, then raised it to her ear.

"Mom, I need you. We're at the hospital. It's the baby."

Jensa sat up, instantly awake. She nudged Eion. "Did you call Vyviane yet?"

"Fiona called her when she woke up with the cramps. She told us to come here."

Jensa was out of bed and tugging a pair of pants out of the dresser. "I'll be there in a few minutes," she said, then disconnected the call. "Eion."

Eion grunted as he woke up. "What?"

"Fiona's in the hospital. The baby." She yanked a shirt over her head. She rushed out of the bedroom.

Eion bolted out of bed. "Wait! I'll come with you." Two minutes later they were out the door.

When they reached the emergency room, they found Julian slumped in a chair in the waiting room, hands clenched, head back, eyes trained on the ceiling. Gregory and Vyviane sat to one side of him, clasping each other's hands for support as they awaited word on their daughter. The grim looks marring their faces told Jensa and Eion everything they needed to know.

Julian straightened as his parents approached. He had started to stand to greet them when the doctor emerged from the hallway. Julian turned toward her. Her blank face didn't portend good news. Julian steeled himself for the dreaded words he already knew were coming.

"I'm sorry," she said. Julian's shoulders slumped. "We did everything we could," she continued, "but we couldn't save the baby. Fiona is going to be all right. She wants to see you. I'll send a nurse to show you back there."

"Thank you," Julian mumbled. Numbing grief descended on him. He reached out for someone, anyone, as his knees went out from under him. Jensa was at his side in seconds. She took him into her arms, holding him like she had when he was a toddler and had scraped his knee, except this was one owie she couldn't fix with a kiss.

Julian didn't notice the nurse's presence until Jensa pulled away and called his attention to her. Gregory and Vyviane offered to go in with him, but Julian thought it would be best if he and Fiona were alone for a few minutes. Their parents nodded and went to sit in the waiting room. Julian followed the nurse down the hall to Fiona's room. He fumbled in his mind for words as he walked. What was he supposed to do? Maybe he should bring her flowers. No. Flowers wouldn't erase what they had lost. What she needed was him.

The nurse stopped at a door. "She's in here."

"Thank you," Julian mumbled again. He stood in front of the door. He took a deep, composing breath, then pushed the button to open the door. He turned to ask the nurse a question, but she was already gone. He stepped into Fiona's room. The sight of her curled up in a ball on the hospital bed, her face turned toward the wall, broke his heart. He crossed the room without a sound and eased into the bed behind her. She slid back into his arms and they lay together. Julian comforted Fiona with his strong arms and gentle touch as sobs wracked her body. "I'm sorry, honey."

"Me, too."

"Our parents are out there. Do you want to see them?"

"No. Don't leave me yet."

Julian hugged her tighter. She nestled down into his arms, letting her grief pull her deeper into it. They stayed in that position until Fiona's doctor came back into the room with instructions and her release papers. Fiona rolled over to take the bottle of painkillers her doctor was offering.

"These are for any residual cramping. Don't take more than one every four hours," she said. She also offered Fiona a sheet of paper listing contact information for a miscarriage support group and a grief help line. "I'm sorry, again. Call me if you have questions." Fiona nodded. "You can stay here as long as you need. There's a wheelchair outside the door when you're ready to go home."

Julian thanked the doctor for her help. After the doctor had left, he asked, "Do you want to stay awhile?" Fiona shook her head no. Julian went to the dresser and retrieved her neatly folded nightclothes. He helped her into her nightgown, being extra careful with her in her weak, drugged state, then walked her over to the wheelchair.

Fiona collapsed in the chair. She held a protective hand over her belly where only hours before there had been a baby, but now all she protected was a gaping emptiness. The gentle clacking of the wheels on the floor announced their progress toward the exit. Fiona prepared herself to see their parents, whom she knew were waiting right outside the door.

The double doors opened and Julian pushed Fiona out into the noisy waiting room. Their parents moved toward them. Fiona looked up into her mother's eyes and saw the tears there, which unleashed another torrent in Fiona. Vyviane leaned down and hugged her daughter, wishing she could take the pain from her. Jensa moved to hold Julian again. He dropped his cheek against his mother's welcoming shoulder while Eion and Gregory stood in the background, waiting to be of some assistance.

After a few minutes, Fiona and Vyviane parted. Fiona attempted to dry her tear-stained face with a tissue as Julian separated from Jensa and took his place behind the wheelchair. No one spoke as the three couples waited for a six-person PRTV. When it arrived, Julian helped Fiona into the first seat while Gregory wheeled the chair to the side of the platform. As soon as Gregory had boarded, Julian entered the destination. The car zoomed away from the hospital. The whisper of the car slipping against the track was the only sound marking their journey. No one knew what to say at this moment.

The PRTV pulled to a stop, and the six of them stepped out of the car. Fiona was still very weak from the medication, and Julian asked Gregory to help him support her as they went up to the apartment. Once inside, Julian took Fiona into their bedroom where he tucked her into the bed they had left in the middle of the night. He straightened the sheets around her, then stroked her cheek for a moment before moving out of the room.

He went into the kitchen. Jensa and Vyviane were making tea and preparing a few casseroles for Julian and Fiona so they wouldn't have to deal with cooking while they mourned the loss of their child. Jensa handed Julian the first cup of chamomile tea to calm his overstressed nerves, then shooed him out to the living room. Gregory and Eion were out there feeling useless, each experiencing the sorrow of the loss of their first grand-child.

Julian joined them on the couch. He reached for Eion's hand and turned to Gregory. "Fiona could use a visit from you."

Gregory responded with a slow nod and left the room. He stopped in the doorway to the bedroom and looked at his only child lying in her bed, her eyes glossed over in a vacant stare. Gregory crept forward, then settled on the bed beside her. Fiona turned to face him. He brushed the hair from her eyes.

"I'm so sorry this happened. I know how much it hurts," he said. He saw the question in Fiona's eyes. "It happened to your mother and me." Shock crossed Fiona's face. She reached out to hug her father. He wrapped his arms around her and brushed his chin across her hairline. She buried her face in his chest. "I guess your mother never told you. It was before you were born."

"No, she never told me."

Vyviane peeked her head around the corner to check on Fiona. When she saw her husband there she backed away, not wishing to intrude. Fiona glanced up and beckoned her in. Vyviane entered the room and sat on the other side of Fiona, reaching out to stroke her long hair. "How are you feeling, honey?"

"It hurts." Tears began to stream down Fiona's face once more.

As she watched her daughter cry, sympathetic tears welled in Vyviane's eyes. She wished again that there was some way she could take away all the pain, both physical and emotional, that Fiona was feeling now and would continue to feel in the days and weeks to come.

Fiona's sorrow receded after a bout of heavy crying. Julian came into the room with a tray of food. Gregory and Vyviane got up to leave the grieving couple alone. Vyviane kissed Fiona's forehead and followed her husband out of the room.

"Are you hungry?" Julian asked as he set the tray on the night table.

Fiona responded with an almost imperceptible nod. She winced in pain as Julian helped her sit up and fluffed pillows behind her back to support her. Julian set the tray on the bed over her lap, then went around to the other side of the bed to sit with her. They sat in silence and ate the casserole their mothers had made for them. When Fiona was done, Julian took the tray and set it back on the night table. She winced as she slid back down into the bed. Julian grimaced, She rolled over onto her side, and he knelt on the floor to face her. He took one of her hands in his, caressing her face with his other hand.

"I'm sorry," Fiona said, fresh tears threatening to pour.

"Sweetie, it's not your fault. I love you as much as I did before." Her tears raised more crushing sorrow within him. He rested his head on the edge of the bed. Fiona stroked his hair while he cried, gently, finally letting himself express his pain over their loss. When his sobs faded, he lifted his head up. They moved their lips together for a gentle kiss and held there, lips touching but not moving, the tender pressure reassuring them that somehow this would all pass.

Their kiss parted, and Fiona rested her head back on the pillow. "Do you want to sleep?" Julian asked. Fiona nodded yes. "Me, too. I'll show our parents out." Julian rose to his feet. Fiona closed her eyes as he went out to the living room.

Their parents halted their quiet conversation. Julian explained that he and Fiona were ready to go to sleep. He thanked them for coming to the hospital and for their help once they got back to the apartment. They each gave him a supportive hug and made him promise to call if he or Fiona needed anything. Grateful for the help, he said he would. He watched the door close behind them and then turned to make his way back into the bedroom.

When he approached the bed, Fiona was already asleep. He undressed as quietly as possible and slid into bed beside her, being careful not to disturb her. He dropped a kiss on the back of her shoulder, then curled up in bed. Despite the sun rising in the window, he fell asleep as soon as his head hit the pillow.

They slept through the next day, only occasionally stirring from the bed to consume cold casserole and water, then returning to sleep away their misery. Their parents were kind enough to call into work for both of them. They were safe in their cocoon, left alone to deal with their sadness. On the third day after the miscarriage, they emerged from bed and went into the living room to find a brief distraction from the grief, but nothing could steal their minds away from the sorrow.

They took turns caring for each other in the most intense moments, and spent the rest of the next week moving between grief and numbness. When Fiona had first decided to have the baby, she'd spent hours imagining what it would look like. Would it have her eyes, Julian's nose? What would they name it? Now she wondered how it was possible to so deeply miss a child that hadn't been born yet. It would never have a name. And she would never know which one of them it would have looked like.

Julian questioned if he would ever feel ready to have a child. He had been unprepared for the strong love he had developed for the baby in the last two months. His sense of loss was incredible. He never wanted to go through that again. He recalled the statistics he had called up the day they had decided to keep the baby. Could his negative thoughts after reading them be responsible for the miscarriage? He wiped away that thought. No, this wasn't his fault, it was just a sad coincidence, and maybe a message that they weren't ready.

***

Three weeks after her miscarriage, Fiona's physical pain was gone, but she still felt empty inside. She decided the best way to fill that void would be to work. She needed something mentally stimulating to distract her from the flood of emotion she couldn't get past. As she called her computer back from its long sleep, she noticed the date on the pop-up calendar. It was late October. Forgetting her work, she went over to the sofa where Julian was reading. He set down his page-viewer and pulled her into his arms when she sat down beside him.

"Honey, I just realized that Samhain is only a week away. I think we should do some kind of ritual to say goodbye to our baby."

Julian kissed Fiona's hair. "I like that idea. Should we invite our parents?"

Fiona thought about that. "No. I know they're hurting too, but this was our baby."

He nodded in understanding. "Okay, just tell me what to do."

"Don't I always?" she joked, smiling up at him.

For the first time in three weeks, he laughed. He hugged her closer to him. After a few minutes, she slid out of his arms. She went back to her computer to start her work while Julian went back to his reading.

They gathered the items they would need for the ritual during the next week, each baby-related item bringing new sorrow. Then Halloween was upon them. Fiona prepared foods that she thought the baby would have liked. She asked Julian to vacuum and to set out the table they would be using for their altar.

Just before midnight, Fiona and Julian went into the bathroom where they took a ritual bath together, cleansing their bodies and preparing their souls for the night ahead. They washed each other with a special soap Fiona had purchased from a Pagan store, then helped each other dry off. They rubbed their pressure points with oil made from neroli and spikenard oils and went out to the living room to begin the ritual. Fiona carried a printout of her ultrasound with her. Julian held a small stuffed animal he had purchased a few days after Fiona had told him about the baby. He had planned for it to be the child's first toy.

Fiona had already set the plates of offering food on the altar, and they knelt before it. A photo-viewer displaying a recent picture of them sat in the center of the altar. It had been taken on the Witches' Thanksgiving, just after they had revealed their news to their parents. The photo brought back memories of the joyous day and the love they had felt for each other and the baby during the brief pregnancy.

They linked hands and took deep grounding breaths, pushing their energy down into the earth to use its support during the emotional rite ahead. Fiona stood, then walked clockwise around the altar to cast the protective circle of energy around them. She welcomed the quarters and asked Persephone, protectress of the dead, to join them. A calm came over Julian as a presence he hadn't known before arrived. As the Goddess took her place in the ritual, Fiona invited the spirit of their lost child to join them. The arrival of the new presence brought a great sadness with it.

The ultrasound printout rested in Fiona's hands. She

placed it on the altar before her. "Sweet baby, this is and will always be my only picture of you, but I will carry you in my heart forever. Be safe as you pass back into the Summerlands—" Fiona's voice cracked. She had to stop. A sob escaped her lips. As the pain welled up in her again, she shuddered. Julian reached out for her. She crumpled in his arms and cried, wetting their skin with her tears. As her tears subsided, she took a deep breath and calmed herself down enough to continue.

Julian turned back to the altar. He set the stuffed animal on the altar beside the printout. "You weren't in our lives for long, but I already loved you more than I ever thought possible. I will miss you for years to come. I hope you will find your way back to us someday." His voice broke as he finished the sentence. He bowed his head in sadness. Fiona reached over and stroked his back while he released it.

After a moment, Julian lifted his head back up and looked to Fiona with a slight nod of thanks. Together they picked up the baby book they had purchased only days before the miscarriage. They placed it on top of the altar. When it had arrived, they had each made one entry. The entries told the baby what the first few weeks of the pregnancy had been like and everything they hoped to share with and teach it. Fiona opened the book to two handwritten letters tucked inside—one from Fiona, the other from Julian—that they had written the day before the ritual. They read their letters aloud to the child and expressed the sentiments they had been unable to speak aloud until this moment. They told the child what it had meant to them and how deeply they mourned the loss of it from their lives. They lit the letters from the black candle burning at the center of the altar and dropped them in a miniature cauldron. As they watched the letters burn, they poured all their pain into the flames.

They sat in the circle holding hands and staring at the unseen child's energy as the fire burned down. When all that remained of the letters was ash, they took a bit of the food Fiona had prepared and offered it to the Goddess Persephone, the baby, and then to each other. They ate the morsels in silence. Then it was time to end the ritual. They focused their attention on the child's energy.

"Sweet child, our first, thank you for coming to us tonight. Go in peace and love," Fiona said. Sensing that the child had chosen to stay awhile longer, Fiona thanked Persephone for her protection and bade her farewell, then dismissed the quarters and opened the circle.

After taking another bite of the bread to ground them back in the mortal realm, they got up from the altar, leaving it set up in honor of the unborn child. Julian reached for Fiona. She moved to him, slipping her arm around his waist as he did the same. Arm in arm, they moved into the bedroom and stopped at the foot of the bed.

They turned to face each other and gazed into each other's eyes, seeing the sorrow still carried deep inside and wondering how best to comfort each other. Julian closed his eyes and lowered his lips to Fiona's, an unspoken question in the gentle pressure. They explored each other's lips as if for the first time. Then Fiona answered his question with a stronger kiss. The kiss blossomed into passion, offering them the pure sensation that could overwhelm their grief. Julian turned and lowered Fiona onto the bed. He looked down at her, another question in his eyes. Her answer was to reach up and pull him over her. With slow, gentle strokes and caresses, they began to make tentative love for the first time since the miscarriage.

With Fiona's orgasm came a fresh flood of tears. The pain of her loss ripped through her once more. She cried and cried, releasing the last well of grief that had been locked inside her, letting go of the sorrow and guilt she had clung to since the night she'd lost the baby. Julian cradled her in his arms while she cried, muffling her sobs with his chest. As the night wore on, the sobs turned to screams of anger as she railed at the Gods for taking her baby, then let go of everything that was left in her.

Just before sunrise, her cries and screams spent, Fiona and Julian slipped into exhausted sleep. They awoke a few hours later and moved together again, resuming their lovemaking without speaking. This time there was no great outpouring of grief as they both reached gentle orgasms. They lay back to rest in each other's arms.

"I feel at peace now," Fiona said. "Or, at least, the crushing sorrow is gone."

"It doesn't pierce as sharply as it did yesterday," Julian murmured.

"I want to make an altar for her—it feels like a her—and leave it up until Yule."

"I'd like that." He climbed out of bed and handed her a robe. "We should do it now."

Fiona followed him out to the living room. They cleared off the top of a small table to make a place for the altar. Fiona found a sheet of black cloth embossed with white stars that would serve as an altar cloth. Julian set the photo-viewer in a corner. Fiona propped the ultrasound against the center of the wall behind the table. They placed a small stuffed animal in the other corner and laid the book in front of the ultrasound. Julian carefully set the cauldron holding the ashes of their letters next to the book. To finish the altar, Fiona went into the kitchen and got a black candle from the refrigerator. She returned to the altar. She and Julian held the candle in their hands to charge it with energy to ease the transition of their baby back into the Summerlands where it would wait for its proper parents.

Fiona lit the candle. They knelt in front of the altar, watching the candle burn. A cold breeze fluttered across their lips like soft baby kisses. Then there was nothing. The room was empty except for the two of them. They were now left to resume their lives without their child.

Julian turned to face Fiona. "She'll be okay. It wasn't our time yet."

Fiona nodded. "I know." She paused. "I did learn something from all this though."

"What's that?"

"Whenever I felt pain or sadness, I asked the Goddess to come to me, and She did. I think Wicca is my path. I'm going to start seriously studying it now."

Julian, too, had felt the Goddess' presence these last few weeks. "I'd like to join you. Is that okay with you?"

A bright smile reached Fiona's eyes for the first time since the miscarriage. "Yeah, that'd be nice."

Chapter 6

Once Upon a Yule Night Clear

There was that sound again. The strange noise emanating from down the hall. First it was a swishy, sliding sound, followed by a woody thump and feminine grunt. Julian swiveled in his chair to investigate the disturbance just as the inner door to the apartment slid open. Fiona stumbled in backwards dragging a seven-foot potted noble fir.

Leaping out of his seat, Julian raced over to help her tip the tree up onto its base. "I didn't know we could buy trees yet." It was only the first week of December.

"I didn't either till I walked past the tree lot." She laughed. "This one cried out for me to make it the first one off the lot."

"You should have called. I would've helped you carry it."

"I didn't need to. They popped it right into a PRTV for me. But I'll tell you what . . . ." Her sentence trailed off with a hint of something exciting to come. "You can have the honor of positioning the tree while I get the decorations." She pointed toward the far corner, then scurried out of the room before he could argue.

Julian stared down the tree, trying to figure out how best to wrestle the large fir into the corner. Taking a deep breath, he bent low at the knees and wrapped his arms around the middle of the trunk. With a grunt, he lifted it an inch off the floor, then tottered rapidly across the room to shove it into the corner. The tree in place, he stepped back and noticed that bits of branch and bark had become attached to his sweater. He swatted at them, attempting unsuccessfully to free them from the knit pseudo-wool. He decided to wait and see if Fiona really wanted the tree there.

A sharp shriek came from the bedroom. He rushed in to see Fiona standing on a foot stool draped in long strands of tree lights that had tumbled from the top shelf. Their box rested on her head. Julian burst out laughing. She glared at him through the tiny lights she was trying to pick her way out of. Julian stopped her.

"Wait! I want to take a picture." He dashed back out of the room. Fiona allowed him to snap only one photo before demanding that he free her from her wire cage.

He lifted the box from her head, then untied the tangled strands of lights, neatly coiling them as he went. The lights tucked back into their box, Julian went up the ladder. He handed the remaining boxes down to Fiona, being careful not to drop one and have an embarrassing photo of his own taken.

They carried the boxes of various sizes out to the tree. Fiona approved the tree location and position. Julian started to brush the tree bits from his sweater again, but Fiona reminded him he had to put the lights on.

"Do you want eggnog?" she asked.

Julian nodded. While Fiona went into the kitchen to pour them each a glass and grab some cookies, he plugged in all the light strands to check for burned out bulbs. By the time she returned, Julian had linked the strings together. All the bulbs glowed brightly, and the strings were ready to be put on the tree.

Fiona set down the tray, then handed Julian his glass. She held hers aloft. "To our first Yule."

Julian smiled. "To our first Yule. The first of many."

They clinked glasses, then set to work wrapping the fidgety strands around the fir's full branches. Once they had finished arranging the lights in all the tree's nooks and crannies, Fiona let Julian pick the pine needles off his sweater. She settled on the floor to unpack her ornaments and eat more cookies.

Julian picked the last needle off his sweater, then joined her on the floor. He unwrapped a particularly dilapidated ornament and was about to put it back in the box when Fiona stopped him.

"No, it has to go on the tree."

"But the paint's chipped, and it's missing pieces."

Fiona took the ornament from him, smiling as she remembered her first ornament shopping trip when she was a child. She had scoured every tree in the store in search of just the right ornament and had found this wooden ballerina, with pink, red, and white feathers sticking out of the top of her cap and frilly lace glued to the bottom of her painted pink tutu. Every year after that her parents had taken her to the store again to buy another ornament. At the end of every holiday season, she had carefully wrapped each ornament in a thick layer of tissue. When the earthquake had come, only one had broken, thanks to the fat cushion of tissue and toilet paper around each one.

She reached up and hung the ornament on the tree, then went back to unwrapping the rest. Each decorated glass ball, carved figurine, or molded metal piece marked a stage in Fiona's growth and reflected her mood and spirit for the year she had chosen it. They served as a telescope into her childhood. She told the story of each one to Julian as it was uncovered, then handed him a few to hang.

Julian protested that the ornaments were special and he shouldn't hang them, but Fiona insisted that he help. They sang Yule tunes as they arranged the ornaments on the branches. Once every ornament was suspended from a strong branch, Julian helped Fiona mount the star at the very top of the tree. Her parents had given it to her the first Yule she had her own apartment. They stepped back to admire their handiwork. "It needs something," Fiona said.

Julian raised his eyebrows. "It looks pretty full to me."

Fiona shook her head and scampered to her backpack. She pulled a tissue-wrapped object from the bag and carried it back to Julian. He took it from her with a questioning look, then carefully unfolded the delicate paper. Nestled inside was a small, bead-encrusted frame holding a printed photo taken of them at Beltane. At the bottom, the pearl seed beads spelled out "Fiona and Julian, Year One."

Julian turned toward the tree with a wide grin. He hung the ornament in the exact center of the front of the tree, then arranged the needles around it just so to frame the ornament. He stood back to admire the tree and pulled Fiona into his arms for a long, loving hug. "Thank you," he said. "That means so much to me."

As Fiona rested her cheek on Julian's shoulder, she noticed that the tree skirt was still in the ornament box. She went to retrieve it. As she unfolded the red and green quilted circle, a smaller cloth she had used in years past to decorate a small table of winter figurines tumbled out of it. She unfolded it. It would make a perfect altar cloth. At the thought of an altar, she stopped what she was doing. She dropped the tree skirt on the floor as she turned to face the altar to their unborn child. Julian followed her gaze. He knew what she had in mind.

She knew from a place deep in her heart that it was time to take down the mournful reminder and replace it with hope for the future. She took one nervous step toward the altar, then looked toward Julian. He moved to her. They clasped hands in support as they approached the altar.

After a silent prayer to the Goddess to give her strength, Fiona plucked the ultrasound from the altar and slipped it inside the unfinished baby book, which she handed to Julian. She lifted the cauldron of ashes from its place on the altar. Being careful not to spill it, she carried it into the kitchen with the black candle that she had burned down over the last month. As she emptied the contents of the cauldron and the candle's remains into a plastic bag, she made a promise she would bury it outside as soon as she found a suitable place. She paused before she returned to the living room, unsure how to proceed. She didn't want to get rid of the altar cloth, stuffed animal, and baby book, but she also didn't want to keep them as a constant reminder of what she had lost.

Feeling much the same way, Julian had already formulated a solution by the time she returned. She watched as he set the baby book back on the center of the altar cloth. He picked up the animal and held it to his chest for a moment, breathing deeply, then set it on top of the book. He turned back the corners of the cloth and moved the photo-viewer and candleholder to the table surface before folding the altar cloth around the book and animal, creating a neat package that could be set aside until they were ready to part with it.

Satisfied with the solution, Fiona took the package from him and tucked it into a box, which she carried to the closet. She placed it way in the back where it would be hidden until a later date. While she was gone, Julian retrieved the altar cloth from the floor and stretched it across the altar table. He meticulously smoothed out the wrinkles. Fiona returned, purposely changing her mood to a more festive one. She dug deep into her box of decorations to find her silver reindeer candleholders and red and green holly candles. She also found painted ceramic figurines of a wintry Mother Nature and Father Time. She arranged the candleholders at the back corners of the altar and set the figurines between them.

She turned back to see Julian rummaging through the box. He unwrapped a faded, tattered cloth that protected a sunwheel. The perfect centerpiece for the altar. Their altar complete, Julian nodded in appreciation, then started to go back to the couch.

"We're not done yet," Fiona said.

He turned back. "What else do we have to do?"

"You need to get a ladder. And I need to get the garlands ready to go up."

While Julian went down to the storage room, Fiona opened the box of preserved fir branches. They had been strung together to make a long strand, wrapped in red velvet ribbon, and tied with large, stiff bows. When Julian returned, she granted him the task of hanging the garlands while she stood on the floor and dictated their placement. As they bickered about how low the garlands should dip, all traces of their grief passed. Their festive moods returned. The remainder of the evening was spent enjoying eggnog spiked with brandy and exchanging teasing hints about possible Yule gifts.

***

A week later, Fiona was hard at work designing the posters for the City Corporation's spring promotion of its new shared garden plots. The plots would be planted at street level, another attempt to draw the nature-shy residents out of their apartments. Fiona's thoughts about what she would do with such a plot were interrupted by the arrival of an e-mail. She flipped over to it. As she read it, her breath caught. She downloaded it into her pageviewer, which she carried to Julian, who sat reviewing project notes on the couch.

With an offhand glance, he took the proffered page-viewer and skimmed the e-mail. He read it again more carefully before looking up at her. "Do you want to go?" he asked.

Fiona couldn't decide whether or not she could handle the emotions a Wiccaning might bring up. Would be too painful to participate in a naming ceremony for a friend's child when she had just lost her own baby? She did love Wiccanings and Suzanne was a good friend. It wouldn't be right to miss such a special occasion. "Yes. I think I do. I haven't seen Suzanne's baby yet," she said, trying to hide the hint of nervousness with excitement.

Julian saw through her bravado and pulled her into his lap. "As long as you think you'll be okay, honey. I'll help you shop for the gift online tomorrow."

Fiona kissed his forehead and slid off his lap. "Thank you, sweetie. I appreciate that. You know they just opened the new stores. Why don't we shop there?" She went back to her terminal to return Suzanne's message before she lost her courage to attend the ritual—and to avoid Julian's eye-rolling at the idea of going to a store.

***

The next afternoon, after much cajoling and coaxing by Fiona and whining and complaining from Julian, Fiona dragged him down to the new shopping quarter. Although everything sold in the stores was available through the network portals, Fiona was eager to visit the new boutiques the City Corporation had opened to encourage residents like Julian to leave their apartments more often. Fiona remembered how much she had enjoyed shopping in Old San Francisco's Union Square. She hoped the shopping quarter would live up to her memories.

As they passed by a Pagan shop Fiona made a mental note to check it out later. She and Julian went into the baby store next door. The little bell over the door jingled to announce their entrance. The sweet scent of baby powder and potpourri greeted them. The white shelves were piled high with fuzzy receiving blankets in soft shades of pink, yellow, blue, and lavender, and with hand-woven quilts crafted from a wide range of fabrics and motifs. Fiona caressed the tiny dresses and boys' suits that hung from the center racks. She should have been buying one for her own child. She took a breath to hold back the tears that threatened to come, and turned in search of Julian. He was standing at a small bassinet painted with stars and moons. Inside was the perfect gift for a Witch baby: a cotton quilt pieced together from patches of sun, moon, and star print fabrics.

As they left the store with their purchase, Julian put his arm around Fiona's waist. He kissed the top of her head. "Are you okay?"

Fiona nodded. "It wasn't too bad, actually."

From behind them, Sarah's strident voice halted their pleasant afternoon. "Don't tell me you're having a child with her!"

Steeling himself for another onslaught, Julian's arm tightened around Fiona's stiffened back. They continued to walk away from her.

Sarah chased after them, struggling to keep the shock and disgust from her voice. "It's not too late! Her demonspawn won't survive, and then you can come to us! We can help you!" The leader wouldn't have sent her on a spy mission to the Pagan store, Sarah thought, if he hadn't had some hint that she would have another chance to save Julian. And then Julian would be hers again.

Fiona's shoulders shook with anger and sorrow. She bent her head. Raising a hand to her forehead, she willed herself not to appear weak in front of Sarah. Julian spun around, placing himself between Sarah and Fiona. "If you upset her again, I will turn you in to the City police. You and your leader. Leave us alone."

"I can't, Julian. Don't you see that we're meant for each other? The leader knows that, too, or he wouldn't have asked for your help."

Fiona turned. "What?" She looked at Julian. He hadn't mentioned that.

"It's nothing," he said to Fiona in a soothing tone. "Just another deranged scheme." He turned to Sarah, his voice becoming strained and angry. "Go, get out of here. I meant what I said." He spun back around and put his arm around Fiona again, leading her away from Sarah. Once they were safely on the PRTV, he explained about the run-in he'd had with Sarah the same day Fiona had told him about her pregnancy. In the stress of that night, he'd forgotten all about it. He assured her that it was nothing. Sarah wasn't dangerous, just irritating.

They returned to the apartment. Julian offered to play a game with Fiona as a diversion from the emotional afternoon, but she assured him she was okay. Besides, she had to bless the gift. She set the quilt on the altar and booted up her page-viewer to scan through her new magick books. She searched the texts for a ritual she could use or adapt as a blessing for the quilt. She settled on one that would allow her to imbue it with properties that would then be passed on to the child.

She asked Julian not to disturb her for the next few minutes, then lit two candles. She cast a circle around herself and the altar. Not yet familiar with the individual Gods and Goddesses for birth and childhood, she invoked the God and Goddess at large and placed her hands on the blanket. After a centering breath, she asked Them to bestow her chosen gifts on the blanket. The energy flowed from her tingling fingers and into the blanket. When the flow slowed, she knew the quilt was charged. She thanked the Lord and Lady for their assistance, then released Them and the circle. She wrapped the quilt back up in the tissue, then set it back in the shopping bag for safekeeping until the day of the Wiccaning.

***

The afternoon of the Wiccaning was clear and beautiful. A light winter frost made the air crisp, but the sun was out and did its best to mitigate the chill. Many of Fiona's pagan friends greeted Fiona and Julian at Suzanne's apartment. Fiona had not most of them seen since Lammas. Fiona made her apologies for having been so out of touch. She chose not to state the reason for her long absence. A few of them already knew, but she didn't want to put a damper on the festivities for the rest, especially Suzanne, the beaming mother of the four-month-old Diana.

After an hour of mingling, Lady Celesta called the jubilant friends and family members to order. They formed a circle with Suzanne and her daughter at the center next to a small altar and chair. Lady Celesta led the gathering through the casting of the circle and the calling of the quarters. She invoked Diana, Suzanne's matron Goddess, and her twin, Apollo. Suzanne held her child out for all to see and said, "I proclaim this child shall be called Diana. She shall be raised in the tradition of the Goddess, until such time as she chooses her own path. May the Lady and Lord bless her now and forever. Blessed be." The guests echoed the sentiments, then began bestowing their gifts on the child.

Lady Celesta was first. She stepped forward from her place in the circle to present the girl with a tiny pentagram. "Diana, I bless you with wisdom and second sight." She was rewarded with a bright smile from the baby.

When the circle came around to Fiona and Julian, he set the quilt on the altar. Fiona said, "We bless you with imagination and creativity." The quilt had been charged with these same traits. The baby flashed another smile and gurgled in a way that made Fiona think she knew this. They stepped back to their places in the circle, and the baby's grandmother stepped forward with her gift of kindness. The ceremony continued until all the gifts had been bestowed. Lady Celesta offered the child a final blessing to seal the gifts and welcome her into the Pagan community.

Following the ceremony, the revelers feasted on warm glazed turkey, honey ham, full-bodied cheese fondue with cubed French bread, rich chocolate fondue with chopped winter fruit, and a crescent moon cake with Diana's name printed across the top in beautiful calligraphy. As everyone enjoyed the feast, Suzanne was afforded several chances to take a much-needed rest by her guests, who clamored to hold the well-behaved child.

Fiona was deep in conversation with another friend when a soft tap on her shoulder called her attention and Diana was placed in her arms. The well-meaning woman smiled, then moved away as a stunned Fiona stared at the gorgeous baby girl. Diana's clear blue eyes twinkled and Fiona's heart started to fold in. Diana reached out and closed her tiny fist around a tendril of Fiona's dark hair. Fiona let out a long, slow breath to halt her tears. She had not been prepared to hold the girl.

Julian was standing next to Fiona's chair and heard the breath. He looked at Fiona. He recognized the pain in her eyes and bent down, whisking the child away. He carried her over to Suzanne with an explanation that Fiona wasn't feeling well and didn't want to make Diana sick. Suzanne accepted the explanation without question. She shot Fiona a sympathetic look as Julian returned to Fiona's side and helped her to her feet. He bent his head, kissing her softly on the cheek as he whispered, "We should go." Fiona responded with a mute nod as she rose. They said rapid good-byes to Fiona's friends and promised to keep in better touch. Julian slid Fiona's arms into her coat, then placed his arm around her waist to guide her out the door.

As they settled onto the PRTV, Fiona rested her head on Julian's shoulder. Her eyes slid closed. He reached over and ran his fingertips over her forehead and her cheek. She looked up at him and answered his motion with a soft kiss, then rested her head back on his shoulder for the duration of the ride. He turned to watch out the window as twilight turned to night. The stars shone brightly above the tall buildings.

Fiona stayed silent as they rode the elevator to the apartment. She tumbled through confusion, fear, desire, longing, and sorrow. None reached out to the forefront and took hold. She had to sort through them together to figure out what they meant. She dropped her coat in a pile at the door, then moved to the couch. She sat with shoulders slumped and her head bowed.

Julian followed her, unsure how to help her. "The Wiccaning really affected you today, didn't it?" He instantly regretted the redundant question.

"I realized what we don't have," she said, her voice flat.

"Honey, it will happen again." Julian reached out to stroke her hair. He tried to pull her into his arms.

Fiona resisted and moved her hand to block the motion of his hand. She curled his fingers in hers, pulling their hands down between them. She gathered up her courage, then looked him straight in the eyes. "I don't want to wait."

The statement startled Julian, but he masked it with feigned confusion. "What do you mean?"

"I want to start trying. Really trying." Even she was amazed by the statement, but she meant it. That was the real reason she had been so upset when she'd held Diana. She searched Julian's face for a glimmer of happiness or agreement, but found none.

Instead, he answered with downcast eyes and a grim pallor. After a long pause, he looked up at her, his eyes barely meeting hers. "I can't."

"It's time. I feel it deep inside me," she said, willing him to understand.

"I . . . I just can't. I'm not ready."

"You were before."

"That was different. We had to make the best choice we could. And after what happened . . . I can't go through that again." He bowed his head.

"It won't happen again," she said, trying to console him.

He looked up at her. "You can't know that."

"But I do. I do. I don't know how, but it's there." She was bordering on pleading.

"No. Not yet. Not now. Let's give it time."

"I can't. And if you don't agree, well then . . . ." She paused. Was she willing to go this far? "Then I don't think we can continue." She looked into Julian's eyes and recognized them as those of a child whose favorite toy just fell onto the PRT tracks. She knew that hurt but couldn't think of anything to make it go away. She was sure about what she wanted.

Julian slumped back onto the couch, defeated. Fiona stood and shuffled out of the room. The bedroom door closed behind her, and although it made the same soft click it always made, to Julian it sounded like the clang of an iron lock. As he sat in the apartment he shared with Fiona, the memories of the eight months that constituted their life together drifted through his mind. He contemplated what his life would be like without her in it. Without them in it. His life had become one with hers in an incredibly short amount of time. She was the woman he wanted. The only woman.

He pictured the joyful look on her face when he had agreed to have the first child. He remembered how excited he'd been when he'd finally accepted the decision and begun to imagine what the child would be like. He had looked forward to the opportunity to pass on his ideas and to see the world through his child's eyes. He had wanted to experience the growth of a life he had created with Fiona and then to grow old with her and watch their child continue the cycle.

When that child had died, he had been heartbroken. Still

was heartbroken. Could he risk that again? He hadn't checked the odds on second miscarriages, and even if he had, would he trust them? But he also didn't know the odds on finding another woman like Fiona. Things had moved so quickly between them that he hadn't had time to think. That had been good, but a part of him wanted to spend more time settling into their relationship before they added another person to it.

In the bedroom, Fiona rolled onto her side and stared at the empty space where Julian should have been. She regretted saying those last words. She loved him. She didn't want to start over with someone new. There had never been a Julian for her before and she didn't think there would be again. If he was truly not ready to have a baby now, she would go along with his choice and wait. They had time together, time to enjoy life with and without a baby. Holding Diana had reawakened her maternal drive, but perhaps it wasn't the right time after all. Maybe it was just the longing for the child she had lost rising to the surface again. That pain had been almost too much for her to bear. She understood why Julian was hesitant to open himself up to that again. It wasn't fair of her to force him to do it. Not yet. The time would come.

She turned onto her other side and mentally practiced her speech of surrender. The soft swish of the door opening sent panic racing through her veins. Julian padded across the room and sat hard on his side of the bed. Her heart racing, Fiona lay motionless on her side of the bed, hoping he hadn't noticed the quickness of her breath.

Julian sat silently, then lifted his legs onto the mattress and lay on his back. One hand slipped under the covers and slid across the chasm of the bed to pinch Fiona's bottom ever so faintly. Fiona smiled in relief and released her breath. She stretched her leg across the bed in search of his calf and her heel made soft contact with it. In the dim light of midnight, Fiona and Julian rolled over to face each other. They moved into each other's arms. "I'm sorry…I didn't mean—we can wait."

The firm pressure of Julian's lips on hers quelled Fiona's apology. "Thank you," he whispered into her mouth. "We have plenty of time. We will get there eventually, I promise." He pulled her back in and rolled her over, crushing her beneath him as her shoulder had crushed the flower on Beltane. Their bodies melted together as they moved against each other to repair the damage the argument had done.

***

Over breakfast the next morning, the glow of a night of lovemaking cast a bright light across their skin. Their conversation turned to the upcoming holidays. Between bites of his blueberry muffin, Julian told Fiona that his family wasn't religious. All they did on Christmas was exchange gifts and have a big dinner. Fiona reached across the table to wipe a crumb off the crevice of his mouth as she explained that her family celebrated the Pagan holiday of Yule. Intrigued, Julian asked what that entailed.

"Well, we start our celebration with a traditional feast, then we make promises to the Gods for the coming year, then we exchange gifts. We finish the evening by burning the Yule log that served as the dinner table centerpiece the year before."

"That sounds nice, honey. I think we should have both our families over here for Yule."

"Sweetie, that's a wonderful idea! I'll message our moms in a little while." She brushed her foot against his shin and reached for his hand. "But first, I think we need to go into the bedroom and make up some more."

"I'm all for more making up!" he said as they scurried into the bedroom.

Following their post-breakfast interlude, Fiona sent invitations to her and Julian's mothers for Yule. She was thrilled when they both said they would come and asked what they could bring. She assigned each of them a course of the feast, then left the rest up to them.

Knowing Julian's need for clear instructions, she typed up the procedure for drilling the candleholder holes into the Yule log and wrapping it in holly leaves and mistletoe. She informed him that it was his task to build it. He accepted it as his duty as the man of the house, in exchange for her promise to take care of the gifts for their friends.

The remaining days leading up to Yule passed in a flurry

of gift-buying and log-hunting, Julian being the perfectionist he was, and brief but merry visits with friends not often seen. Fiona and Julian spent much of the two weeks bustling from one event to another and shopping in between. They received an invitation to attend Lady Celesta's Yule gathering, but Fiona regretfully declined. It was the same night as her first family dinner party.

***

The morning of the dinner, Fiona dragged Julian into the kitchen bright and early to help prepare their portion of the feast. Everything had to be perfect. She wanted to make a good impression on their parents, even though she knew that their mothers wouldn't care how the meal turned out. The two of them danced around each other in the kitchen as Fiona stuffed the big bird, then put Julian in charge of maneuvering it into the oven under her watchful eye.

Once the turkey was in the oven and cooking, Fiona moved into the dining room to set the table for the occasion. She asked Julian to get down the good dishes that her parents had given her when she'd first moved out of their home, while she laid out her favorite holiday tablecloth. Fiona flipped her page-viewer to a place setting diagram, then arranged the glasses and silverware as shown. For the final touch, she retrieved the Yule log Julian had painstakingly drilled and decorated from the mantle and placed it on the table for her centerpiece.

Fiona went into the bedroom to dress for dinner. As she slid on her shoes, she glanced at the clock. Their parents were due any moment, and she still hadn't set out the ornament bowl. She dashed into the kitchen for a glass bowl, then out to the living room. She arranged the glass ball ornaments she had purchased for this purpose inside the bowl with six strips of parchment paper. The outer door opened, announcing the arrival of her guests.

Julian slid open the inner door and greeted their gift and food-laden parents. He took their fathers into the kitchen to drop off the food while Fiona ushered their mothers into the living room to unload their bags of brightly wrapped packages. Fiona's mother held out another bag with their special Yule ornaments and the Yule log from the year before. While her mother placed the ornaments on the tree, Fiona set the log on the mantle over the fireplace.

Gregory, Eion, and Julian emerged from the kitchen. Hugs were exchanged around the room as the three families settled in the living room. They feasted on warm brie baked inside puff pastry and slathered in French bread. Vyviane's eyes rolled back in pure pleasure as the delicious morsel melted on her tongue.

The holiday chatter began with brief updates on what everyone had been up to since their last gathering, then turned to a round of storytelling. Jensa was the first to mention the old days as she recalled the year Julian, determined to see this Santa he had heard so much about, had tried to stay awake all night. He had arranged a stiff chair next to the fireplace and loaded himself with books and video games. He'd positioned a bright light to shine on the chair so he wouldn't fall asleep, then ever so precisely rigged the fireplace with bells that would wake him when Santa arrived, should the light fail to keep him awake. The next morning Jensa and Eion had found him curled up on the floor, the milk and cookies he had set out gone, and a carrot clenched in his hand for the reindeer.

Vyviane countered with a story of the time an eleven-year-old Fiona had decided to decorate for Yule on November 1st. While Vyviane and Gregory were out for the evening, Fiona had dragged a tall ladder over to the storage closet where she had pulled down box after box of Yule decorations, even managing to dig out the boxes stuffed deep in the back and coated with several seasons of dust. Fiona had popped a batch of popcorn, then strung it together with frozen cranberries. Vyviane and Gregory had returned home to find the resulting garlands hung in every doorway and window, but at Fiona's eye level, which was chest level on Gregory. Every visible surface was layered with garish gold pinecones and tinsel. Since they didn't have a tree yet, Fiona had hung their ornaments from lighting fixtures and the fichus tree. Holiday music blasted from the sound system. Empty boxes and wadded up tissue paper were strewn all about. Vyviane and Gregory had gently explained that while they appreciated all her hard work, it wasn't quite time to decorate. Fiona hadn't been happy about it, but she had allowed them to remove all the decorations except those in her room, which she had left up until March!

At the conclusion of Vyviane's story, Fiona ushered the laughing group into the dining room for dinner. She started the meal by picking up a warm biscuit and breaking off a bite-size piece. She turned to Julian, who was sitting to her left, then placed the morsel on his tongue, murmuring "May you never hunger." Julian repeated that to Jensa, who was at his left, and so they went around the table. When the biscuit had been passed all the way around, Fiona lifted a goblet of wine from the center of the table, then handed it to Julian, who took a sip as she said, "May you never thirst."

Once the blessings were completed, the feasting began in earnest. They enjoyed the holiday turkey, winter squash, and mincemeat pie. The dining room was a cacophony of laughter and chatter as all six of them talked at once and deepened the family bond they shared.

Julian turned to Jensa. "How's Mariah doing?" he asked, referring to an aunt who had recently battled cancer and won.

"Still in full remission," Jensa said with a grin. "She's about to pass her one year milestone, which is a good sign, I think."

"I should call her this week."

Jensa's grin softened into a tender smile. "She would love that, Julian."

The meal came to a close, and the sated group moved back out to the living room to exchange gifts and enjoy an after dinner glass of wassail. Eion presented Julian with the first present. Julian neatly unfolded the petite package from his parents. When he saw the ornate pocketwatch resting in the folds of tissue, he was struck speechless. It had been Eion's and Eion's father's before him. Tradition stated that the watch was passed from father to son when the son had embarked on a new life with his wife. By giving the watch to Julian now, Jensa and Eion were giving his relationship with Fiona their blessing. Julian stood and hugged his parents tightly, touched by their gesture and amazed by how much that blessing meant to him.

Fiona watched them embrace, knowing he would later

explain why the gift had affected him so much. Once he had seated himself, Fiona's parent's handed her a gift. She ripped into the paper, then pried open the box, eager to get inside. She couldn't help but squeal with delight when she saw the beautiful blue glass vase that had been her grandmother's. It had held a special place on her mother's mantle since they had discovered it in the attic after the quake. For years she had admired it and wondered if it would ever rest on her mantle, but she had never expressed those sentiments to anyone. Somehow Vyviane always knew what she really wanted.

She reached under the tree and pulled out the gift she had labored over. Her mother and father exchanged a questioning glance when Fiona presented them with the wide, shallow box. Vyviane lifted off the lid. When she saw the handmade Yule wreath tucked inside, she released an awed breath. Vyviane and Gregory had been looking for a new wreath for a few years but had never found one that was just right. Fiona had created a new one out of freeze-dried gardenias and red roses. Interspersed with the flowers were tiny printed photos from past Yules, scraps of gift wrap, and small wooden ornaments that had decorated Vyviane and Gregory's first tree. When the quake had come, they had been rescued along with everything else in the attic but had then been stuffed in a dark corner of Fiona's closet after the move to New Denver. That box had moved into this apartment with Fiona and gone back into the closet. She hadn't opened it and learned its contents until she'd needed to make room for Julian. Fiona and her parents hugged each other, then returned to their seats for the last gift.

Julian handed his parents the tall box holding the gift he had agonized over, as he did every year. This year he had selected a pair of silver deco candlesticks he knew they had wanted for several seasons. He had seen his mother eyeing them in the network catalog during visits to their apartment. Fiona had related how his mother had hefted them in the store and set them back on the shelf during a recent shopping trip. When Jensa oohed over them, Julian knew he had made the right choice.

Excusing herself, Fiona went into the kitchen to get dessert. She returned to the living room bearing a tray with the traditional Yule log cake her mother had prepared, plates, and a decanter of wassail. As she set the tray on the table, she asked Julian to take the old wooden Yule log off the mantle and put it in the fireplace. Julian set the log aflame. As it started to burn, Fiona explained to Julian and his parents that the Yule log served as a symbol of hope and a reminder that the days were once again lengthening and the warmth of summer would return. Fiona went to the tree, then removed the three glass balls she and her parents had wished on the year before. The three of them stood before the hearth, each thanking the universe for the gifts it had brought, and tossed the balls into the fire to burn away.

They waited for the flames to catch the parchment slips inside the broken glass balls, then returned to their seats around the coffee table. Fiona handed each of her guests and Julian a slip of fresh parchment. She asked them to inscribe the papers with their wishes and promises for the coming year. Despite her promise to Julian that she could wait, she still hoped they would be ready in the next year and wished for a successful pregnancy and a healthy baby. She promised to honor all the sabbats from that point on and to teach any child she had to do the same. Julian wished for peace and love in his relationship with Fiona and promised to honor the Lady and Lord each day. Fiona looked up from her writing to see five pairs of eyes looking at her. She reached for the ornament bowl, which she handed to Jensa, asking her to choose one and pass the bowl on. She then showed them how to carefully remove the metal cap, roll the parchment so it would slide into the ball, and snap the top back on. She instructed them to hold their ornaments to charge them, then place them on the tree when they felt ready.

One by one, the ornaments were hung on the tree until they were all dangling from the full boughs. The ritual complete, they resumed their conversation as they enjoyed the wassail and Yule log cake. As the evening waned, both sets of parents decided it was time to leave. Fiona and Julian helped them retrieve their dishes and pack up their gifts for the ride home. Fiona also reminded them to take their ornaments from the tree to be hung on their own trees. Next year they could bring them back. Julian presented each with a plate of leftover Yule log and another hug before they left.

Julian slid an arm around Fiona. They watched the inner door close behind their parents. They didn't need to tell each other how happy they were that the evening had gone well. "Why don't you put another log on the fire?" Fiona asked as she slipped out of his arms. She went into the kitchen to pour them some eggnog.

They settled on the carpet in front of the blazing fire and spent a moment sipping their eggnog and reflecting on the evening before they decided it was time to exchange gifts. Fiona presented Julian with his gift first. He took the triangular package from her and opened it. The gleaming athame tucked inside was stunning. Fiona had commissioned a good friend to craft it for her after Julian had decided to take up the study of Wicca with her. He had done a magnificent job engraving the runes for Julian's name into the onyx handle. The curved steel blade was polished to a shine. Julian ran his fingers over the carved handle. "Thank you, my love. It's perfect," he said with a kiss.

Julian carefully set the blade back in the box and handed Fiona her gift. She tore back the paper to reveal a small oak box, with an ornate pentacle interwoven with leaves carved into the lid. Inside the silk-lined box she found a deck of tarot cards she had been drooling over for months. "Sweetie, I love it! How did you know?"

He winked. "I have my sources."

With a laugh, Fiona leaned in to kiss him. She wrapped her body around his. They rolled to their sides and made love in front of the fire. Afterwards, they decided to spend the rest of the night there, to pretend they were waiting for Santa as Julian had done as a child. They lay in each other's arms, buried under a warm cotton blanket. Fiona slid one hand down to her belly, wishing it were full with child and held it there as Julian pulled her closer.

Chapter 7

The Winter of Their Joy

Julian gazed out the window of the PRTV as they passed through the City. Now he understood why Fiona spent so much time on the roof of their building. The beauty of white winter was astounding. Although the City Corporation kept the walking paths and PRT tracks clear of snow and ice, icicles hung from the window ledges, and snow blanketed the rooftops, giving New Denver the feel of a winter wonderland. Snow enveloped Mount Komo in the distance. An expanse of unbroken white stretched across the plains and hills leading to the mountain.

Fiona hadn't told him why they were aboard the PRTV swaddled in scarves, mittens, and parkas, but he knew as soon as he spotted the sledding park out the front window. Julian was on his feet before the car came to a full stop, bouncing from one foot to the other until the door swung open. Brimming over with boyish glee, he raced onto the platform, down the escalator, then dashed toward the hill. About a quarter of the way to the top, he stopped, raced back down, and pressed his cold lips to Fiona's. Before she had a chance to catch her breath and return the kiss, he turned on his heel and ran toward the snowy sledding hill once more.

Fiona let him run ahead while she enjoyed a more leisurely walk to the top, taking the time to experience the chilly air around her and the crunch of icy snow under her feet. By the time she reached Julian, he already had a sled waiting for them. She put their thermos of hot chocolate in the warmer in the observation area, then walked toward Julian. He eagerly motioned for her to get on the sled first. She arranged herself with legs straight at the front of the sled. He sat down behind her and wrapped his legs around hers. Then without warning, he shoved off the embankment, sending them tearing down the steep hill at breakneck speed, both screaming with exhilaration as the frigid wind stripped away their adult personas and transformed them into carousing five-year-olds.

As they reached the bottom of the hill, the sled slowed to a stop. Fiona and Julian spilled onto the hard snow. Fiona leaped to her feet and pulled Julian to his, throwing her arms around him. She planted a hard kiss on his freezing lips, then spun him around and pushed him up the hill with a playful shove, crying, "Again, again!" Laughing, Julian raced up the hill, the sled bumping along behind him as Fiona ran to catch up. As soon as they reached the top, they scrambled back onto the sled and shoved off again. They careened down the hill over and over, until all the children in the park were watching and begging their parents to get them faster sleds.

After several runs, an exhausted Fiona and Julian went back up the hill to return the sled. Fiona grabbed their thermos from the warmer and poured a mug of the piping chocolate nirvana. She took a long sip, sighing with contentment as it warmed her insides. She passed the cup to Julian, who took a warming pull, then passed it back.

They cuddled and shared the cocoa as they watched other City-dwellers ride down the hill in groupings of all kinds. Fiona wondered when they would able to do the same with their own children. She couldn't wait any longer. It was time for her to start a family. She only hoped that Julian was more ready now than he had been two months earlier. "Are you ready to go?" she asked.

Julian turned to her and nodded, wondering about her sudden change in mood. He had his answer as soon as they returned to their apartment. Fiona led him over to the couch. He could tell from the look in her eyes that he was not going to enjoy this discussion. And he had an idea what it was about. "It's only been a month," he said.

Fiona looked down at her feet and took a deep breath. "I know." She lifted her head. "But I feel it more strongly than ever. I can't wait any longer."

"I'm just not ready for a baby," Julian insisted.

"Why does this always have to be about what you're ready for? Why not what I'm ready for? How long do you expect me to wait?"

Stunned by the attack, Julian reeled, then roared back on the defensive. He jumped off the couch. "Don't pressure me! I'm confused. My life has changed so much so fast, I don't know what I want!"

"Well, make up your mind already or I'll find someone who will."

"Fine!" Julian stormed out of the apartment, then out of the building. He turned in a random direction to walk and clear his head. Why had he become so angry? She didn't deserve that. And maybe he wasn't being fair to her. But what could he do? He wasn't ready.

Julian continued walking, turning those thoughts over in his mind. The hours passed as he walked the city in circles, with no clear destination in mind. As darkness fell, he looked up to get his bearings. He was in front of the cult's enclave. Was someone trying to tell him something?

The door to the house opened and one of the elders stepped out, a man by the name of Frederick whom Julian had become good friends with when he was a member. "Hey, Julian! Glad to have you back."

Julian started up the walkway. "Hey, Frederick. I'm not sure I am."

"What brings you here then?"

Julian shrugged. "I was just kind of walking."

Frederick motioned for Julian to come inside. "Want to talk about it? Let me get you some coffee."

With a nod, Julian followed Frederick into the house. He went into the living room. He had spent a lot of time in that room before he had started to have doubts about the cult. Maybe it had just been a crisis of faith. Maybe Sarah was right. Frederick returned with two mugs of coffee and sat down opposite Julian.

"Sarah tells us you've fallen in with the Pagans." When Julian didn't respond, Frederick continued. "She's very worried about you."

"Yeah, I noticed."

"She may have gotten carried away."

Julian sighed and nodded vigorously.

"Is that what has you down?"

Julian's shoulders slumped. "No, it's Fiona. She had a miscarriage a few months ago, and now she wants to try again, but it doesn't feel right."

Frederick placed a sympathetic hand on Julian's knee. "You know, God doesn't like for children to be born out of wedlock. Maybe that's why she miscarried. If you marry Sarah, you will be rewarded with many children."

Those words shot through Julian like a spear. He looked up at Frederick. "I have to go."

Frederick stood, blocking Julian's path. "Wait. Where are you going? Let's talk this through. We can help you."

Julian shook his head and smiled. "Believe it or not, you did." Julian walked out of the enclave to return to the apartment. He finally knew what to do.

***

Fiona had perched a chair in front of the window so she could stare out at the city and think. She had pushed him too far. She knew he wasn't ready. Why had she gotten so angry? Why had she lashed out at him like that? And now he'd been gone for hours. She had no idea where he was or when he would come back. *If he came back.* He wasn't answering his satellite phone, and he wasn't at his parents' apartment.

As the inner door slid open, she jumped. Julian walked in. She turned to face him, steeling herself for the goodbye she knew was coming. Instead Julian wore a smile on his face.

He walked toward her without a word, then knelt in front of her, taking her hands in his. "I'm sorry. I'm ready."

She looked down into his earnest face. "Are you sure?" His nod was the only reply she needed. She swept down into his arms, pressing her lips against his and drawing him into a passionate embrace to celebrate his decision.

***

A few days later, Fiona had just left their apartment to make her daily prayer on the rooftop when Julian heard the outer door open. Thinking it was the delivery Fiona was expecting, he pushed a button on his terminal to open the inner door. "Julian," said a familiar voice from the doorway. Alarmed, Julian spun in his chair. Sarah stood just inside the door. "I came to get you," she said, crossing the room toward him in a few quick steps.

Wary, he rolled back a few inches and tilted his gaze up to her. "I'd prefer that you leave right now. Fiona will be back soon."

Ignoring him, Sarah placed a gentle hand on Julian's shoulder. She surveyed the room, her gaze falling on the new white Imbolc altar Fiona had arranged after the sledding trip. She shuddered. "This has gone on long enough."

Anger roared through him. He plucked her hand from his shoulder, dropping her wrist as if it was a venomous snake. "You have no control here. Get out."

Sarah persisted. "But I do. I could have come to get you long ago, but I decided to let you have your fun. It's time for you to come back to the truth. You know that or you wouldn't have come back to the house."

"I was confused, but now I've found my truth. It's not with you. You're delusional."

Sarah shook her head sadly. "No, Julian, you've found nothing but lies. Your truth was with me and the leader."

Julian struggled to remain calm. "Get out! I don't want to see you again." Julian snatched his satellite phone from his belt. He punched out the number for the local police.

Bowing her head, Sarah sank to her knees. She placed one hand on Julian's thigh and looked up, her eyes deep wells of pity. "I'm so sorry I allowed you to be led astray. Call me when you're ready to be saved, and I'll come for you. There is always a place for you with the leader."

Julian shoved her hand away as the police answered the call. "I have an intruder," he said into the phone. The inner door opened, and he looked up toward the sound.

Sarah followed his gaze. Fiona skipped into the apartment, her cheeks flushed from the brisk winter air, her face peaceful from meditation. She came to an abrupt stop when her eyes met the cold determination in Sarah's. Sarah rose to her feet, moving toward Fiona.

Cold steel sharpened in Fiona's eyes. She straightened to her full height. Her voice came out in a low growl. "Get out of my house!"

Sarah nodded. This fight was not over, but she would concede this battle. It would be better to get Julian alone. She skirted past Fiona, who didn't move an inch to make way for Sarah's passage. Fiona trained her gaze on Julian. She could see the plea to stay calm in his eyes. Sarah stopped in the doorway and turned her head, drawing Julian's attention to her. "Think about it," she said. The inner door closed behind her.

"Nevermind. She's gone," he said into the phone. Julian disconnected the call. He stood, then rushed toward Fiona as she took a few faltering steps toward Julian. He kissed her forehead, her cheek, then buried his head in her shoulder. His reassurances tumbled out in ragged whispers, "Don't worry. I'm not going to let her hurt you. She's never going to have me. I love you. I want you. *You* are my truth."

"Oh, Julian, sweetie. I love you." Fiona moved her head and placed a sweet kiss on Julian's lips.

He answered her kiss with a stronger embrace. Guiding her with his arms, he moved them toward the floor. His anger at Sarah turned to desire for Fiona as her welcoming body opened to him and her love poured from her lips.

They let the confrontation with Sarah drift away from them as lust swept through them. The soft rug became their bed. Their bodies molded into each other as they had many times before. They slipped their hands over each other's skin with unconscious familiarity until each had reached a climax and declared their love in the greatest moment of ecstasy.

Their passion sated, Fiona lay in Julian's arms. Her gaze drifted toward the coffee table where a sheaf of damp wheat was awaiting her attention. She nudged Julian. "We didn't make the corn dolly yet," she said.

He grunted at being disturbed from his post-coital nap. "Do we have to do it now?"

"Yes. We do. Get up." She poked him in the ribs.

"All right. All right," he grumbled. He tugged on his pants as he moved toward the sofa. Fiona pulled his shirt over her back, then joined him on the couch to make the dolly. They would dress it as a bride to represent the Goddess in the Imbolc ritual Julian had suggested they perform. She gave Julian a piece of red cord, an acorn, and a twig that would become a priapic wand. It would serve as the God in their ritual.

"Do you want to go to the Winter Festival?" Fiona attached the arms and head.

Julian wrapped the cord around the twig to secure the acorn he had glued to the top. "We could do that, but when will we do our ritual?" He had plans, and he didn't want to miss the perfect moment to carry them out.

"We can do it after sunset the day before Imbolc. That's the Celtic tradition, I think."

Relieved, Julian put down the finished wand, then pulled Fiona to him. "Good plan." He nuzzled her neck.

Giggling at the featherlight caress, Fiona wriggled out of his arms. She stood up, tugging him to his feet, a lewd suggestion in her eyes. He started to close in on her when she stepped back, holding up one finger. "Before we get to that, we have some baking to do." She giggled and darted into the kitchen with Julian chasing after her, intent on punishing her for being a tease.

Fiona used every maneuver she could think of to keep Julian's tickling fingers away from her sensitive spots. First she put Julian to work reading the directions while she mixed the batter. Then she had him knead the dough. While he worked, the perfect way to carry out his surprise came to him. Julian set aside the kneaded dough to let it rise.

He crossed to Fiona and kissed her forehead. "How long is this going to take to rise?"

"About an hour. Why?"

Julian smiled. "I'll be back in a little while."

"Where are you going?" she asked.

"It's nothing. I'll be back before the bread goes in the oven." Julian walked out of the kitchen, leaving Fiona to wonder what he was up to.

She went out to her terminal to work on a new creation. An hour later, she went back into the kitchen. The dough had risen, and she now rolled it into a long rope. She folded the rope into a braid to continue the Imbolc theme.

Julian returned just as she was about to put it in the oven.

"Wait, I'll do that."

Fiona stood up, closing the oven door. "Too late."

Fiona set the timer, then left the kitchen. Julian waited until she was back in the office, then stepped across to the oven. He opened the door and slid out the pan. He tiptoed to the door and peeked out. Fiona was still in the office. Walking back to the counter, he slipped a small object out of his pocket, then tucked it into the bread. He quietly put the bread back into the oven. Fiona wouldn't be the wiser.

While the bread baked, Julian settled on the couch to catch up on the new developments in network design. Both were startled when the timer went off in the kitchen, but Julian jumped up first. "I'll get it!" he cried. Fiona watched him race into the kitchen, amused by his sudden eagerness for baking, then went back to work.

Julian slid the pan out of the oven and inspected the surface for visible clues of the surprise tucked inside. Seeing none, he poked a tiny hole in the crust until it met with the secreted object, leaving a mark to direct him to it later. He set the loaf aside to cool and strolled back out to the living room to remind Fiona of some unfinished business their baking had interrupted.

***

The following evening, as the sun dipped behind Mount Komo and cast a pinkish-orange glow over New Denver's white expanses, Fiona and Julian arranged the temporary altar for their Imbolc ritual. He moved their spare table in front of the window to add to the ritual the magic of sunset and the view of the red-tinged white cap of the mountain. After smoothing a white lace cloth over the altar, Fiona put a cut-crystal vase of white roses in the upper center. She took the silver candlesticks from the permanent altar, replaced the white candles with one silver taper for the Goddess and one gold taper for the God, then set them on either side of the vase. Julian handed her his onyx-handled athame, her small cauldron-shaped incense burner, and a sterling silver chalice inlaid with rose quartz and amethyst. He watched as she arranged them in their proper places on the altar. In the very center, she laid the corn dolly and the acorn-tipped wand. Below the altar she placed a basket wrapped in decorative white and silver ribbon and filled with a cushion of white fabric that would later serve as the bed for the maiden and the God. At each of the four quarters, Fiona set jar candles in green, blue, red, and yellow.

Satisfied with the altar, Fiona sent Julian into the bathroom to take a cleansing bath while she went into the kitchen to make the Imbolc incense from sandalwood, cinnamon, and frankincense. She ground the first two ingredients into powder with her marble mortar and pestle, although she could easily have purchased them that way, then mixed the ingredients together in equal parts. His bath complete, Julian went naked to the living room to fill the chalice with mead while Fiona took her ritual bath. For the final touch, he set the braided bread on the altar, turning the plate so her surprise was on his side of the altar.

He kneeled before the altar and bowed his head in meditation until Fiona emerged from her bath. She soon joined him naked at the altar. They took a few minutes to ground and center themselves before beginning the ritual. Fiona alerted Julian that it was time to begin by lighting the quick-catch charcoal. She dropped incense on it. The sweet smoke drifted up from the altar, and Julian rose. Carrying his athame in his right hand, he held the ritual blade aloft and moved clockwise around the outer candles to mark the boundary of the sacred circle.

The circle cast, Julian knelt again before the altar and set the athame back in its place. Fiona stood. She turned to the East where she lit the yellow candle and called in the element of Air. She continued around to the South, West, and North, inviting each into the circle, then returned to her place beside Julian. Julian handed her the lighter, and she held the flame beside the silver candle as she invoked the Goddess. "Lady, we call upon you this winter eve to join us and ask you to bring us your fire and awaken the earth." Fiona touched the flame to the candlewick. The flame swelled, then separated into two distinct flames. Fiona handed the lighter to Julian, who held it beside the gold candle as he invoked the God.

"Lord, join our Lady in the circle and spark new growth within her." He set the gold candle alight, then turned to face Fiona.

Fiona took the corn dolly from the altar and slid the basket out from beneath it. She set the bride into the basket with the words, "Welcome, lady, to your maiden bed."

Julian placed the acorn wand over the bride and said, "Blessed be the maiden." They covered the bride and wand with a soft cloth and slid the basket under the altar, saying, "Maiden, may your bridehood be sweet and bring with it warm spring."

Reaching for the braided bread, Fiona tore off a small chunk, which she handed to Julian. "May you never hunger." Julian placed the morsel in his mouth and took up the loaf, searching for the tiny marking he had made. He pulled a chunk out, squeezing it to make sure the secreted object was tucked inside. He placed the bread in Fiona's hand and repeated her words.

She put the bread between her lips. When she bit down, her teeth met with something hard and metal. Puzzled, she pulled the foreign object out of her mouth. She was surprised to see a simple square emerald atop a gold band.

Julian plucked it from her hand and wiped the ring with a wet cloth he had hidden under the altar. She stared at him wide-eyed as he reached for her left hand. He slid the ring onto her finger. "Fiona Rowan, will you do me the honor of becoming my wife?"

"Yes! Of course! I love you!" She pulled him into a hug. Julian arched his neck down and tipped her chin up to him, bringing his lips down on hers for a long, slow, kiss that expressed the deep currents of their love for one another. After an extended embrace, Fiona pulled away, smiling giddily and laughing. "We still have to finish the ritual."

Julian nodded. He turned back to the altar, yearning to end the ritual and quell the desire that kiss had stirred up. Fiona lifted the chalice from the altar, and, tossing him a playful glance, peeked inside to make sure no further surprises awaited her. She offered the chalice to him with the words "May you never thirst." He took the chalice from her and drank deeply from it, then handed the cup of honey wine back to her, again repeating her words.

As Fiona replaced the chalice on the altar, Julian picked up the candle snuffer. He held it beside the gold candle and said, "Lord, thank you for attending our circle. Farewell and blessed be." He extinguished the candle, then handed the snuffer to Fiona, who held it next to the silver candle.

"Lady, we thank you for attending our circle. Farewell and blessed be." She snuffed the candle, then stood to release the quarters. She moved to the West, thanking the element of water for its part in the ritual. She extinguished its flame, then continued around to the South, East, and North. She returned to the center of the circle and resumed her place beside Julian.

He picked up the athame and walked counter-clockwise around the circle to release it. As he finished, he said, "May the circle be open, but unbroken."

Julian took his place beside Fiona. He set the athame on the altar, then she pushed him onto his back and moved over him, her lips meeting his with a hungry kiss. He responded in kind. Once more, passion overtook them, leading them to make love in front of the altar.

***

The next morning, still reveling in the bliss of being engaged, they went to the City Center for the Pagan Coalition's Winter Festival. Although it looked like a plain New Denver building on the outside, inside it was a winter wonderland. As they passed through an archway made to look like carved ice, they saw sparkling three-foot snowflakes hanging from the ceiling. Small tables draped in white silk were placed around the outer edge of the room. Crystal bowls of white floating candles had been placed on top of each table and decorated baskets were tucked underneath. Fiona and Julian were surprised and delighted to see so many people had chosen to attend the event, many of them drawn by the advertisement posters Fiona had designed. Members of the Coalition fluttered from small group to small group explaining the meaning behind the celebration and pointing out the activity schedule posted near the door.

Lady Celesta approached as Fiona and Julian were reviewing the schedule, debating which activity to participate in first. As they exchanged a warm greeting, Lady Celesta noticed the stunning green stone adorning Fiona's delicate ring finger. She turned to Julian. "Does that mean what I think it means?"

"It certainly does," he said with pride.

"Congratulations!" She hugged Fiona and then Julian. "Have you set a date yet?"

Fiona glanced at Julian. They hadn't discussed it, but she had an idea what she wanted. "I was thinking Beltane would be nice. We would be honored if you would perform the ceremony."

"I was hoping you'd ask," Lady Celesta said. Another guest waved from across the room, and Lady Celesta waved back.

Fiona noticed the exchange. "I know you have a lot to do today, so I'll get in touch tomorrow about planning the ceremony. We're thinking of a formal handfasting."

"Wonderful!" Lady Celesta started to move across the room in the direction of the person who had waved. "Enjoy the festivities," she said as she walked away.

Once Lady Celesta was out of earshot, Julian turned to Fiona. "Can we plan a wedding in three months?"

Fiona flashed a determined grin. "We sure can. We have to start now, though."

Her excitement was infectious. Julian swept her into a hug and twirled her around in a circle. "Beltane it is, my love. I'll do it whenever you want as long as you promise to be mine."

Laughing brightly, Fiona bent her head and kissed him. "I will. But for now, we have merrymaking to attend to." Julian set her back on her feet. The happy pair headed off hand in hand to the candle-making area where they would dip their spell candles for the coming year. Unsure of what their needs might be, they decided to make two each of red, blue, green, purple, pink, yellow, orange, white, brown, and black—all the colors that were available.

Julian had never made candles before, so Fiona showed him how to dip the folded wicks in the hot, bright-hued wax until they had become pairs of six-inch tapers, the perfect size for spell work. As each pair of candles reached their full lengths, Fiona hung the middle of the wick over the drying rack with a label bearing her name. While the candles hardened, Fiona and Julian went to the feast area to munch on the delicious home-baked goodies the Pagan Coalition had provided. There was such an assortment of cookies, brownies, and fruit that they didn't know where to start. Fiona finally chose a brownie but stole bites of

Julian's cookies.

As they ate their snack, they went to the children's craft area to watch the young ones make corn dollies, using the same simple method Fiona had shown Julian. Other children dressed their dollies in tiny scraps of lace and bits of ribbon. Next, Fiona and Julian moved on to the adult craft area where vendors created more ornate corn dollies and decorative candles right in front of them. They admired one craftsman in particular and purchased a pair of his elegantly wrapped white and silver beeswax tapers. They returned to the drying rack where they had left their candles and found them hard enough to remove. Fiona carefully lifted their hand-fashioned tapers off the rack so as not to break them, then turned to Julian. "We need to bless these. I think there's a ritual about to start over there." She pointed. "Why don't we do that and then go home to celebrate our engagement again?"

Julian smiled. "Honey, you're my kind of woman. Lead the way."

They crossed the room to one of the small tables, arriving just as a member of the Coalition was preparing to lead the rite. Fiona slid one of the decorative baskets out from beneath the altar, carefully arranged the candles inside, then put the basket back under the alter. The leader signaled she was ready to begin.

As a circle had already been cast around the entire City Center, she did not recast a smaller circle. Instead she called the quarters with a specific invocation that asked the elements to bless the participants' candles with the energies of earth, air, fire, and water. She then lifted her crystal wand from the altar and raised it over her head. She drew it down towards herself as she said, "Lady Brid, maiden Goddess of the flame, come be our muse and lend us inspiration as we cast our magick on these candles. Bless them for right purpose and charge them with the strength to bring us all we desire."

She set down the wand. Each participant took a moment to present their baskets of candles to the Goddess and make a personal request for their blessing. After the last person had made her request, the priestess reached out and linked hands with the person on either side of her. The remaining participants followed suit. Fiona was confused by the odd pressure on her left hand, then remembered she now wore a ring on her finger. Smiling to herself, she squeezed Julian's hand, then focused her attention back on the ritual. The priestess led them in a toning "oh." Their voices raised as their arms lifted skyward and the cone of power was raised over them. With a shout, they released the tone and, swinging their arms down, sent the energy into the candles under the altar.

The priestess thanked Brid for joining them, then released the quarters, thanking them also for their part in the rite. Fiona and Julian wrapped their candles in tissue and placed them in a bag that was also under the altar, then went in search of Lady Celesta to thank her for the wonderful event and promise to contact her the next day about the wedding.

They rode the PRTV home in silence, both making wedding plans in their heads. Fiona reached across the seat and took Julian's hand in hers. He turned his head and smiled, then abandoned his thoughts. He leaned closer to Fiona, placing his lips on hers. She opened her lips and returned the kiss with greater heat.

The car came to a stop just as their arousal threatened to overtake them. They jumped out of the car, carrying their bags of candles with them, and ran toward the elevator. Fiona wrapped herself around Julian as they rode up to their floor, her lips searing his with their vigor. The elevator doors slid open. Julian carried her down the hall to their apartment, their mouths still locked in the heated embrace.

Fiona had Julian's shirt off before the second door had closed behind them. He made the snap decision that the bedroom was too far to walk and deposited Fiona on the couch, bending over her, his fingers fumbling with her buttons to expose her skin to his touch. She moaned softly and arched her back against his fingertips, pulling him closer. Julian reached out for Fiona's hand. As he twined his fingers around hers, he brushed the cold surface of her engagement ring and remembered that Fiona had scheduled their wedding date only three months hence. He pulled back and reminded Fiona of that imposing fact.

She giggled and said, "I know sweetie. And tomorrow we'll get started . . . ." With that, she pulled him back down. She traced her tongue along the outline of his ear. Any thoughts of the wedding were driven from his mind for the rest of the evening.

Chapter 8

With Spring Comes Change

Despite her looming ad deadline, Fiona went straight to work sketching her wedding dress the very next day. In addition to finishing her paying work, she had wedding vows to write, flower arrangements to select, and a menu to plan, but she wouldn't be able to focus on any of that until she had designed the perfect dress. She used a light pen to draw the outline on her touch pad and watched as the lines of the gown she had designed years ago in her imagination appeared on her screen.

Julian came into the room, clucking at her for avoiding her work. She turned to him with her best scowl. When all it got out of him was a chuckle, she was disappointed. But he was right. She really shouldn't blow her deadline. With a sigh, she saved the preliminary dress design, then opened the newest poster.

***

Three days later, the assignment was completed. She could turn her attention completely to the wedding she had less than three months to plan. The next few weeks passed in a flurry of activity. They found they had little time to do anything that wasn't wedding related, and even less time to spend together just having fun. In the midst of the chaos, Fiona received word from the New Denver Housing Bureau that the two-bedroom they had requested was available. She fired back a message that they would accept the apartment, then tried to figure out how they would squeeze time to pack into their already hectic schedules.

When she told Julian the news, he suggested that they move within the week to get it out of the way. Fiona thought it was a good plan. She also thought it would be a good time to purge themselves of any old belongings that were no longer of value to them. Always one to do things the organized way, Julian set up three boxes in the living room. One was for give-aways, one was for recycling, and one was for the maybe-keeps they would have to decide on together.

Fiona's first stop was her bookcase. She pulled out the dusty volumes she had purchased on a volunteer mission to Old Savannah after the hurricane. She had rescued the books from a destroyed store. The owner had been so grateful for her help that he'd given them to her as a thank you. She had kept them as a reminder of the trip and how good it had felt to return the favor of help her family had received after the earthquake, but she had no use for these books now. These would better serve an historic library, where old books were collected and the text transferred onto the network for all to share. The physical books were then preserved in vaults that would protect them for posterity. As she deposited the books in the give-away box, she noticed Julian was sitting on the couch reading his page-viewer. "Don't you have some packing and purging to do?"

He looked up at her, a guilty look spreading across his face. "Yeah, but I can't decide where to start."

She raised her eyebrows. Mr. Efficient didn't have a plan? She glanced at the box sitting in one corner of the apartment. It had been there since he had moved his stuff in. "You can start with that. Odds are you don't need anything in it."

He glanced at the box. "No, I need that stuff."

"What's in it?"

Julian's face twisted as he tried to remember what he had put in it. "I don't know."

Just as she had suspected. "Then you don't need it."

Julian ambled over to the box and, with a deep sigh, folded back the flaps to reveal a jumble of old printed magazines protected by plastic envelopes. He slid one magazine out of the sleeve and flipped through it.

"That's not going to get you anywhere," Fiona teased.

"I can't get rid of this. It's a collectible," he said.

"To whom?"

"Me."

Fiona sighed with resignation. "Okay, you can keep it, but do something with the rest of that stuff. We're not moving all your junk again." She went back to work purging herself of all the excess stuff her life had collected. After the turmoil that had filled the last turning of the wheel of the year, she wanted to make a fresh start in the new apartment. Out of the corner of her eye, she watched as Julian closed the magazine he had claimed was a collectible and crossed the room with it.

He watched as it settled at the bottom of the give-away box with Fiona's old books. It had been one of the few things he'd managed to salvage from his parents' home. At nineteen, it had seemed important to keep it. Now he didn't feel the need. He turned back to finish sorting through his box of random belongings. Deep down he knew if he really wanted to get rid of the dust bunnies of the last year, he had to get rid of the junk filling his home and make room for the new things he really wanted, things he wanted to share with Fiona.

The bedroom closet was next on Fiona's agenda. Julian followed her into the room as she prepared to sort through the belongings that had accumulated on the top shelf. She pulled down a box and opened it up. Inside were some of her girlhood clothes that had been in her mother's attic, trinkets from vacations taken since moving to New Denver, and letters she had written and never sent. She sank into the mattress and sighed. She looked up at Julian as he came into the room. "I don't think I can get rid of any of this," she said, disappointed with herself for clinging to the past.

"Then don't. I have an old trunk in the storage room. We can put our mementos in that."

"But I don't need this stuff." She held up the sheaf of old letters as an example, then fingered the baby clothes. "And I certainly don't need these."

Julian took the baby clothes and letters from her. He sat on the bed facing her, then reached one hand out and placed it on her stomach. "You will soon enough, love." He kissed her gently.

His words sent a warm rush of affection through Fiona. She returned the kiss. "You're so right, sweetie. I'll put the baby clothes in another box marked 'For the Future'."

Without a word, Julian left the room. He walked out to

his desk in the living room, slid open the bottom drawer, and removed a small envelope he had tucked in the back. He returned to the bedroom and set the envelope in the box with the baby clothes.

"What's this?" Fiona asked, picking it up.

Taking it from her, he put it back in the box. "Just something for the future."

***

They still had a wedding to plan amidst all the packing, so they took a break early the next day for the first of two visits to the couples' counselor. The City Corporation provided her services to all residents planning to formalize their commitment to each other. In their first session, Fiona and Julian discussed their expectations for the marriage and were pleased to find them similar. Before they left, the counselor asked them each to make list of the qualities and actions of the other that they were grateful for. They were to bring the lists to the next meeting.

On the way home, Fiona and Julian stopped in at the caterers to discuss the reception menu and sample one or two appetizers, then went to the park where the ceremony would be held to map out the seating. As they walked around the white gazebo figuring out where the sun would be during the wedding, Fiona came up with a new idea for the flowers. She made a mental note to e-mail the florist when they got back to the apartment.

While Julian was noting the measurements of the gazebo in his network notepad, Fiona wandered a short distance from the gazebo to look at the spring flowers just in bloom. She had the odd sensation of being watched. Chills went up her spine as she turned to meet the frigid gaze of Sarah, who was standing on the other side of the park. They did not have time to deal with her today. Fiona joined Julian in the gazebo and warned him that they were being spied on. She suggested they go home. He nodded, taking her arm as they walked away from the gazebo and Sarah.

Their second appointment with the counselor was scheduled for the next day, so Fiona and Julian put the incident out of their minds as they prepared their lists. They made a game of it, protecting their network notepads from intruding eyes the same way they had hidden their test papers from the other children in grade school.

***

The counselor hadn't told them what the lists were for, so the next afternoon, they were surprised to learn that they would indeed be sharing their lists with each other. The counselor called them gratitude lists. She used them as the first line of defense against damaging fights. "Every couple fights," she said, "but some fights are worse than others. I want you to keep your lists in a place you'll remember. Whenever you're angry with each other, take out your lists and remind yourselves why you're together in the first place. Why don't you each share one item now?"

Fiona called up her list, a faint pink coloring her cheeks as she looked over the mushy items. She scanned it until she found one she thought was more profound than the little things that took up much of the list—like washing the dishes. "I am grateful for that look in your eyes when you say you love me." Her skin grew warmer from the memory of that look.

Touched by her words, Julian searched his own list for something of equal depth. "I am grateful for all the ways you support me, every day." He gazed at her with the very look she was grateful for. Fiona leaned forward and kissed him gently.

The counselor asked them to finish reading their lists to each other that night. Fiona suggested they turn it into a ritual. Julian thought it was a grand idea. Sunset was fast approaching, so they returned home to perform the ritual at the magic hour. Fiona removed the white candles from the holders and replaced them with pink candles. She added a red intention candle to bring passion to the ritual, then set dried rose buds on the incense burner to add a romantic air. Julian joined her in the circle. They sat cross-legged facing each other. They each took a large sheet of white parchment and a red ink pen, then opened their lists on their network notepads. They copied them neatly onto the parchment, each adding a few new items that came to them as they wrote. When they were done, Fiona read the first item from her list aloud. "I am grateful when you put the dishes away," she said.

Julian grinned and kissed her, then started with the first item on his list. "I am grateful when you kiss me awake in the middle of the night."

Fiona smiled. She would have to do that more often. Fiona leaned in to brush her lips against his, then sat back and looked down at her list. "I am grateful for the way you stroke my hair."

"And I'm grateful for your understanding when I get lost in my work and forget to come to bed." He ran one hand over her thigh. They continued reading their lists in this way, stopping repeatedly to exchange soft kisses and tender caresses.

The pink spell candles had burned almost all the way down by the time they finished reading their lists. They set the papers on the altar, then asked the Goddess Aphrodite to bless their sheets of parchment with romance, love, and passion, and bless their lives with the same qualities every day they were together. They would leave their lists on the altar until the full moon three days hence to allow the energy invested in them to grow stronger as the moon grew larger.

Fiona moved to sit astride Julian, her legs wrapped around his waist. They gazed deep into each other's eyes, bringing their breathing in line and experiencing the pure connection between them until the candles had burned out. Their lips met in a smoldering kiss to complete the ritual. As they continued their embrace, Fiona got an idea for the perfect wedding gift for Julian.

***

The day before they were scheduled to move, Fiona and Julian planned a visit to the new place for the first time. Julian asked if they were going to clean it while they were there. Fiona said yes, but rather than a dust cloth, she loaded her backpack with white candles, all her candleholders, and two sage wands. She was planning a spiritual cleansing, not a physical one.

The PRT ride was a quick one, but it took them almost to the edge of New Denver. Only a few stops remained between their building and the last building, with the rest of the track leading out to Mount Komo. When they got out of the PRT, they could just see the mountain peeking out from behind the corner of their new building. They stepped onto the elevator. Julian checked the apartment number, then punched the eighth floor button. Fiona's backpack grew heavier. She jiggled it from shoulder to shoulder as they rode up to their new floor.

They reached their door, and the outer door opened with a rush of air. They entered the code in the interior chamber that would open the second door, then stepped inside their new apartment for the first time. The unit was larger than their old one. Fiona walked straight to the west-facing wall where blinds covered the window. She pulled them open and caught her breath at the unobstructed view of Mount Komo rising from the hills outside the City, its snow-capped peak reflecting the light of the full moon overhead.

"Julian, come over here."

Julian focused his wandering and made his way over to her, wrapping his arms around her waist. He shifted his gaze out the window. "Wow," he said. They stood awestruck by their good fortune for several minutes until a cloud passed by the moon, dimming the glow of the mountain.

Fiona turned in Julian's embrace. "I can't believe our luck. This is amazing." Julian nodded his head in response, then lowered his lips to hers, his desire stirred by the majesty of the mountain and the power of the full moon. Fiona returned his kiss briefly before pulling away. "We have to cleanse the space first."

Slipping away from him, she retrieved her backpack from the spot where she had dropped it by the door. She carried the pack from room to room, setting a candle and holder in the exact center of each room's hardwood floor. She went back to the living room where Julian waited, pulled the two sage wands and lighter from her pack, then dropped it back on the floor. With her lighter, she lit the candle in the living room and set the wands ablaze from that. Once the wands had developed strong flames, she blew them out, letting the dried herbs smolder.

Julian took one of the wands from her. He followed Fiona as she walked to the front door, dragged the smoke around the entrance, then drew a banishing pentagram across the center. She turned back to face the apartment. She began to prance through the living room, with Julian mimicking her steps. The two of them chanted, "Happy! Happy! Joy! Joy!" as they moved through the apartment. They saged every window and doorway they came to, and even the most minor inlets of energy into their space, including the network connectors.

When they reached their office, Fiona blessed it for good work and good fortune. They moved next to the master suite and blessed it to bring them joy, restful sleep, and great sex. They continued into the kitchen and blessed it for sustenance and health. They continued next to the smaller bedroom, which they hoped would be their child's bedroom, and blessed it to bring their child happiness. Finally they returned to the living room. Julian stood silent, awaiting Fiona's words to bless the room.

Rather than verbally bless it, Fiona instead went back to her backpack and pulled out a blanket, which she laid across the middle of the floor. She moved the candle out of the way, then turned back to Julian, reaching out a hand for him. As she led him to the blanket she said, "I have a special way to bless this space."

"Mmmm. The perfect way to break in a new apartment."

Fiona moved to her knees. Julian joined her there. "Exactly," she murmured as they came together. Julian lowered her onto her back, his body moving over hers and guiding her into the familiar rhythm of give and take that fueled their desire for each other. Their passion pervaded the living room. As the heat between them intensified, the blessing expanded into the outer rooms, making the entire apartment a sanctuary for the lovebirds and all who entered. They became enveloped in the blessing they had created. It drove them toward the peak of excitement, the final explosion of energy blessing their home with love and happiness for all the days they would live there. The energy also created a new blessing for both of them, but neither would be aware of it for some time.

Still holding Fiona in his arms, Julian rolled onto his side and turned his head to look out the window at the mountain. "I like the effect this place has on us. We should stay all night."

"We still have that closet to pack," Fiona reminded him.

They returned to their old apartment to stay there one last night and to finish packing. Against his will, Fiona dragged Julian to the hall closet and forced him to help her go through it. It had become the catch-all for whatever items had found their way into the apartment without an obvious home. Now those things had to be dealt with. Most of the stuff could be thrown away, but a few objects reminded them of their first few months together. They decided to keep them.

In the very back of the closet, buried under a pile of clothes, Fiona saw the box she had placed there a few months before. She had almost forgotten it amid the busyness of planning the wedding, trying to conceive a new child, and packing to move. She bent down, lifting the box out of the corner as if it held a delicate crystal vase.

"What is it?" Julian asked. Fiona handed him the box without a word and left the closet, head bent. Julian watched her walk away, then opened the box and peeked inside. When he saw the bundle of fabric he recognized as the altar cloth from their mourning altar, he closed the box. He went to Fiona, who stood nearby, arms crossed over her chest as she remembered the pain of the previous October.

"I'm sorry. Should I get rid of it?"

Shaking her head, Fiona took the box from him. "No. We should save it. I'll put it in the keepsake trunk." Julian nodded his agreement. Fiona carried the box to the trunk, then threw herself back into cleaning the closet, wanting to put that sorrowful experience back out of her mind.

***

The next morning, the intercom buzzed, alerting them to the arrival of the Moving PRTV. Fiona rolled over and nudged Julian awake. "It's time to get to work." Julian groaned, them slid out of bed, trudging toward the shower for a quick wake-me-up blast of hot water. Fiona pulled on some shorts and a T-shirt, then started carrying the lighter boxes down to the van. Julian soon joined her, fresh and bright-eyed, to load the heavier boxes while Fiona took her last shower in the old apartment.

When she emerged from the shower, there was nothing left to carry but the furniture. Through much cursing and struggling, the pair managed to lug their bed, couch, armchairs, and dining table into the van, then finished off with the bookcase and the smaller furniture. When they were done, the van was filled to the roof and threatening to overflow. Julian shut the door, then followed Fiona back up to their apartment for a last check.

Fiona wandered through the unit, opening all the built-in drawers, closets, and cabinets to make sure they hadn't left anything behind. Julian checked their terminals to make sure everything had been downloaded and the machines reset. Satisfied that they hadn't left anything behind or unfinished, they met in the middle of the living room. Julian pulled Fiona to him.

"This is it," she said, looking around the empty apartment.

"There's no turning back."

"You can still back out . . . ." Fiona teased.

"Yes, love, now that the van is packed, I'm leaving you . . . ." His voice trailed off as his lips explored the cleft of her neck and shoulder.

As his tongue met her sensitive spot, Fiona giggled and squirmed away. "Don't start." She laughed. "We have to unpack the van on the other end."

"Okay, okay. Let's go." He grabbed her hand. Together they walked out of the apartment, the inner and outer doors closing behind them for the last time.

They unloaded the van at the new place as fast as they could, then began the difficult business of unpacking and debating what should go where. Fiona went first to the picture window and pulled open the blinds, eager to see the daytime view.

Inspired by the bright late afternoon sun glinting off the pure white snow, Fiona decided to set their altar up near the window. She placed the altar table along the wall perpendicular to the window, then retrieved the box of altar decorations. As the Spring Equinox was in two days, she used a light pink cloth embroidered with flowers. She had recently purchased white candles adorned with a chain of molded flowers. She mounted the candles in silver candlesticks and set them on the altar. Tomorrow she would find a flowering plant to add to the altar, but for now she arranged their tools and put a feather in the east, a rock in the north, a shell in the west, and a chunk of red lava rock in the south.

The altar complete, Fiona joined Julian in the bedroom

where he was unpacking. As she helped him make the bed, she remembered they had an appointment with Lady Celesta the next day. "We're supposed to start planning the ceremony," she said to Julian. "Oh, and the Ostara ritual is in two days. I told her we'd go."

Julian smiled. The Spring Equinox would be the last new sabbat he experienced before starting over again at Beltane. "Sounds good." He tossed a freshly cased pillow onto the bed. "I'm tired of unpacking. What do you say to a picnic on the floor and some cuddling?"

Fiona rewarded his suggestion with a kiss. "Great idea. You get the food, I'll find the dishes." Julian went down to the local convenience mart while Fiona dug through the kitchen boxes. By the time Julian returned, she had unearthed the plates and silverware. Then after a quick dinner, they retired to their new bedroom to break it in as they had the living room.

***

Early the next morning, Julian left to get the rest of his belongings from storage. Fiona went to the garden center in search of plants for her new rooftop garden. It was a little late in the season to be planting seeds, so she settled on plants that were already flowering or just about to flower.

By the time Fiona had made her choices and returned to the apartment, Julian had already transported his boxes from storage and was sorting the contents into keep and give-away boxes. Tomorrow they would call the charity that would sort the goods and deliver them to the appropriate places, including several Midwestern cities that had recently been destroyed by a deadly swath of tornadoes like the one that had leveled Chicago.

Seeing that he didn't need her help, Fiona went up to the roof to plant her flowers. She lost track of the day as she became immersed in the rich new soil of her garden. She planted lilacs, tulips, and daffodils. She interspersing bunches of rosemary, lavender, and thyme with the flowers. These were all herbs she used often in cooking and magick. As she worked, she had a vision of her wedding bouquet. Tucked into it was one of each flower she was planting. That thought reminded her of the appointment with Lady Celesta. Fiona glanced at her watch, then rolled to her feet to brush the dirt off her knees. She dashed down to the apartment and took a quick shower to clean off the garden soil.

Then she and Julian went to Lady Celesta's to plan Julian's wedding attire and write the script. Lady Celesta also recommended that they write their vows soon, so as not to run out of time or forget in the hectic days ahead. They promised they would have their vows ready a week before the ceremony. As the hour grew late, Lady Celesta shooed them away, saying she had to put the finishing touches on the Ostara ritual for the next day. Fiona and Julian thanked her for her help and went on their way, promising to say hello at the Ostara Fair the next morning.

***

Daylight streaming in through the bedroom window woke them early again the next morning. They rose to take ritual baths before going to the sabbat celebration, then took extra care dressing in their spring finest. They stopped at the convenience mart on their way to pick up some early spring fruit for the potluck feast at the fair.

Giddy with excitement, Fiona grinned broadly and peered out the window for the first glimpse of the fairgrounds as they rode the PRT. Beside her, Julian chattered away about how much he had loved his first trip to the fairgrounds the previous Beltane. The car pulled into the station, then they bounded out of the car, joining several other revelers heading to the fair. Once again, protestors met the celebrants as they walked toward the gates. Fiona took Julian's hand, and they walked toward the blooming archway that served as the entrance. As they passed by the zealot group, Sarah called out to Julian to join her.

Julian didn't stop walking or even look in her direction; instead he held firmly to Fiona's hand and called back to her. "I'm one of them now!"

Infuriated that Fiona had won him, Sarah dropped her placard. She chased after them, but security at the gate stopped her as Fiona and Julian passed through it. Sarah screamed after them. "I'll have you still, Julian! You're mine!"

Fiona and Julian strode into the fairgrounds in search of something to help them forget the uncomfortable incident. Spring flowers dotted the grass. Festive booths offered flowered crafts and refreshments. Festival-goers eager to add a spring flair to their faces surrounded a face-painting booth near the entrance. Julian pointed toward it. "I think that's what we need."

Her grin returning, Fiona nodded. Julian had a sun painted on one cheek and a rainbow on the other. Fiona chose to have a chain of daisies painted across her forehead. She pulled back her dark hair with another chain of live daisies to show it off.

As they stepped away from the booth, Julian swept Fiona into his arms as he had that first Beltane all those months before. "You, my love, have made me the happiest man alive."

Fiona giggled and kissed him. "And you've made me the happiest woman in the world."

Julian crushed Fiona closer to him and moved his lips over hers. They continued their affectionate embrace until the bells called them to ritual. They joined hands, then strolled to the place of ritual, both aware that this was their last sabbat as an unmarried couple. In six short weeks they would make the leap from betrothed to wed. They joined the circle, eager to see what results the ritual might hold for them this time. Little did they know of the future already growing inside Fiona.

Chapter 9

Handfasted Bliss

One week rolled into the next. The date of the wedding approached. Fiona struggled to edit the vows she had written into something that would take less than an hour to read. Julian had finished his quickly and efficiently, as she had known he would. She wished she had some of his skills in that area. But she had them done a week before the wedding as promised. She e-mailed them to Lady Celesta just in case she forgot to bring them to the ceremony.

A few days before their wedding, Julian was wandering through the apartment, mentally going over everything they had to get done, when he noticed a flat, wrapped package resting on the altar. It hadn't been there hours before. His interest piqued, he crossed over to it. He was about to pick it up when Fiona stopped him with "Don't touch that!"

Startled, he yanked his hands away and turned to her. "Why can't I touch it?"

Fiona slid between Julian and the package on the altar. "Because it's not time yet. Now I'm sure you have something you need to be doing." She shooed him away from the precious present.

***

Two days later, Fiona was awakened by the sunlight shining on her face through the window. Looking forward to a relaxing day at home with Julian, she rolled over to check the time. Then it hit her. She wasn't going to have a relaxing day at all. This was her wedding day! And her mom was going to be there in an hour. She leaped out of bed and threw back the covers with a mix of exuberance and panic. She pounced on Julian, startling him Julian awake. "We're getting married today!" she cried.

Julian grunted and peeled open his eyes, stretching his neck up to kiss her. "I know. In a few hours you'll be my wife."

"And you'll be my husband."

"I never knew I could be this happy," he murmured.

"I knew, but I was waiting for you to come along and share it with me," Fiona said with a teasing lilt. She climbed off him, then walked out of the bedroom, calling over her shoulder, "Mom will be here in an hour. If she catches you here, we're in for another lecture."

Julian shuddered at the thought of having to listen to Vyviane tell him why he shouldn't see his fiancée before the wedding. He hopped out of bed to shower and hightail it out of the apartment before she descended.

Fiona unconsciously hummed a wedding march as she fixed herself a cup of herbal tea in the kitchen, then carried the steaming mug over to the window. She stared out at Mount Komo. She sipped her tea, letting the calming herbs quell her rising anxiety about everything being perfect on her wedding day. She heard the water from the shower turn off. A few minutes later Julian surprised her by slipping his arms around her waist and dropping a kiss below her ear.

"I'm leaving now. I'll see you in a few hours."

Fiona turned and hooked one arm around his neck. "Give me one last kiss as a fiancé before you go."

With a smile, Julian complied, granting her a long, sweet kiss. They parted and gazed into each other's eyes for a moment, both filled with a stronger love than they could have imagined. Julian hugged her and whispered "I love you" into her hair.

"I love you," Fiona said, then swatted his butt lightly. "Now get out of here." Julian saluted and turned on his heel, making his way out of the apartment as Fiona went into the kitchen to steep her mother's tea. Vyviane and Gregory arrived moments later.

"I saw Julian leaving," Vyviane said. "He wasn't supposed to see you this morning."

Fiona shared a smile with her dad over her mom's superstitious nature. "Don't worry, Mom. We have more than enough luck on our side." She held up the cup of tea as a diversion. "I made tea."

"Thank you. Now go get showered. We have to do your hair."

Fiona wrapped her parents in an impulsive hug, then scurried towards the shower. She spent a long time under the hot spray, grounding and centering herself in preparation for the excitement of the day ahead. After she had dried herself with the fluffiest towel she owned, she applied a special lotion that she had created to bring the blessing of joy and love to her handfasting day.

She pulled on a robe, went out to the bedroom, and took the garment bag holding her dress out of the closet. She hooked it onto the edge of the closet door, then unzipped the bag to reveal her stunning wedding gown. She spent a long moment looking at it, amazed that the dress she had dreamed of for years was in her bedroom, waiting for her to slip into it. She was as happy as she'd imagined she would be. She looked forward to spending the rest of her life with Julian and discovering all that life had in store for them.

Vyviane came into the room and interrupted Fiona's reverie to help her step into the pool of royal blue silk. The high empire waist and Celtic knotwork runner edging the bottom of the A-line skirt conformed to Fiona's slim shape as if she had been born in it. The rich blue set off her dark hair and bright green eyes, lending them a shimmer.

Vyviane laid the matching cape over the bed, then draped a towel over Fiona's shoulders before combing Fiona's hair as she had when Fiona had been a child. Gregory slipped into the room to watch this moment and admire his daughter who was about to give him a son-in-law. When Fiona's hair had been smoothed and arranged, she stood to face her parents, twirling in front of them to show off the gown. Her parents offered her their blessings on her union, then hugged her between them.

Over at his parents' apartment, Julian was making similar preparations for the long day ahead. Before dressing, he spent several minutes meditating about how much he loved Fiona and the personal metamorphosis he had undergone since meeting her a year before. Now he was ready to marry her and join his life with hers. Thoughts of everything he wished to manifest for their life together drifted through his mind. After another moment of quiet contemplation to get focused on the day, Julian rose to his feet. He walked over to the suit bag he had dropped off the day before. With a slight nervous tremor, he slid open the bag and removed the light gray Victorian summer suit he had chosen. He dressed with extra care so as not to wrinkle the fine fabric, smiling with affection for his bride as he tucked the white gloves Fiona had insisted he carry into his pocket. After a few frustrating attempts at fixing his tie, he called his parents to help him. Eion had some previous experience with this sort of thing and fastened the antiquated ligature around his neck.

Julian's parents stepped back to take in the sight of their son, dressed in his finest, and about to embark on a new life. They expressed their hopes for a good marriage and told him how happy they were with his choice in brides. Julian thanked them and wiped a small tear from each eye, then gave them each a firm hug, promising he would give them more to be proud of soon. Jensa glanced at the clock. If they didn't leave right away, they were going to be late. Julian took one last look in the mirror, then turned and followed his parents out the door.

Sarah reached the park before them. She secreted herself behind a bush where she could watch the ceremony without being spotted, hoping she would find some way to stop the wedding or that Julian would end the charade before his union with Fiona was made legal.

Fiona and her parents arrived at the park next, unaware anyone was planning to foil the day. They met Lady Celesta at the gazebo. Vyviane gasped as she took in the beauty of the place Fiona and Julian had chosen for their nuptials. A quilt of vibrant spring blooms and ribbons of bright silk interwoven with the same violet petunias Fiona had worn the day she and Julian had first met trailed down the sides of the gazebo. Chairs decorated with nosegay favors for the guests were arranged on one side of the gazebo. A small table with a guest book and basket of small scrolls waited at the end of the white carpet running down the center aisle.

After exchanging greetings with Vyviane and Gregory, Lady Celesta took Fiona's cape from them, then led her into the waiting room. Julian arrived soon after and was shown into the same room. Lady Celesta reminded them they had twenty minutes before the ceremony, then left to greet the wedding guests as Fiona and Julian waited in the small room together, at a loss for words to express their feelings about this day.

Outside the small room, Fiona and Julian's friends and loved ones were arriving, some having traveled from other cities to attend the wedding. As the guests took their seats before the gazebo, Sarah realized she would not be able to do anything to stop the proceedings. Too many people stood between her and the small room where Julian waited with Fiona. Instead she would have to watch this debacle happen, powerless to do anything except pray that Julian would come to his senses before he said "I do."

Julian was fully aware of what he was doing. This was the beginning of a life lived in perfect attunement to his true desires. He was eager to start that life. The time passed with racing speed and aching slowness as he waited in the little room with

Fiona for the initial strains of music that were their cue. When the first notes drifted into the room, they sprang from their seats. Julian placed Fiona's wreath of irises on her head, attached the long cape at her shoulders, then slid his white gloves over his hands. They linked hands and waited for Lady Celesta to come get them.

Fiona was suddenly aware that her life was about to change forever. Her life would be linked to Julian's. They would experience all of life's troubles and triumphs together, for better or for worse, as the old vows said. She was both petrified and excited by that idea. "Ready?" she asked with a quivering voice.

"I've never been more ready," Julian said, squeezing her hand in reassurance.

"Then let's do this."

Lady Celesta slid open the door and motioned for them to follow her out to the gazebo. She walked around the outer edge of the gazebo and chairs to cast the circle and bring everyone into sacred space. Fiona and Julian walked a few steps behind her and as stopped at the end of the white carpet while Lady Celesta continued up to the gazebo. She turned to face their gathered guests.

"Welcome all who have come today to witness the union of Fiona and Julian as they formally promise themselves to each other and, through their handfasting, join their lives together as one," Lady Celesta said. "Please stand now as Fiona and Julian join us in this celebration of their love."

Their guests stood, turning to face the end of the aisle where Fiona and Julian waited. In unison, Fiona and Julian took a step forward and glided down the aisle toward the gazebo. They mounted the steps to the platform, then stood hand in hand facing Lady Celesta.

She called the quarters to join them and bring the blessings of their elements to the union. She raised her hands skyward and invited the Goddess to join them. "O Great Lady, from whom all love is derived and for whom is known the greatest love, please join this couple today on the occasion of their handfasting. Grant them the blessings of your wisdom as they prepare to spend the remainder of their days together."

A moment of silence followed as white energy filled the gazebo and stretched out over the guests, enveloping all in the circle. Lady Celesta lowered her arms and held them out at her sides as she invoked the God. "O Great Lord, you who are derived from the Goddess' love and desire, please join us today as we bless the union of this couple before you. Grant them the blessings of your passion as they prepare to spend the remainder of their days together."

The God joined them in a burst of deep red energy that stretched out over the guests, filling them with joy. Then one of Fiona's friends read the Charge of the Goddess followed by one of Julian's friends reading the Charge of the God. Lady Celesta turned her attention back to Fiona and Julian. "Do you both come here today of your own free will to be joined before the Gods and all who are present here?"

Fiona and Julian turned to face each other. They clasped each other's hands as they answered "Yes" with certainty. Lady Celesta invited Fiona to make her vows first.

Fiona lifted her gaze to meet Julian's fully and extended her heart out to his. "Julian, I thank the Goddess every day for bringing you into my life and for the myriad ways you have added to it. I have come to know true joy and peace with you and experienced a love that I have never known before. I would not sacrifice a single day we have spent together. I love you and promise to honor our love for as long as we are together. I promise to support you and be honest with you. And I promise to be always true to myself, you, and our future."

Holding back the tears of love welling in his eyes, Julian took a deep breath. "Fiona, I have never met a woman like you. You fill my life with love and joy. Every day I thank the Goddess for blessing my life with yours. I promise to stand beside you and support you in whatever way you need. I promise to be honest with you and myself and to love you in every way I can. During our time together, I have experienced the greatest joy and greatest sorrow I have ever known. I promise to stand by you through both for as long as our love shall last. I love you."

A warm flutter rolled through Fiona at his words. She reached forward and pulled Julian into an impulsive hug to the applause of their guests. Julian dropped a kiss on her lips. Lady Celesta cleared her throat to get their attention, and he pulled away.

Lady Celesta held aloft two simple gold bands. "These rings symbolize the circle of life and the circle of love. By wearing them, Fiona and Julian recognize that love and life have their ups and downs, but they always come back to the beginning." She turned to Fiona and placed the larger band in Fiona's outstretched hand. "Fiona, place this ring on Julian's finger as a symbol of your dedication to him." Julian removed his gloves. He held out his hand as Fiona slid the gold ring onto his finger with a shaky hand. Lady Celesta turned to Julian and set the smaller band in his palm. "Julian, place this ring on Fiona's finger as a symbol of your dedication to her." Julian took one of Fiona's hands in his. He slipped the matching gold band onto her finger with a sigh of relief as it met with no resistance.

"Fiona and Julian will now bless each other with sustenance and prosperity through the ceremony of cakes and ale," said Lady Celesta, handing Fiona the ale horn.

Fiona held it out for Julian and said, "May you never thirst." Julian took a sip of sweet mead, then offered the horn back to Fiona with the same wish. She took a sip and handed the horn to Lady Celesta, who then offered Julian a small plate bearing two tiny bites of wedding cake. ·

Julian placed one morsel between Fiona's lips with the words, "May you never hunger." Fiona returned the sentiment.

Lady Celesta took the offering plate from Julian and set it on the altar, then removed a woven cord from around her neck. She held the cord above her as she explained to those gathered that Fiona and Julian had chosen to weave together strands of red silk to bring them passionate love, blue to bring them good fortune, and green to bring their lives continued growth. Fiona and Julian crossed their wrists and took each other's opposite hands. Lady Celesta wrapped the cord around their wrists three times, binding their hands, then knotted the ends together. She bade them to solidify the union with a kiss. The couple tipped their heads forward to touch lips for the first time as a handfasted couple. They stepped back, slipping their hands out of the cord, but leaving the knot intact as a symbol of their promises to each other and the bond of marriage between them.

One of Lady Celesta's coven members laid a handcrafted broom at the top of the stairs. Fiona and Julian clasped hands as they turned to face their guests and stepped over the broom, thereby ensuring them a fertile marriage. When they reached the bottom step, they continued to face their guests as Lady Celesta announced, "These two stand before you today joined as one. They now ask for our blessing."

Their guests unrolled the scrolls they had taken from the basket when they arrived and stood to read aloud the words printed inside. "Fiona and Julian, we served today as witnesses to your blessed union. Now we offer you this wish: may you be healthy, wealthy, and joyous for all the days of your lives."

The guests retook their seats, and Lady Celesta made her final pronouncement. "I declare before the Gods that you are joined in a sacred union as husband and wife," she said, concluding the ceremony of handfasting. She thanked the Lord and Lady for their attendance and bade them farewell, then repeated her thanks to the quarters. Fiona and Julian kissed one more time within the sacred circle, then moved back down the aisle and released the circle together.

The ceremony was complete. Fiona and Julian were legally married. Shoulders slumped, feeling the heavy weight of defeat, Sarah slunk away from the park to return to her cult's enclave and seek solace and guidance from the leader.

Still unaware of Sarah's presence, or that anyone had ill wishes for the newlyweds, the guests adjourned to the private wedding garden where the reception was being held. Lady Celesta showed Fiona and Julian back to the waiting room to sign their marriage certificate and make their union official under civil law. The embossed certificate was laid on the table. Fiona took a decorative pen from its holder and signed the document with a flourish. She watched as Julian signed the paper with equal exuberance.

"Now, there is just one more thing. Someone wishes to speak to you privately," Lady Celesta said. Fiona and Julian stared after her as she left the room, wondering what she had in store for them. They were surprised when the door reopened and Julian's aunt Mariah walked through it. She was a round woman in her mid-fifties, white hair woven into a braid down her back, cheeks ruddy from working in the garden. She was the earth mother incarnate.

Julian rose to his feet and hugged his aunt, who had come to the wedding from New San Francisco. Julian had told Fiona about Mariah many times, and she often recalled that Julian had once said she reminded him of Mariah. She hoped that Mariah would like her as much as she already liked Julian's aunt.

After Julian's introduction, Mariah gave Fiona a hug and said, "I've heard so much about you. Welcome to the family."

Comfort and familiarity filled Fiona. She returned Mariah's greeting and thanked her. They took their seats at the table.

"I hope this isn't bad news," Julian said.

With a chuckle and a wave of her hands, Mariah alleviated his concern, "No, dear, everything is as it should be." Seeing the two confused faces looking at her, she explained why she had wanted to see them alone. "I have looked into your future and want to share what I have seen." She saw the question about to spill from Fiona, and with a pat on her hand said, "Julian may have neglected to mention there are seers in our family. I am one of them. The only one in our family who still practices the old ways, I believe."

"I'd love to hear what you have to say," Fiona said.

Mariah leaned back in her chair with a wide smile, knowing that neither was expecting her next words. "Your union is much blessed, and you will have a very successful and joyous life together. You will, however, see much change in your lives, and very soon. In a little more than seven months."

Fiona and Julian glanced at each other, trying to puzzle out what that meant. "Mariah, you're speaking in riddles again," Julian said.

Mariah's smile grew deeper as she said to Fiona, "You are pregnant."

Shock jolted through Fiona. She clenched Julian's hand. "Oh, my Goddess. I didn't know." She turned to face him. "I thought my cycle was still off from the miscarriage!"

Julian jumped out of his chair and pulled Fiona to her feet, whisking her into his arms. He held her tight to him as tears of joy flowed from her eyes. "I love you. Now we are truly blessed," he said. As they kissed and hugged, Mariah slipped out of the room, leaving the two lovebirds to rejoice alone.

Their wedding day even more blessed by the news, Fiona and Julian rejoined the reception. The party continued long into the day as their guests mingled with one another and enjoyed the exquisite Beltane day on which Fiona and Julian had chosen to be handfasted. They greeted each of their guests and thanked them for being a part of their special day. Then they invited everyone to get a piece of wedding cake, the same cake from which Fiona and Julian had shared pieces.

Once all their guests had enjoyed a bit of cake and champagne, Fiona and Julian called them over to the Maypole erected nearby. The guests formed a circle around the tall white pole adorned with bright silk ribbons and offered Fiona and Julian gifts of love, peace, joy, fertility, growth, and abundance. Fiona and Julian thanked their guests for the gifts and promised to weave those gifts into their future. Then Lady Celesta began the dance of couples as the guests wove the ribbons around the pole in pairs, merging the gifts and binding them to Fiona and Julian.

The afternoon turned to dusk. They decided it was time to make their escape. They said goodbye to Lady Celesta, thanking her for performing their beautiful handfasting rite, then sought out their parents and thanked them for their blessings. Fiona and Julian returned to the waiting room to retrieve their marriage certificate and flee out the back. Upon sneaking out a back door, they discovered that their friends had figured out their scheme and were waiting outside with tulips filled with birdseed. Fiona and Julian ducked their heads and ran hand in hand through the cheering crowd to escape the shower of birdseed that followed them.

They continued to run all the way to the hotel where they had reserved the honeymoon suite and then raced laughing down the hall to their room. To keep with wedding tradition, it was the only room in the hotel with an old-fashioned, non-electronic door.

Fiona turned the knob. She was about to swing open the door when Julian stopped her, lifting her into his arms and kicking open the door with one foot. Fiona giggled and begged him to set her down. He did, but only after he had carried her into the large room overflowing with fragrant flowers. A bottle of sparkling cider, fresh strawberries, and two crystal glasses waited for them on a small table. Julian uncorked the wine as Fiona settled on the bed. He carried the full glasses to the bed, handing one to Fiona, who toasted their marriage.

After her first sip, Fiona leapt up from the bed, startling Julian, who almost choked on his cider. "What are you doing?" he asked.

Fiona continued to the dresser. She slid open the top drawer where the concierge had hidden Julian's present. "I have a gift for you." She lifted out the flat package Julian had seen on the altar.

"Oh, I have something for you, too." Julian rose and moved toward the closet where the concierge had secreted a square package.

They came back to the bed and exchanged their gifts. Fiona insisted Julian open his first. He unwrapped it quickly, curious to see what Fiona had been keeping secret for three days. With a gasp, he set the box down on the bed and lifted an antique gold frame out of the box. Inside the frame were their gratitude lists rewritten on white parchment in calligraphy and surrounded by a painted border of their wedding flowers. He leaned forward and kissed Fiona to thank her. "We'll hang it on the wall in the bedroom to remind us every day why we are together."

Fiona smiled, happy that he liked the present, then looked down at her own gift. Julian told her to open it. She ripped open the paper, then folded open the top flap of the box. With a bright smile, she took out a small birdhouse hand-painted with moonlight cosmos and oak leaves. "Those are the flowers and leaves we wore at our first handfasting," Julian said. Fiona nodded, remembering that romantic day a short six weeks after they had met, when they had known already that they were to spend the rest of their lives together. Fiona turned the tiny cottage in her hands, tracing a finger over the door where their names and the year were inscribed.

"Did you make this?" she asked.

"I built it and my friend painted it. It's to remind us of our first year together."

Touched, Fiona granted Julian a delicate kiss as a thank you. "I love you," she said. "We'll put it in the roof garden where it will be blessed by the birds who use it." Fiona set the house down beside her, then slid the frame out from between them. She leaned in to kiss Julian with more vigor. They lowered themselves to the bed to perform the Great Rite as a final promise to the Gods and each other.

Chapter 10

Litha Promises

Warm sunlight streaming down onto his face through the skylight stirred Julian from his restful slumber on the second day of his honeymoon. He rolled over in bed and gazed down at his beloved wife, who was still asleep. Admiring the gentle curves of her body, he watched her sleep and imagined how it would change over the next few months. He slid over to her peaceful form and wrapped his body around hers, lowering his lips to her forehead. He placed a soft kiss on her silky skin. "Good morning, Wife." His eyes flickered with a tender gleam as he lifted the covers, then slid underneath. His lips met with her bare belly, which he also graced with a soft kiss. "Good morning, baby."

Fiona stirred. Julian slid back up to her head as she opened her eyes and looked up at him. "Good morning, Husband," she murmured. She reached up to pull him into a more amorous embrace. Their lips pressed together and their tongues roamed the familiar crevices of each other's mouths, enjoying the experience of the old tinged with the excitement of a new marriage.

A soft knock at the door prevented Fiona and Julian from continuing further. Julian slipped out of bed to see who could be calling on them at this early hour. He returned with a platter of chopped fresh fruit. He climbed back into bed, then fed Fiona a morsel of ripe mango. She moaned with delight as the sweet fruit melted in her mouth. She sat up against the headboard to stare out the window at the undulating water before them. The waves crashing on the beach below their bungalow added natural music to their meal as they took turns feeding each other from the generous platter. "Goddess, it's amazing," Fiona said.

Julian glanced around their thatched hut outfitted with all the modern amenities. "It really is. I'm glad we decided to go with the beach villa."

Fiona elbowed him softly in the ribs. "They're all beach villas, silly! The whole island of Paradise is for honeymooners. And anyway, I meant the ocean." She nodded toward the window and the view of the rolling sea. Julian turned his gaze in that direction and was instantly transfixed by the power of the ocean, something he never would have noticed before Fiona had come into his life.

After their tropical breakfast, Fiona slipped into a bikini and wrapped a simple sarong around her waist while Julian pulled on a pair of shorts and a T-shirt. When she stepped out of the villa onto the pristine white beach below, her toes sank into wet sand and the warm waves lapped at her heels. Fiona jumped in surprise. She hadn't seen the ocean since she'd left Old San Francisco, and this was the first time she'd ever felt tropical waters on her feet. She glanced at Julian. The look on his face told her it was his first time, too. She took his hand, and they walked down the beach at the tide's edge. As they strolled down the sand, she maneuvered around to the shore side, then, with a sudden shove, dumped him into the ebbing water.

Laughing, he held firmly onto her hand as he fell and pulled her down with him. They tumbled over each other, scrambling through the rolling waves crashing over them to be the first one out of the water. Neither seemed a likely winner until Julian pulled Fiona to him and slipped backwards through the water, bringing them to rest on the sand. He pulled her mouth down to his and led her into a new lovemaking experience.

***

Early on his first day back from the honeymoon in Paradise, Julian yawned awake. He opened his eyes, expecting to see a thatched roof, and instead his gaze was met by a plain white ceiling. He remembered that their week-long sojourn of romance and lovemaking was over. They were back in the real world and starting work again today. Hoping to extend the honeymoon a little longer, he rolled over and nuzzled Fiona's sleeping body. Caressing her belly, he grazed her cheek with his lips. Fiona stirred against him as the sensation brought her one level closer to being awake. "Good morning, Wife," Julian whispered in her ear. He slipped his head under the covers and kissed her belly through her silk camisole. "Good morning, baby."

Through muffled sleep, Fiona murmured, "Good morning, Hus—." She lurched out of bed and raced for the bathroom. After a quick calculation, Julian followed her in, recalling what the early stages of her last pregnancy had been like. He found her kneeling over the toilet. She muttered something about morning sickness and asked him to please get her a glass of water and her phone. Pained at seeing Fiona's discomfort, Julian quickly returned with both items. Fiona took them from him. She leaned back against the wall, ordered the phone to call her mother, then took a sip of the water. Julian soaked a hand towel in cool water, then draped it over Fiona's sweat-dampened skin while she waited for Vyviane to answer.

"Hi, Mom. I started the morning sickness today," she said into the phone. "The doctor I saw before we left for Paradise confirmed what Julian's aunt said. I was expecting it around now." Fiona handed Julian the empty glass. "Juice," she whispered before turning her attention back to her mother. "Okay, thanks, Mom. I'll see you in a little while." She depressed the disconnect button, then set the phone on the floor beside her. Moments later, Julian was back at her side with a glass of grape juice.

"It's all we have. I can go get something else if you want," he said.

"No, it's okay. Mom's bringing over the tea she gave me last time. Goddess, six more weeks of this!" She dropped her head back against the wall.

Julian crouched on the floor beside her and reached out to hold her. "I'm sorry. I'll do anything you want to make this easier, babe."

"Thank you, sweetie. I appreciate that." She collapsed into his arms.

Later that afternoon, Fiona sent Julian to the store to find the exact brand of ginger cookies that had soothed her tummy during her last pregnancy. Their convenience mart didn't carry them, but the one a few stops down did. Julian went to the store, only to find that the aisles had been rearranged. He was going to have to hunt for the cookies. As he wandered the store, he heard Sarah's voice coming from another aisle. She was speaking to another member of her cult about their upcoming protest plans. He could tell from their voices that they were moving in his direction. Scurrying around the corner to avoid another confrontation with them, he found the cookie aisle. He grabbed five boxes of the cookies Fiona wanted, then hurried to the check-out. As he passed the boxes through the scanner, Sarah and her companion stepped into line behind him.

"What are you doing at this store?" Sarah asked.

His only thought was on getting home to Fiona quickly and without having another argument with Sarah. "I only live a couple stops over."

"But you have a mart in your building, don't you?"

Julian shrugged, trying to remain nonchalant. "Yes, but I wanted these cookies." He waved the box as he dropped it into a canvas bag to carry home.

Sarah's companion recognized the brand. "Those are the kind I ate when I was pregnant." Julian stiffened, then realized he had given himself away when he saw the shock on Sarah's face.

"She's pregnant?" Sarah asked.

Julian turned to her, his face blank, his tone blank. "Yes. And we're married." He turned back to the register so the computer could scan his retina and deduct the total from his account. "Good day."

He hastened out of the store, then turned down the street in the direction of his building. He was determined to get home to Fiona without being bothered by Sarah again, but she followed him out of the store, leaving her friend behind.

Sarah called after him. "Julian! Julian! Don't do this. That baby isn't yours."

He stopped. He had to put a stop to her trouble-making before Fiona had the baby. The police had said they didn't have enough to arrest her with yet, so he would have to take care of her himself. Sarah stopped a foot back from him. He turned to face her. "It's mine," he said.

"It may be your seed, but it is not your soul. It's a demon," she said with conviction.

Fury raced through him. He had tried to ignore her, to not let her get to him, but now she had gone too far. "Don't ever come near me again," he yelled.

Sarah fell to her knees, keening like a woman whose husband had just died. She reached out to touch his leg. "Please, Julian, I only want to save you. Can't you see what this woman is doing to you? If you have that child with her, you will never get free."

His face magenta with rage, he slapped her hand away, then grabbed her shoulders, yanking her onto her feet. "Listen to me!" he screamed, shaking her. He could see the terror in her eyes and loosened his grip. He lowered his voice to a low snarl. "Leave me alone. Leave Fiona alone. If you ever come near our child, I will kill you. Do you understand that?"

Sarah shrugged his hands away and stepped back. Her terror became rage. "No! I will not leave you alone! You are mine!"

Julian howled in frustration and anger, then turned on his heel and dashed away from her before he struck her, or worse.

"I will kill her before I let her have your child!" Sarah screamed after him as he raced down the street toward his apartment building.

He darted into the lobby where he fell against the wall, panting and shaking. Never in his life had he been so out of control. Sarah's last words echoed through his mind. She couldn't have meant that. He hadn't. They were just threats made in anger. He wouldn't tell Fiona about the confrontation. It would only upset her. He looked down at his feet. The bag from the store lay next to them. He should get those cookies up to Fiona.

He rolled his head back against the wall and called upon the Goddess to take his anger as he slowed his breath and calmed his nerves.

When he entered the apartment, he heard laughter coming from the office and followed the sound. Fiona and Vyviane were at her terminal looking at images of teddy bears and balloons. Fiona turned to him, grinning cheerfully.

"Hi sweetie. Want to help pick out some wallpaper?"

"For what?"

She laughed. "For the nursery, silly."

Her happiness was infectious. Julian joined his wife and mother-in-law at the terminal to choose a theme for the nursery, effectively banishing all thoughts of the exchange with Sarah from his mind.

***

Six weeks later, Julian awoke to the sound of Fiona in the bathroom dealing with her morning sickness again. He eased out of bed and padded into the kitchen to fix a cup of the soothing tea her mother had blended. While there, he grabbed the ginger cookies, once again remembering the argument with Sarah. She hadn't made another threat. In fact there had been no further contact with her since that horrible day. He shook his head to clear his mind of such thoughts, then set the cookies and tea on a tray. He carried the tray into the bedroom, set it on the bed, then continued into the bathroom to check on Fiona.

She came to the door. Julian slid his arm around her waist to help her move through the bedroom. "After all I'm going through, this baby had better be healthy," she said, only half in jest.

Julian helped her settle back in bed and stroked her cheek. "You know it will. Mariah promised us." He handed her the tea. "Now drink this. It's good stuff."

Fiona granted him a wan smile to show she appreciated his mothering. After Julian had gone back out to the living room, she leaned back against the fluffy pillows. She sipped at the tea, feeling its warmth pool in her belly. She munched on a cookie and rested one hand on her stomach. "It's okay. Settle down. We're here to keep you safe," she said to the baby inside her. By the time she had finished the cup of tea, her stomach had calmed. She set the empty cup aside.

Julian came back into the room. He took the tray off the bed and set it on the floor, then joined her under the covers to cuddle. "Are you sure you want to go hiking today?" he asked as he stroked her soft hair.

She turned to face him, then gave him a peck on the lips. "Yes. It's the one-year anniversary of our first handfasting, and we have new promises to make. The nausea is getting better, anyway."

"Okay. As long as you feel up to it."

Fiona nodded. She nestled down into his arms, and they faded back to sleep for a few more hours.

***

Fiona reawakened around noon, her stomach settled. She meandered out to the office to check her e-mail and snack on more ginger cookies. The most interesting message was from her mother. Fiona had just finished reading it when a smiling Julian walked into the room rubbing his eyes.

"I can't believe we slept so late," he said.

Fiona stood and hugged him. "I think we needed it." They held each other close for a long moment, the deep connection between them swelling in a rush of love. Fiona spoke again. "I got e-mail from my mom. They were approved for one of the new village homes. They move next week."

Julian leaned back to look at Fiona. "I thought the lots were booked up months ago."

"They were, but since I designed the ad campaign, I was able to get Mom and Dad an early application. Mom says to plan on celebrating Mabon there."

Julian hugged Fiona close again. "Our second Mabon. What an amazing year it's been. I love you."

Warm fuzzies washed through Fiona. "I love you," she murmured, then pushed him away with a playful shove. "But if we don't get dressed we're never going to make it on that hike today." Julian clicked his heels together and turned with a mock salute. He left the office to shower while Fiona went into the kitchen to pack a light lunch of fruit, thick-crusted bread, cheese, water, and the ginger cookies she carried with her everywhere.

She had just finished packing her backpack when Julian sauntered into the kitchen, dressed and ready to go. He wrapped an arm around her and patted her belly. "You two had better head off to shower or we won't get there till sunset." Fiona laughed and kissed him once more before skipping into the bedroom. A half-hour later, Fiona came back out of the bedroom arranging her T-shirt. "Ready?" he asked.

"Ready," she said, mimicking his earlier salute. She glanced down at his belt and noticed the absence of his phone. "You're showing improvement."

Julian smiled. "I'm learning." She went to sling the backpack over her shoulder, but he reached for it and snatched it out of her hands. "I'll carry that," he said.

"Julian, I'm pregnant, not an invalid," she protested, to no avail.

As she started to move toward the door, he whirled her into another hug. "Happy anniversary of our first handfasting," he said. "I would have downloaded a card, but I don't think they make them for this."

Fiona giggled as she kissed him. Julian returned the kiss, then whirled her back toward the door. "Now, march!" Fiona laughed harder as she high-stepped out of the apartment and down the hall with Julian following behind in lock-step. They continued the military pretense all the way to the PRT station, then collapsed aboard the car in a fit of laughter.

The PRTV pulled to a stop at the Mount Komo station. They hurried onto the platform, eager to reach the overgrown path that led to the hiking trail. They stopped at the foot of the meandering way to gaze up at the mountain in all its glory. Even though they had a perfect view of it from their apartment window, the fresh air filling their lungs and the soft rustle of the breeze brushing the fields of yarrow made it more breathtaking than either had recalled. Julian took a deep breath, giving his lungs a refreshing taste of country air, then reached out for Fiona's hand to guide her toward the mountain. So deeply had the previous Midsummer affected him, that although he had only traveled the path once before, the way to the waterfall was etched on his memory.

As they walked, Julian reeled off the names of the plants Fiona had taught him the year before, as well as some new ones they had learned together. She began to wonder if he had been keeping a photographic memory from her. He assured her that he didn't have one, but he made a point of memorizing everything she taught him. He knew how important those things were to her. He helped her pluck some of the herbs from the ground and echoed her thanks to each plant for its generous gift.

The sound of rushing water grew louder as they followed the path up the mountain. They rounded a bend and were stunned by the sight of the magnificent falls tumbling into the churning lake a short distance ahead. "It's more amazing than I remembered," Julian whispered.

Entranced by the power of the water, Fiona took his hand and pulled him toward the waterfall, yearning to rest her feet on the sandy bank beside the lake. Within minutes they had moved off the path to the small lakeside beach. Julian took a small blanket out of the backpack. He spread it on the ground, then arranged their food onto the blanket. Suddenly feeling ravenous, Fiona ripped apart the bread and started to devour it before Julian had a chance to get settled beside her.

Julian teased her as he took some of the food for himself. The bubbling water brought a meditative calm over Fiona, and she slowed her eating to a more reasonable pace. The couple ate in silence, each content to enjoy the meal and listen to the soothing sound of the water pounding over the cliff above. After they had finished, Julian stood and stripped off his clothes, whooping as he leaped into the frigid lake. He spun in the water to face Fiona. "It's great. Why don't you come in?"

Fiona kicked off her shoes and wriggled out of her clothes. "Tell you what, I'll meet you on the other side of the waterfall." She tempted him with her bare flesh as she scampered over the wet rocks at the edge of the fall. After she had disappeared behind the wall of water, Julian climbed out of the lake and went to their pack, retrieving the dried, year-old handfasting cord from a zippered pocket. He draped it around his neck, then made his way across the rocks to the cove behind the waterfall.

Fiona awaited him on the mossy bank where they had made love a year before. She sat up in surprise when she saw the chain of flowers around Julian's neck. "I can't believe you brought it! How did you get it here without me noticing?"

"I packed it while you were showering." He lowered his body down to hers, and they reclined on the soft moss. He joined his hand with Fiona's and wrapped the chain around their wrists, securing it so it wouldn't come off as they made love. His lips met hers in a burst of desire, and his body molded over hers. She slipped her free hand over his back and pulled him tight against her.

She reveled in the pleasure of his cool skin against hers. Fiona dipped her head back. He grazed his tongue over her neck in the familiar motion that never failed to bring her to the brink of ecstasy. With fevered lust, she pushed Julian up into a sitting position. She mounted his hips and brought him into her, their hands still bound together at their side.

Their eyes locked as the sexual connection between them deepened. Their energy centers opened to each other as they had countless times before, exchanging energy and heat and spurring each other on to greater heights of passion, until they brought their lips together again and exploded in climax.

Fiona rested her head on Julian's shoulder, and he on hers. They loosened their hands from the cord, then let it fall to the moss so they could tighten their arms around each other. They relaxed into the deep love flowing between their heart chakras, re-energizing the spiritual and physical connection between them.

They lay back on the bank and fell asleep still twined in each other's arms. After they awakened from their brief naps, Julian gathered up the chain. Then they swam across the lake to the patch of wildflowers where their first handfasting had taken place. They knelt on the grass, facing each other, and Fiona reached for Julian's hands. "I thought we could meet our child today," she said, "and make our vows to it so it will know it is loved before it comes into this world."

Julian looked at her with confusion. "How?"

"All we have to do is meditate and ask the Goddess for an introduction."

Julian nodded his agreement. They repositioned themselves to sit cross-legged and linked hands again. Julian slipped into a trance, as Fiona had taught him, by counting his breaths, drawing each one deep into his lungs and holding it before releasing the breath and letting his mind become blank.

Fiona chose to concentrate on the soothing sound of the rushing water. It drowned out the chaos of her mind and brought her into her spiritual center. The deafening falls faded into the background as her third eye opened. She asked the Goddess to please let them meet their child.

A rustling in the leaves at the edge of the clearing drew Fiona's and Julian's attention. They turned to see a doe emerge from the woods beside the waterfall. Fiona recognized the animal as one of her spirit guides. The doe approached them on the grass and Fiona reached up to stroke her flank. The doe bowed her head to Fiona, then turned to sniff Julian. She looked long into Julian, then turned again and disappeared back into the grove. Fiona started to rise to her feet to follow, but her intuition told her it would be better to wait behind. As she settled back onto the grass, the doe returned with the spirit of a baby on her back.

The doe knelt before them. Fiona lifted the baby off its back, holding it close. Its spirit couldn't speak, but Fiona knew who it was. She stroked the girl child's downy skin and whispered into her ear, "You're the baby I lost, aren't you?"

The girl nodded her head yes. Fiona handed the baby to Julian, who was beside her. He took their daughter in his arms. "I hope you are the child Fiona is carrying. I want you so much. You're such a beautiful girl."

The baby waved her head from side to side, indicating she was not to be their child. With a rustling of leaves, the doe emerged from the woods. Fiona and Julian had been so intent on the baby that they had not heard the doe leave. They looked up to see another child on her back. Julian held their almost-daughter to him, wishing she could somehow be theirs.

Fiona leaned over to stroke her face. "Whomever you belong to, I know you will have a good life. They will be blessed by you. Goodbye, sweet child," she said through choking tears.

The doe came to them, and Julian placed the baby girl on

the doe's back while Fiona picked up the other child. As they gazed at the baby she cradled in her lap, she realized she was holding a boy. She cuddled him to her chest, falling in love with the tiny soul, amazed by how right he felt in her arms. "Are you ours?" she asked, but before the child nodded yes, they knew he would indeed be their son.

Fiona released the child to Julian, who took the strong little man in his arms, positioning the child so he could look into his big eyes. "I promise to protect you and teach you the ways of the world. I treasure you already and love you more than I thought I could love anyone except your mother," he said.

As Fiona watched her husband make vows to their un-born child, fresh tears welled up inside. He looked up at her and planted a soft kiss on her tear-soaked lips. "I love you. Thank you for him."

He handed the child back to Fiona so she could make her own promises to her beloved baby boy. She held him in her lap and looked into his innocent eyes. "I promise to love you and raise you to be a good man like your father, a strong person, and a gentle soul. I will never stop loving you. You can't possibly know what you mean to me, but I will try to show you every day."

Astonishing love spilled out of Fiona and Julian. They stared in awe at their son, who stared back at them with perfectly formed, dark green eyes. Their heart centers sent waves of energy to the child, and he returned the energy. It joined and merged with theirs to seal their bond.

Without a sound, the doe returned barebacked. It knelt before them, but Fiona wasn't ready to relinquish the child. Julian reached over and lifted him out of her arms. "Soon you won't have to," he said. Fiona nodded and understood that he was right. He set the baby back on the doe, and they watched her disappear into the woods, carrying their child safely on her back.

The woods closed around the doe, and Fiona and Julian lay back on the grass, hand in hand, to stare up at the cloudy sky. They watched their future unfold in the white clouds overhead. They saw images of Fiona pregnant, Julian holding their tiny squalling child at birth, both of them playing with him as he aged into a toddler, Julian teaching him how to use a terminal, Fiona showing him how to garden, and on through the years. As the pictures faded, they drifted off to sleep on the grassy patch surrounded by wildflowers.

The sun moved behind the waterfall. Fiona stirred. She rolled over to nuzzle Julian awake. With a soft moan, he stretched and blinked, then gazed into Fiona's clear green eyes. The same eyes he had seen on their son. He smiled and hugged her. Fiona returned the gesture and murmured, "It's getting late. We should be going." She moved up onto her knees and pulled him up into a sitting position. He glanced at the sky.

"I guess you're right." He sighed. "I wish we could stay here forever."

"Me, too. But the real world beckons." She skimmed her hand across her belly. "And this little boy needs to eat again."

Julian rolled to his feet and helped Fiona the rest of the way up. They swam across the small lake to their belongings, then dressed and packed up the remains of their picnic lunch, being careful not to leave anything behind that might damage the environment.

As they hiked back down the mountain path, Julian took the lead, stopping to survey the downhill slope whenever he thought it might be too difficult for Fiona. She reminded him that she had hiked this path many more times than he had and would be fine, but she did appreciate his protectiveness.

They emerged at the end of the path as the sun was setting below the horizon. They called a PRTV, then boarded the car. Collapsing inside it, they realized just how exhausted they were, despite taking two naps on the mountain. They linked hands again and rested their heads on each other, reliving the images they had seen in the sky and the vision of their son in their arms.

Peace from the knowledge that their son would be healthy soothed them. Even though Mariah had promised them he would, both had feared deep down that Fiona would suffer another miscarriage. Their anxiety turned to anticipation as they looked forward to the day their son would arrive and they could begin sharing their world with him and living the vows they had made to him in the grassy clearing beside the waterfall.

Chapter 11

The Wake

When he returned home from his sojourn on the mountain with Fiona, Julian had a message from his mother on his satellite phone. Jensa wanted him to call her as soon as he got the message. As he waited for her to answer, a variety of reasons for the urgent request ran through his mind. What if his dad was sick? What if she was sick?

"Hi, Mom. You said to call?"

There was a long pause before Jensa answered, then she said, "It's Mariah. Her cancer has returned. It's in her liver now."

He hadn't thought of that one. His stomach knotted into a ball. He sat down on the chair next to him. "What are they doing for her?"

Jensa explained that they were going to do some chemotherapy and radiation to try to force her into remission, but she had probably a year left. Julian promised to call his aunt soon and pray for her every day. He disconnected the phone and went to find Fiona. She was in the bedroom emptying her backpack. He sat on the edge of the bed and told her the news, his head down, his voice barely audible.

She hugged him. "We'll get her something to help. Maybe a crystal," she said. Julian nodded.

***

The next morning Fiona and Julian went to the Pagan store and asked for a stone to help with cancer. The shopkeeper advised them to get apophyllite. She had just received a gorgeous green cluster of it that day. After quickly blessing it to bring Mariah healing energy, they wrapped up the package and shipped it off to her. She called the next day to tell them how much she appreciated it, and that she wasn't going anywhere soon. She was going to beat the cancer again.

Julian spoke to his mother almost daily on the phone after that, getting updates on Mariah's condition. It wasn't going as well as her doctors had hoped. Six weeks later, she slipped into a coma. The family knew there wasn't much time left. Julian lit a candle for her and spent several hours watching it burn. He did his best to project energy into the candle in hopes that it would transmit his love and support to his cherished aunt.

***

Fiona stood at the sink washing dishes while Julian spoke to Jensa again. The sharp increase of pain in his voice drew her attention away from the task. She stood at the ready to go to him.

He hung up, turning to her with a heavy sigh and a lump of choking tears in his throat. "My Aunt Mariah died this morning. The cancer took her." He forced the words out one at a time as their gravity sank in. Fiona crossed over to him to take him into her arms as the first wave of grieving sobs rocked his body. Together they sank to the floor. She cradled him while he cried.

When his tears had run out, he lay spent in her arms on the kitchen floor and stared up at the ceiling. She stroked his hair, her light touch soothing his twisting mind. "The memorial is in three days," he said. "She left detailed instructions. This is going to be something very different for my family."

Fiona looked down into his eyes. "I'm coming with you."

Julian turned in her arms and caressed her gently sloping belly. "Are you sure it's okay for you to travel?" Fiona nodded. Julian accepted that without argument.

***

Three days later, Fiona and Julian arrived in New San Francisco by superjet, a high-speed natural gas powered airplane. Julian's parents had arrived a day earlier to make arrangements for the memorial and they met Fiona and Julian at the arrival gate. After a sober greeting, the four of them made their way out to a PRTV.

The foursome boarded a car and sat in silence. They stared out the windows as the car zipped toward the mortuary where they would join the rest of the family before departing for the mountaintop with Mariah's ashes. As Fiona watched New San Francisco pass by her window, she recognized a few of the old landmarks she remembered from her childhood beside the high-tech buildings the City Corp had built. A part of her wished her parents had never left the beautiful city, but it hadn't been beautiful when they'd left. New San Francisco had taken years to become what it was now. Her parents had made New Denver their home rather than cling to what had been. And if they hadn't moved to New Denver, she might not have met Julian.

The PRTV pulled up to a small, low building set away from the rest of the City. It housed the City's Death Services Department. As soon as the car stopped, an attendant swung open their door and whisked away their bags. Jensa and Eion followed him into the building. Julian stopped before they went in and turned to Fiona. In a hushed tone he said, "I wish we were at the Lammas campout right now."

"I do, too. But if it helps, in a way we're honoring the wake aspect of Lughnasadh instead."

Julian nodded. "I know. But that doesn't make this any easier," he whispered as he bowed his head in sorrow.

Fiona slid her arms around him and held him as his body went slack against hers and another sob rolled through him. They stayed that way until several minutes had passed. His tears subsided. He lifted his head to look into her eyes. "Thank you," he said.

"I love you."

Julian reached for Fiona's hand as they went into the building to wait for the departure vehicle with the rest of his family. While they waited, he reintroduced Fiona to his aunt and uncle, their daughter, and her six-year old daughter. Those four people comprised his entire extended family. After a moment of stilted conversation, the attendant came in. He ushered the family outside. They boarded the van that would take them to the site Mariah had chosen for her memorial.

In silence, the family members rode the solar van to the top of the mountain where they would mourn the passing of their beloved matriarch. Julian peered out at the scenery moving by the window and reflected on Mariah's life. She had chosen not to marry and instead had served as the knot that held the family together through everything. She had acted as mother to both Julian and his cousin whenever their mothers had been sick. She was the best person he had ever known, and he had spent his life striving to achieve the peace she carried naturally within. Now he was joining his family to cast her ashes to the wind. It was a time for saying goodbye and a time for celebrating her life.

The van pulled to a stop in a plateau clearing just below the peak. The attendant came around to open the side door. Eion stepped down onto the earth. After a few hushed words with the attendant, he pointed to the spot where their camp should be set up. While the attendant pitched their tents, the family members scattered across the mountain clearing. Some walked to the edge to peer into the woods, half expecting Mariah to come walking out of them, while others wandered a brief way up the path they would later follow to the top.

Julian took Fiona's hand again, leading her toward the far edge of the clearing. They stopped at the bottom of a cliff wall and gazed up at a retreat house perched peacefully at the edge of the earth. "She took me there when I was a child," he said.

Fiona was surprised to learn he had been to old San Francisco. "You never told me that."

He nodded. "I had pretty much forgotten about it until now. I was only seven. She wanted to teach me to meditate, but all I wanted to do was run around the house in circles. Finally she gave up. I loved every second of that trip." Julian turned and took Fiona in his arms. "I wish you'd gotten a chance to know her better. You have so much in common with her . . . had so much . . . I'm not sure what's right . . . ."

Fiona leaned in closer and tightened her arms around him. "I know what you're trying to say, sweetie. I wish I'd known her better, too. At least she was able to come to our handfasting."

Julian nodded, taking only slight comfort in the thought. "Yes, at least."

He pulled away and, after another glance up at the retreat house, Julian and Fiona went back to the center of the camp. The attendant carried baskets of food and offerings to the table. The attendant spoke to Eion once more, then got back into the van and drove away, leaving the family members to deal with their mourning period in solitude. Jensa asked Fiona and Julian to help her set up the altar according to Mariah's instructions.

With reverence, they approached the small table the attendant had left. Jensa picked up the box of offerings on the ground beside it. The table would hold trinkets that represented Mariah's pastimes, photos of her life, and objects that bore special significance to her or her family. She had chosen each item carefully in the weeks after she had been diagnosed. All would be burned later in a ceremony, then sent off with her ashes to give her solace on her journey toward the Summerlands and her next life. Julian spotted a photo of his aunt and himself as a child. Overcome, he collapsed on a nearby bench as the memories of those days came rushing back. Fiona started to go to him, but he waved her back to help Jensa with the emotional task of arranging a tribute to her beloved sister-in-law.

As darkness fell, Julian helped Eion build a fire in the stone circle beside the altar. The family gathered in a circle around the altar and fire in dark cloaks. Eion read aloud Mariah's instructions for her memorial. When he was done, the family members reached out to grasp one another's hands. They took a moment to quiet their hearts and focus their minds on the ritual they were beginning. One by one, they stepped up to the altar to choose an offering. They spoke of what it meant and of what Mariah had meant to them, then placed it into the blazing fire. After the individual offerings had been added to the flames, Jensa gathered the remaining photos and objects from the altar and set them in the fire. They watched the offerings burn, carrying treasured memories away with them.

The family members watched in silence, tears streaming down their faces as their memories whipped through them and tore at their souls. In testament to their love for Mariah, they experienced the pain wholly and without chagrin. When midnight approached, they picked up the drums and rattles the attendant had supplied. With faltering hands, they began to drum a chaotic rhythm until their emotions overtook them and an ancient knowledge surged forth, guiding them into a tribal rhythm of mourning, ushering their sorrow of out of the depths where it hid and clung to their souls. They hammered out their pain on the drums as it swelled inside them again and again, letting the beat absorb them, becoming one with the rhythm. Moaning and screaming into the night, they let their pain escape into the darkness. The wind picked up as the drumming became more fervent, carrying their grief away on its gusts. They continued through the night until their hands ached and their arms screamed from fatigue.

As dawn rose, they dropped their instruments to the ground and the remnants of the mourning music echoed through the trees until silence once again reigned over their vigil to the matriarch. The new day's sun quelled the wind, and Eion stepped to the fire pit to gather the ashes in a stone urn. As the last remnants of Mariah's life dropped into the urn, he lost his strict self-control and set the urn down, his shoulders shaking with fresh anguish. He motioned for Julian to come forward and asked him to carry Mariah's urn as he could not do it himself. Julian nodded. He gingerly lifted the urn from the bench. Fiona came forward, and Jensa handed her the urn bearing the ashes of the offerings without a word.

Julian and Fiona led the silent procession out of the circle toward the path to the mountaintop. The family members worked their way to the peak in quiet meditation. There was no rush. This was a time of recollection and sorrow. As they approached the peak, the wind picked up again, and it seemed to Fiona that Mariah was making the wind to carry her away to the Summerlands.

They reached the top and formed a half-circle around the edge of the cliff. Julian stepped to the very edge, then unscrewed the lid of his aunt's urn. He held the jar aloft and tipped it forward until the ashes began to fall from the lip. The wind grabbed at his cloak and lifted the ashes away from him, carrying them off the mountain and into the sky. Light from the setting full moon and rising sun streamed through the ashes, creating a glow around them and allowing the family to witness their matriarch's ascension. When the urn had released the last of the ashes, Fiona joined Julian at the edge with the second urn. She held it over her and tipped it so the ashes contained inside could follow the path of the first.

Still in silence, Fiona and Julian watched the ashes drift away from them, new tears flowing over their already damp cheeks. They offered prayers of safe passage to Mariah. Julian realized that after this mourning period, he would not have many more chances to say goodbye. Mariah had made peace with her death. She would depart for the other side immediately after the memorial was completed. She had only stayed to witness the farewells from her family. Julian centered on her spirit as Fiona had taught him and spoke with his soul about the love he felt for Mariah. A gentle breeze caressed his cheek. He could almost hear her whisper, "I know," in his ear. A deep peace came over him. Although his grief would last a long time, the worst of it had gone from him.

The wind began to drop down and the family members took it as their cue to leave the mountaintop. As he followed his family down the path, Julian began to remember the happy times with Mariah, times when she had helped him experience life at its richest. By the time he reached the camp, the wind had died away, leaving only a gentle breeze to whisper through the trees around him. Once again he joined his family around the fire circle. They cast off their dark cloaks to reveal the colorful cotton tunics, pants, and dresses Mariah had requested they wear. Eion wore rich royal blue, his sister's favorite color. Julian wore ruby red, the color Mariah had worn when she had taken him to the retreat house. Fiona wore white to signify Mariah's pure heart. Jensa wore violet, a power color Mariah had often worn herself. Eion's brother had chosen forest green, to signify Mariah's love for nature, and his wife had selected golden yellow as her tribute to Mariah's reverence for the sun. Their daughter wore orange, a color Mariah had said gave her vibrancy, and her young daughter wore silver in honor of Mariah's connection with the moon.

They sat on benches surrounding the fire pit and took turns telling stories about Mariah. Julian recalled a time when she had helped him out of trouble without chastising him. His cousin retold how Mariah had helped her see a truth she had missed in her anger. Jensa told of the gatherings Mariah had held in her home and of all the happy times she had spent there. After each member of the family had told a story, Julian's cousin picked up a harp. She began to play the tune Mariah had sung to her, which she had then in turn sung to her daughter. The song flooded

Julian with joyous memories of the time long ago when he had felt safe and at peace. Times when his aunt had cradled him in his bed, rocking him to sleep so the monsters couldn't come.

As the song continued, Fiona noticed that Eion had remained silent though all this and Jensa was having too difficult of a time with her own sadness to comfort her suffering husband. Fiona patted Julian's hand and nodded toward Eion. Julian followed her nod. They crossed over to sit beside Eion. "Do you want to talk about it?" Fiona asked in a hushed tone.

Eion looked into Fiona's supportive face. His tears poured forth as he explained that he couldn't get past his sorrow to summon the joyous memories the rest of his family were sharing. Instead he felt all the pain of having to live out the rest of his days without his best friend to confide in. He longed for the days they had spent as children without a care for the future. Now he could only remember the pain of watching her die. The image of her passing, the sensation of her hand in his at her last moment, had stayed with him throughout the memorial. He recalled her final words to him before she fell into the coma. He played them over and over in his head, wishing there had been time to answer her.

"You can do that now," Fiona reminded him.

Eion nodded. "You're right. Thank you." He stared at her for another moment. "You're so much like her, you know."

Fiona's lips spread in a small smile. "Julian said something like that when we first met."

At the mention of Julian, Eion turned and reached out for his son. They held each other close as another wave of grief crashed through them. "I know, Dad. I know. I'll miss her, too."

Eion rose. "It's time to carry out her last wishes," he said, then went back to his tent. He emerged with a large box. He struggled with it as he carried it back to the fire circle. Julian rushed over to help him, but Eion insisted on carrying the box himself. It was his duty. Mariah had requested this favor of him when she had first learned that her cancer had returned. He set the box down by the fire, and, when the circle quieted, repeated to his family his sister's words in her last moments. She had wished they would remember the happy times. She had hoped

Julian and his cousin would pass what she had taught them on to their children. She had wanted her traditions to live on in them. As Mariah had approached her death, she had told Eion where he could find the items she wanted to give her family members to remember her by. She had written a note to each of them explaining the meaning behind the gift. Eion called them up in turn.

He lifted a wooden humidor out of the box and presented it to Julian. Julian took it from him, then recalled for his family the time from his childhood when she had taken him rock-hunting. She had given him the box to keep his treasures in. She had sat with him in her kitchen and explained the name and healing properties of each rock. He had forgotten about the box before the year was out, but Mariah had obviously kept it. He opened the box. The rocks he had found that day were still inside their compartments, neatly labeled in his careful childish printing. Julian sat down next to Fiona and unfolded the note to read through his tear-blurred eyes.

My sweetest Julian,

I saved these rocks for you because I knew you would someday want them for your own son. Teach him what I taught you and give these rocks to him when the time is right. You will know when that is. I can't tell you how I elated I was when you found Fiona. I see so much of myself in her and yet she is so much more. I will be watching over you from above. Call out whenever you have need of me. I will miss you.

Love always,

Mariah

Eion continued distributing the gifts to his family. When he came to the last gift, Fiona was surprised to hear him call her name. She went to Eion and he handed her a thick, leather-bound journal. She carried the heavy volume to her place beside Julian, then opened it to the first page. It was Mariah's old herb lore book. Within its pages, she had written everything she had learned over the years about specific herbs, their properties, the appropriate time to harvest them, and how to grow them. Fiona's name had been printed at the bottom of the list of five names on the front page, indicating that it had been passed down for five generations. Fiona flipped through the book and read a few of the entries, fascinated by what each woman had chosen to share about an herb and how their attitudes had changed and evolved. The last two hundred pages were blank, awaiting Fiona's contributions and those of generations yet to come. As she turned the pages, a note slipped out from between them. Fiona opened the letter and read it to herself.

My dear Fiona,

I worried about what would become of my knowledge once I passed away until Julian brought you into the family. I recognize myself in my younger days in you and I know that you will continue to pass on the knowledge of the old ways that I learned over the years. Much of what I know you have already learned on your own, but I hope there is something between these pages that will be of value to you. Your contributions will lend another sensibility to the book, one I am sure is needed, for we are old women when the book is passed. It is in need once more of a fresh viewpoint. Please teach the child you carry all you know, and pass this book on when the time is right.

All my love,

Mariah

Fiona failed to notice the tears slipping from her eyes until one fell on the note and began to blur the ink. She quickly wiped up the wet spot before it could further smudge Mariah's words, then tucked the note back inside the book for safekeeping. She silently vowed to do as Mariah had asked in the letter.

The gifts distributed, Eion announced that it was time for the feasting to begin. All of Mariah's favorite foods were there. All the little secrets she had passed on to them had been used in preparing the sumptuous meal. The family asked Fiona to bless the feast as she had more experience in these matters than they did. She stood at the head of the table and lifted her arms into the air, blessing the food in Mariah's name and the name of the Great Mother. Then she prepared a plate for Mariah and set it in the place of honor at the head of the table. After she returned to her seat, the feasting began in earnest. They passed the ale around the table and toasted to Mariah. Then they devoured the food with gusto after their long fast, just as they always had when Mariah had prepared it.

Sated after the hearty meal, the family retired to their tents to sleep for the night. Fiona and Julian lay in each other's arms, reflecting on the previous twenty-four hours and how Mariah's memorial had affected them. Fiona now felt more a part of Julian's family than she had even at their wedding.

She turned to look at Julian as he ran his hand over her round belly. The little boy inside her responded with a sharp kick. "Oh my Goddess! I felt it!" Julian said.

Fiona smiled and patted her tummy. "He's a very active little boy."

Julian lay his head back on the pillow and pondered the circular nature of life. His aunt's life had just ended and his child's was just beginning. That thought brought him comfort through his mourning, and he knew that he would meet his aunt again one day.

***

In the morning, Fiona, Julian, and Julian's family awoke to a clear, warm day. Their hearts were still heavy, but not as heavy as they had been when the family had arrived on the mountaintop two days before. They gathered around the table for their morning feast before they departed for home. While they ate, they shared their dreams. Mariah had joined each of them during the night to share some final words of wisdom, words they would all cherish until the end of their own days.

Once the meal was completed, the family members packed up their belongings from the tents, retrieved the instruments from the fire circle, and gathered the leftover firewood. They scoured the site for any last trace of their visit, determined to leave nothing behind as Mariah would have insisted. Satisfied that the site was clean, they took down the altar table.

They had a little time before the attendant arrived, so Julian took Fiona's hand and led her toward the path to the retreat house. Something was drawing him up there for a last look at the place he had once visited with Mariah in his childhood. As they walked, Julian reflected on the similarities of his wife and his aunt.

Fiona spotted an herb she had seen in the book and picked it. She slipped one hand down to her baby and reiterated her promise that she would teach him everything she knew about herbs and pass on all the knowledge Mariah had left her in the book.

They wended their way up the path to the place where they had scattered Mariah's ashes. Julian didn't understand what had brought him there until he spotted a tiny scrap of photo that had escaped the flames of the offering fire tucked into a crag of rock. The tiny scrap bore only Mariah's bright smile. As Julian bent to pick up the small scrap, a crow flew down from the tree-top overhead and snatched it out of his hand. Fiona and Julian watched in awe as the bird flew away with the scrap, following the path Mariah's ashes had taken. Mariah had been with them to witness their grieving, storytelling, singing, and peace-making. Now she was departing for the other side. A deeper peace came over them. With a silent prayer, they turned and made their way down the path to the camp where the attendant was just arriving to carry them back to the City.

The family members hugged and bid one another farewell while the attendant packed all their gear into the van. Just before boarding it, they each turned back to the mountain for a final goodbye to their beloved matriarch. Fiona looked to the top where Mariah's ashes had been released, and placed a hand on her lips, blowing a kiss to Julian's aunt. Mariah returned the gesture with a gentle brush of air against her cheek. Fiona bowed her head, wiped the tears from her eyes, and stepped into the van.

As the van started the journey down the mountain, Julian leaned over and murmured in Fiona's ear. "Thank you for coming, love."

She turned to him. "You don't need to thank me. You're my husband."

Julian leaned back against the seat. "I wish our child had known her," he whispered, his shoulder slumping at the new revelation about his aunt's death.

Fiona reached across for his hand and gave it a reassuring squeeze. "He will."

Julian sat up. He looked into Fiona's eyes and realized

154 - *Selene Silverwind*

that she was right. He would teach his child the lessons Mariah had taught him, and she would never truly die as long as they remembered her. Relieved by this thought, Julian sat back against the seat and began to make a mental list of everything he needed to teach the child inside Fiona.

Chapter 12

A Thanksgiving Feast

When they returned home from the memorial, Julian made a beeline for the bedroom. He collapsed on the bed, exhausted by the wide range of emotions he had experienced over the last few days. Fiona wanted to sleep too, but she was hungry again. She went to her terminal to check her e-mail while she snacked on cookies and juice.

She had several messages waiting for her after her three days away. A few of them were from the City Corporation and she guessed they were new assignments. She would get to them later. Right now she was in the mood for chit-chat. A friend had attended the Lammas camp-out with a new boyfriend and had promised to send details. That was just what she needed to read. As she scrolled through the list, she spotted a message from an unknown address with the subject, "Painting Purchase." She had recently told the gallery owner that she was interested in selling a few of her pieces. The owner must have given her address to a buyer. Making a sale would be good for her mood. She opened the message.

"You will release Julian from your spell and free him to return to the one he belongs with," it said. Stunned by the vile words, Fiona stopped reading. She stood, then padded into the bedroom. She should get Julian to read it with her. It had to be from Sarah. As she entered the room, she saw Julian sprawled across the bed, breathing deeply and evenly. Lines of exhaustion were etched into his face despite his sound sleep. She couldn't bring herself to wake him.

She went back out to the office and sat down at her terminal again. After a deep breath, she continued reading. "Your child will die whether or not you do this, but you will die too unless you unbind him from your web of deceit and lies." Every muscle in Fiona's body clenched. How did Sarah know about the baby? "Julian is mine. Only I can have his rightful child. You are carrying the seed of evil, and it is my duty to stop you from unleashing it on the world. The day is coming." The message rambled on with more hateful words, but Fiona stopped reading. She skimmed to the bottom. As she had guessed, it was from Sarah.

Fiona's mind reeled. Was Sarah really planning to carry out her threat. No, she couldn't do that. She wouldn't do that. It was an innocent baby, and Fiona had done nothing wrong. Her child was safe. Her child had to be safe. Mariah had promised them. Sarah was just spewing her hatred in another attempt to break them up. She wouldn't tell Julian about it. The last week had already been too emotional. She wouldn't upset him more by telling him of Sarah's empty threats. But she would be more careful when she went out.

She forwarded the message to the police to add to the case already pending against Sarah, then went back into the bedroom and climbed onto the bed. Settling beside Julian, she reached out to stroke his hair. He turned over in his sleep and put his arm around her, as if he knew she needed him. Fiona slid closer to him, letting his protective arm soothe her fear and lead her toward sleep.

The phone ringing jolted Fiona from her sleep. She sat up, heart pounding, mouth agape until she realized what the sound was. She snatched it up. It was Vyviane, calling to make sure they had gotten home and offering her support. Fiona thanked her mother for the offer and said she'd call back later. She hung up the receiver, then looked at Julian. He hadn't been awakened by the phone. Fiona lay back down on his arms, laughing at herself for being so panicked by the simple ringing of the phone.

***

Fiona spent the next few weeks peering over her shoulder whenever she left the apartment, searching for some sign of

Sarah attempting to follow through on her threat. She checked her e-mail daily for another threat, but none came. When Julian noticed Fiona's odd behavior and asked her about it, she waved it away as a symptom of her raging hormones. She never told him of the hateful message.

The weeks slipped by until the fall equinox was just a day away. A very pregnant Fiona bustled in the kitchen preparing the batter for a loaf of bread she planned to bring to the Thanksgiving festival being put on by her parents' eco-village. She poured the batter into a pan, then groaned quietly as she bent to open the oven door. How was she going to get the bread into the oven without leaning over too far? She had folded herself only a few inches when Julian, who seemed to have developed ears that rivaled a dog's, raced into the kitchen.

. "No, you don't!" He whisked the pan out of her hands.

"Julian, I can do this. I'm not that big!" she said, her conviction flagging.

Julian chuckled, displaying his mother hen plumage. "No, you need to go rest while I put this in the oven. You've been slaving in here for hours. Go! Now."

Fiona shrugged, a slight smile that Julian had once again come to her rescue crossing her lips. She shuffled off to the living room to finish reading the rest of the Pagan parenting magazine she had downloaded. She eased her heavy body down onto the soft sofa cushions with a relieved sigh, then raised her aching feet onto the coffee table.

Julian came out into the living room and moved to the couch where Fiona sat. He lay on his side, then rested his head on her lap, facing her pregnant belly so he could have a chat with their son. "Listen, there are a few things I need to say while your mom is busy reading...consider this a little advice for later in life." Julian paused and glanced up at Fiona. She looked down at him with raised eyebrows, then went back to her reading. "Sometimes your wife will be thickheaded and try to do everything herself when she knows she's too pregnant to do it. Help her no matter what. It'll be worth it later." He paused again as he became aware of Fiona's gaze boring down into his temples. He looked up at her, eyes full of innocence. "Yes, dear?"

"Thickheaded?"

"Oh, did I say thickheaded? I meant . . . um . . . ."

Fiona chuckled and stroked Julian's hair. "Okay, okay, I get it. Thank you for being such a sweetie. I love you and—" A strong kick from their son interrupted the rest of her sentence. Julian jolted from his position in front of her stomach, staring at the spot where the kick had come from. "I think that's his way of saying he does, too."

"He's a strong one. My own personal field goal kicker," Julian said.

"Too bad we don't have football in the Cities."

"Hey, I can't let that stop me from being optimistic."

"You don't even like sports!"

"Once again, I can't let that stop me from being optimistic."

***

The next day, on the afternoon of Mabon, Fiona wrapped up the fresh loaf of bread, then set it in her backpack. "Julian," she called. "It's time to go. We don't want to be late."

Julian came out of the bedroom dressed and ready to go. "Okay. Let me get that for you." He swung Fiona's backpack over one shoulder, then took her arm as they walked out of the apartment. "Where are we going again?" he asked as they reached the PRT station.

"The Harvest Adobes station."

"Harvest Adobes? Sounds like a relic from Old Albuquerque."

"I know. I've hated that name since they decided on it," she said. "But it fits on the sign better than self-sufficient, single-dwelling residence village."

Julian laughed. "That's very true."

They boarded a PRTV. Julian punched in their destination, then the car took off. They watched out the window as the car zipped through the City. Gleaming buildings surrounded them on all sides until they neared the edge of the City. They could see a group of smaller houses up ahead. The car disconnected from the track, pulling into their destination.

After Julian helped Fiona step out of the car, they stopped

on the platform to look out at the village below. Fiona admired the small enclave's design, which she had only seen in artist's renderings up to that point. She recognized the recycled clay roofs and solar heating panels on the single-level homes from the blueprints she had consulted while planning the advertising artwork for the City. She pointed out to Julian the greenhouses and gardens behind each pueblo. The food had already been harvested, and the glass huts and patches of earth were being prepared for the winter freeze. They turned their attention to the main road, which was dotted with small gatherings of people, all moving toward the meeting house at the very end of the road.

Another PRTV pulled into the station behind them. They turned to see a car stop at the platform. Eion stepped out of it followed by Jensa who was carrying a basket of fall pies. Fiona and Julian waved at his parents, then waited for the couple to join them at the escalator.

Jensa greeted Fiona with a familiar hug made cumbersome by Fiona's pregnant belly and Jensa's basket. "You've gotten so big since the last time I saw you!" Jensa said.

Fiona smiled. "I know. I notice every time I stand up," she said. The four of them took the elevator down to street level, where Gregory was waiting for them with a solar-powered cart modeled after a turn-of-the-twentieth-century buggy. He extended a festive greeting as he took Fiona's bag from Julian and Jensa's basket of pies. He set them in the back of the cart while his guests climbed aboard.

The ride down the paved road to the village was a short one. As Gregory pulled the cart to a stop in front of his house, Vyviane came to the front porch to wave hello. Julian helped Fiona slide out of the cart, then the five of them walked up the path toward Vyviane. When they reached the porch, she wrapped Fiona in her arms, amazed at how wonderful her little girl looked with the child growing inside her. "I've missed you," Vyviane said.

"I've missed you, too. I promise to visit more often after he comes," Fiona said, motioning toward her pregnant belly.

"You won't have to, darling. I'll be camped out in your entryway."

"Make room for me, too," Jensa chimed in. The three women laughed, then Vyviane offered to give everyone the grand tour. "I'd love that," Jensa said.

Vyviane led her guests on a quick circuit through her new home, which had been designed to be self-sufficient and low-maintenance. First they passed through the simple living room where a large fireplace served as the centerpiece of the room, as well as the main heat source for the house. In keeping with the pueblo theme, Vyviane had kept the furniture very simple and comfortable. Her old twill couch worked perfectly, as did the oak coffee table. As they left the room, Fiona noticed a small weaving hanging on the wall near the door. When she was very small, her grandmother had taught her how to make it from yarn and a Styrofoam meat tray fashioned into a loom. Somehow Vyviane had saved it after the quake. She remembered those old times with sweet pleasure. Fiona's hand dropped down to her pregnant belly as she added that weaving to her list of things to do with her son. She'd have to find something to replace the Styrofoam, but otherwise it was a good craft.

They continued into the den, which featured a smaller fireplace and two comfortable leather chairs. Tucked into the corner was a terminal that controlled the functioning of the house and served as their link to the City.

Next on the tour was the bedroom, where an east-facing window warmed the room with morning light. Again, Vyviane had kept to the pueblo theme. A throw tossed across the bed caught Fiona's eye. She stepped over to pick it up. Fiona recognized it as one she had made in art class after they had moved to New Denver. She turned to her mother. "You still have this?"

Vyviane nodded with a sentimental smile. "Of course, darling. I would never get rid of that."

Fiona's hormones launched a surge of tears, which she choked back, not wanting to appear overly sensitive. "We'd better keep going," she said, covering with saccharine happiness.

The next stop on the tour was the efficient yet homey kitchen. "It's beautiful," Jensa said, admiring the large cooking space. It was much larger than the kitchen in her apartment. She turned to look out the window, which had a view of the plains.

"But how can you stand being all the way out here?"

"We're not that far out," Vyviane said, pointing out another window through which she could see the buildings of New Denver. "And we can take the PRT into the City any time to get the things we can't grow. I haven't given up my chocolate addiction yet!" She took them beyond the kitchen to her indoor garden and then out into the greenhouse and back garden. She pointed out the last of her fresh tomatoes and the herbs that grew year-round with particular pride. "I love having all this fresh food growing within arm's reach. Reminds me of the old days. And wait until you taste it." As she mentioned eating, Vyviane recalled why her guests were there. She glanced at her watch. "We should get down to the meeting house. The feast will be starting soon."

Gregory offered Fiona a ride on the solar cart, but she wanted to walk. As they went down the lane to the end of the village, they fell into two groups: men and women. Jensa asked Fiona if her pregnancy was affecting her work.

Fiona sighed with contentment. "It's fantastic. The baby brings out so much creative energy in me, and the City Corporation has been great, giving me extra time on my deadlines and offering me a lot of pregnancy resources."

"You're lucky to have so much here," Vyviane said.

A few steps behind them, Eion asked Gregory how he maintained his career all the way out in the village. "I work from home now," Gregory said. "Since I do financial planning, my clients can send me their data through the network if they don't want to come out here. You'd be surprised, though, how many city-dwellers do want to."

"I wouldn't." Julian laughed. "I remember the first time Fiona took me to the waterfall on Mount Komo. It was incredible."

Fiona heard his words and glanced back at Julian with a secret smile. She loved the way he had changed since they'd met. And from what Jensa had told her, Fiona had succeeded where no other woman had; she had managed to get him away from his terminal. Now if only she could get him to move out here.

As Fiona fell back a step, Julian caught up to her. He could tell just by looking at her what was running through her mind. He leaned down to whisper in her ear. "You want one of these, don't you?"

Fiona replied with a simple nod. It had been her lifelong dream to share a house, a garden, and children with the man she loved. After the disasters, she'd given up on the first two parts of that dream. They hadn't seemed very likely, but now the City Corporation had given the complete dream another chance at becoming reality.

The walk to the meeting house was short, and they reached it a few minutes before the feast was to begin. Gregory opened one of the large double doors and held it for his guests, who entered the small building bustling with village-dwellers proudly showing off the results of their first season in residence. Sturdy tables built from wood salvaged from recently destroyed cities were piled high with baskets of bright yellow corn, ripe red tomatoes, thick potatoes, and heavy pumpkins. Loaves of thick-crusted bread and fresh pies, many baked from fruit grown in the village graced a few other tables. A large golden-brown turkey sat on the center table waiting to be carved and served to their families and friends who had come out from the City to join in the celebration of the first harvest.

Fiona breathed deeply to take in the new scent of farm-grown food, something she hadn't smelled in years. The hearty aroma awakened her appetite. Vyviane dropped off their contributions while Gregory led their guests toward a table. Julian helped Fiona into the high-backed chair at the end of the table. The others settled on long benches running the length of it.

No sooner had they seated themselves than the village-dweller who had organized the feast stood. He welcomed his fellow village-dwellers and their guests to the celebration, then he lifted a carving knife and sliced into the juicy turkey. A cheer went up, then the village-dwellers and their guests lined up to fill their plates.

Fiona asked Julian to prepare a plate for her. She didn't want to maneuver out of the chair and then back into it again. Following her instructions, he filled her plate with heaping servings of homegrown acorn squash, thick green beans, fresh bread, and a few slices of delicious farm-raised turkey slathered in gravy made from the turkey's juices.

Once everyone had returned to their seats at the table, Vyviane started the circle of thanks. "I give thanks for all that has been provided for me and my family this year. For my beautiful new home and the wonderful bounty of the earth, for my new son-in-law and soon-to-be-born grandchild, and for all that will come in the future." She smiled at Fiona and Julian and then prompted Eion to go next.

Eion took a long moment to think of something to say. He still hadn't gotten past the loss of his sister, but he finally voiced his thanks for the support of his family during the trying period. Jensa mimicked Eion's thanks, then Gregory repeated Vyviane's words almost verbatim.

It was Julian's turn. He gazed at his pregnant wife beside him as he spoke. "Lord and Lady, I've said this before, but I will say it again. Thank you for Fiona. Thank you for bringing her into my life and for all the changes her arrival has brought." He paused and laid a hand on her belly. "And thank you for the healthy child growing inside her."

Fiona sniffled. She bowed her head, then lifted her eyes to meet Julian's again and offered her own thanks. "Lord and Lady, there is so much I'm grateful for this year. Thank you for bringing me the new life inside me. Thank you for sending Julian my way at the perfect time. And thank you for your support during the difficult times this last year has brought." After Fiona finished speaking, they all paused to let their thanks reach the heavens, then lifted their glasses of water and wine. They clinked them together at the center of the table in toast before setting them down and digging into the mounds of food on their plates.

While their guests devoured the succulent dishes, Vyviane and Gregory regaled them with tales of their first days in the house. The water from the faucets had run an interesting shade of puce and the house climate maintained by the computer was set a hair too warm for human comfort, but they couldn't access the program that would allow them to make adjustments. Now that they had gained control over their residences and the kinks had been worked out, they couldn't get over their good fortune in having been selected to live there.

"Do you think you and Eion will move out here, Jensa?" Vyviane asked.

Jensa found the idea amusing. "Oh, no, I'm a City girl. Have been since the day I moved to Old Chicago as a child." She glanced over at Fiona and Julian who were trying to hide their wistful glances out the nearby window. "It looks like those two might be putting in an application, though."

Fiona and Julian smiled and blushed. "You got us," Julian said.

"I think it will be awhile for us," Fiona said, patting her belly. "I want to make sure we have all our little ones in the City where the birthing center is close." There were murmurs of agreement from around the table. After her miscarriage the previous year, there was no need to tempt fate.

The main course finished, the pies were passed around the meeting house. Their table was graced with an assortment of apple, pumpkin, rhubarb, and pecan. Vyviane dished out small slices from each. All of her guests were equally amazed as the full flavors burst in their mouths. The food was much better than anything found in the City.

As the evening wound down, Fiona grew tired. She glanced at Julian. "We should get home," she said. Julian stood and helped her to her feet. Their parents followed suit, then they all made their way back to Vyviane's and Gregory's house to say goodbye. Jensa and Eion decided they had best be going as well. Gregory drove them all back to the PRT station. Both couples waved goodbye as they stepped into PRTVs for the ride home.

Julian started to enter their destination, but Fiona asked him to set it a couple of stops early. She thought walking a couple blocks would help her digest the large meal. "Are you sure you're up to it?" he asked. Fiona nodded. He shrugged, then set the PRTV as she had requested. The village faded into the distance as the car moved back toward the City. Julian reached out and took Fiona's hand. "Someday," he said.

Fiona nodded. "And someday not too far away." She turned to face him. "I want our children to know what the country is like before they get to be our age."

Julian was in complete agreement. Before he'd met Fiona, he had never thought experiencing nature was important, but now he saw how right Fiona was. "They will," he said, glancing down at the current home of their child.

The PRTV changed tracks and slowed to a stop. They stepped off the car, then rode the elevator down to street level to walk the rest of the way home. Both Fiona and Julian had forgotten the stop was near Sarah's enclave. In their sated and happy moods, they had also forgotten her threats against Fiona. As they rounded the corner, their chatter was brought to an abrupt halt by a commotion in front of Sarah's cult's house. They watched as a police officer dragged a shackled, screaming man from the building.

Sarah was dragged out next. Julian took Fiona's arm, remembering the look in Sarah's eyes when she had made her threat. Fiona suddenly recalled Sarah's vicious message to her and hurried her pace to keep up with Julian as he pulled her away from the scene.

They hadn't moved soon enough. Sarah saw Julian. She called out for him. Some force he didn't understand compelled him to stop and answer her. As he turned around, she broke free from the officers who held her. She ran towards him, screaming something in gibberish.

Fiona stopped walking when she realized Julian was no longer at her side. She turned to see him frozen by shock as Sarah darted toward him. Fiona started to go to him, to pull him out of the way.

Sarah suddenly altered her course, barreling toward the pregnant Fiona, determined to end the life of the child inside her. If she could just get rid of it, Julian would be free to come back to her.

The enraged woman ran towards her. Fiona screamed. She crossed her arms over her stomach to protect her child and turned her back to deflect the attack. Julian jumped in front of Fiona, tackling Sarah. He forced her to the ground, then held her there. Sarah continued to scream garbled threats and confused declarations of love until several officers came to take her back into custody. One officer shielded Fiona from harm as two others pulled Sarah to her feet.

Sarah struggled against her captors. "She's a sinner and whore!" she shouted. "Why can't anyone else see that?" The officers dragged her away from Fiona and Julian, but she didn't relent. "She is going to give birth to the devil, and then Julian will be hers forever. I'm trying to help." As the officers forced her into their vehicle, she swiveled her head back to Julian. "I promise it's not yours, Julian. She's only using you to continue her evil. I'm the one who is meant to bear your child. Come get me. We'll be together!" The door slammed shut, silencing Sarah's screams.

Julian backed away from the horror Sarah had become. Fiona shuddered at what had almost happened. As they rapidly walked the rest of the way back to their building, Julian shook his head in sorrow and shame, repeatedly muttering apologies for ever becoming involved with Sarah.

Once they were back inside their apartment and safe, Fiona crumbled in tears. "I should have told you," she said.

"Told me what?" Julian pulled her into his arms.

"About the threat. I got it when we got back from the memorial. I'm so sorry. I didn't think she actually meant it. I didn't even know she knew I was pregnant."

Julian's blanched. "Goddess, I should have told you before.

"What?"

"I ran into her when I went to get the ginger cookies. That's how she knew. Her friend recognized the brand and told her. She threatened you then, but I didn't tell you because I didn't want to upset you. I'm so sorry. I'm so sorry."

Fiona snapped her head up. "She wanted to kill our child. She wanted to kill me." Her fear roared back full force. She began to shake uncontrollably.

Julian pulled Fiona closer and stroked her hair. "I wish I'd never known her. I'm so sorry for dragging you into this. I will be sorry for the rest of my life."

"It's not your fault. But we can never keep these things from each other again."

He kissed her forehead. "Agreed. I'll protect you and our child. She can't hurt you. I won't let her near you again," he declared. His gaze flicked up to the view-screen. "Why don't we watch something to take our minds off it?"

Fiona nodded. They went to the couch, and she sat back against the seat. He clicked the view-screen on. It came alive with the recorded images of the violent struggle at the enclave and they watched the incident replayed in crisp color. Julian flinched as Sarah darted past the camera, her face marred by vicious hatred. The camera panned around and he watched himself tackle her, his own face displaying his fierce desire to protect his wife.

The announcer's voice came on over the images, reassuring them the violence had ended. All the cult members had been taken into custody. The City Police had uncovered evidence that the leader had been planning to assassinate Lady Celesta and several other local residents to protect New Denver from their heathen ways. The announcer assured viewers all those mentioned in the assassination plans were safe. The arrests had been made before any threats had been carried out. The newscaster went on to say that all members of the cult were being held until each member's involvement in the plan could be determined. Many would be placed in counseling centers for deprogramming. The cult had been deemed a hate group, and therefore its members were subject to a minimum of four weeks of rehabilitation. Then they would be evaluated by professionals trained in dealing with cults before they were released back into society.

"Do you think I should forward the threat to the counseling center?" Fiona asked.

Julian turned to her. "You kept it?"

Fiona nodded. "Just in case." They went to her terminal, then she opened the message. As she read the words once again, her feet went out from under her. She reached out for Julian.

"We should get you to the hospital."

Fiona shook her head and motioned toward the living room. "I just need to sit down. I have an appointment tomorrow morning anyway. I'll be fine."

Julian helped Fiona back to the couch and held her close

to him. "She can't hurt you. The police got her. I'll forward them the message." Fiona's shaking had subsided, but Julian continued speaking, more for his own benefit than hers. "Don't worry. Don't worry."

Fiona looked up at him. "Thank you."

"What if it doesn't work? What if they can't deprogram her?"

"We should bind her," Fiona said. "Then we'll be sure we're safe."

Julian nodded. It was the right thing to do. "How?"

"I'll show you." She reached for his hand. He rose and followed Fiona to the case where they kept their magickal supplies. She removed a small black candle, a small black plastic canister with a lid, and a small square of parchment. Julian got her a chair and arranged it in front of the altar. She lowered herself onto the seat, then instructed Julian to go into the kitchen and fill the canister three-quarters full of water.

Julian returned a moment later with the canister. He handed it to Fiona, who set it on the altar. She bowed her head for a moment to center her energy, then lifted her arms up. "Lady, please join us tonight as we bind Sarah Morgan," she said. Fiona handed the parchment paper to Julian. She asked him to write Sarah's full name on it, then roll it up. When he was done, he handed the paper to Fiona, who dropped it into the canister and sealed the cap. Fiona lit the black candle. "Lady, we bind Sarah Morgan from harming either of us or the child I carry. We do this for the good of all and by this act, prevent ourselves from bringing harm or malice upon Sarah through our thoughts or actions. As we will, this spell is done. So mote it be." Fiona asked Julian to put the canister in the very back of the freezer and then return to her.

Once again, Julian was back in an instant. Fiona raised her arms once more, thanked the Goddess for Her help, and bade Her go in peace.

"That's all we have to do?" Julian asked. Fiona nodded. She held out her hands and he helped her out of the chair. "What about the candle?"

"We'll let it burn the rest of the way down to seal the

binding."

Julian looked down at her. "Thank you for being nothing like Sarah." He kissed her forehead, then rested his head on hers. "A part of me feels like singing 'Ding, dong, the witch is dead.'"

"Somehow I think Sarah wishes she could do the same thing." Fiona sighed. She ran her hands down Julian's side and interlaced her fingers with his.

"How could I have so misjudged her?"

Fiona kissed his neck. "You didn't. She changed."

Julian banished his disturbing thoughts. "Let's not talk about it any more. I want to take you to bed and hold my family."

Fiona nodded, then they went into the bedroom. They stripped off their clothes, slipping beneath the covers to create a cocoon where they would be safe from the outside world. Fiona rolled onto her side and Julian cuddled up behind her, wrapping one arm around her stomach and placing his hand over her belly in a protective gesture. Fiona rested her hand atop his. They lay together in silence, both knowing sleep would be a long time coming.

Chapter 13

Sorrows and Celebrations

With only a few weeks left before Samhain, Fiona waddled through the apartment arranging the Halloween decorations she had amassed over the last few years. A large, glowing ceramic jack o' lantern bedecked one corner, while a natural branch-handled broom swaddled in an orange and black ribbon garnished the opposite corner. An old-fashioned apple doll dressed like a hag witch from children's fairy tales took the place of honor on the dining room table.

Julian's startled shriek announced his entrance. Fiona turned from the window. His face was planted in the center of a large, black paper maché spider dangling from a string of black crepe paper. Suppressing a smile, Fiona went back to work using a long pole to hoist a string of pumpkin lights onto curtain hooks. Julian stepped to the side, raising his eyebrows in amusement and curiosity, then turned to inspect the spider that had hit him. His gaze followed the strand of paper leading from the spider's bottom up to the crepe paper web clinging to the ceiling. "Well this is quite different from last year's décor," he said. He took a second look at the web, which also had a Happy New Year banner hanging from it. "I get the spider, but what's with the banner?"

"You haven't been doing your reading," Fiona teased without stopping her decorating.

"You turned me into a rebel."

"Well, if you had, you would know that the other half of Samhain is the Witches' New Year. I thought we should focus on the fun half this year."

Julian nodded. It sounded like a good idea to him, although he had been hoping to participate in another mourning ceremony so he could say a final goodbye to Mariah.

As if reading his mind, Fiona piped up with the rest of the plans she had made. "Lady Celesta invited us to her dumb supper. You'll be able to say goodbye to Mariah there. Then there will be a champagne toast and dancing at midnight."

Crossing the room to his wife, Julian hugged her. "How do you peer into my head so easily?"

"It's all your DNA coursing through my body right now." She grinned and planted a soft kiss on his cheek. "It's leaking into my brain." She slipped out the embrace. "Now come help me with the pumpkin." They went into the kitchen where Fiona pointed to a large round pumpkin that was resting in the middle of the floor. With a grunt, Julian hefted it onto the counter.

"How did you get this up here?"

Fiona giggled and smiled into his confused eyes. "I rolled it!" she said, making a pushing motion with her foot. She sat down at the table, then grabbled an electronic sketchpad on which she drew a sweet pumpkin face with soft round eyes and a simple smile. Julian thought it was too sweet, so she told him to try his hand at a sketch.

While he drew, something occurred to Fiona. "You have no idea what a dumb supper is, do you?"

Julian glanced up at her sheepishly. "I was hoping you would explain at some point." He handed her the drawing. Shaking her head at his childish scratches, she lifted the pen to merge their two designs into one. Julian watched Fiona's hand swirl across the pad, awed as always by her artistic abilities.

She explained the dump supper while she sketched. "Everyone brings the favorite foods of those who have recently passed on. The table is set with extra places for them and the entire meal is spent in silence. Oh, and you should bring a token of Mariah with you for the altar." She turned the drawing around and slid it over to him. "How's this?'

"Nice," he said. The fiendish trapezoidal eyes, demonic, jagged-toothed grin, and sweet triangular nose fit precisely with his idea of what the perfect pumpkin face looked like. "I say we start carving."

Fiona copied her drawing onto the pumpkin's skin with a black marker while Julian fished a carving knife out of the utensil drawer. They started the messy task of scooping out the pumpkin's guts, but were interrupted by the sound of the outer door opening. Fiona glanced at Julian. "Were you expecting anyone?"

Julian shook his head. Wiping his hands, he walked out to the door to see whose name was on the announcement screen. "Sarah!" he said, surprised. He walked back into the kitchen. "It's Sarah. I don't want her anywhere near you again."

Panic shot through Fiona. "I thought she was in treatment." Fiona wiped her hands on a towel while she breathed deeply to calm herself down. "Find out what she wants. She's bound. She can't hurt us. But don't tell her I'm here." As Julian went back to the door, Fiona moved into the bedroom as quickly as her heavy body would allow. She stopped in the doorway, then turned to face the front door so she could hear what Sarah said through the intercom.

Julian pressed the intercom button. Sarah's polite voice drifted through the speaker. "I'm not here to hurt anyone," she said.

He turned to look at Fiona, who nodded her head. She slid the bedroom door closed and flattened her ear against it. Satisfied Fiona was safely hidden, Julian turned back to the door. He steeled himself against the possibility of another attack, then pushed the button. The door swished open in front of him. Sarah stood a foot back from the entrance.

"May I come in?" she asked, her voice soft.

Julian looked her over, trying to get a feel for Sarah's attitude. She appeared calm and the lunatic glimmer was gone from her eyes. He stepped out of her way. "Yes, come in."

Sarah stepped through the doorway and looked around the apartment. "Is Fiona here?"

"What do you want?"

Bowing her head, Sarah scuffed the toe of her shoe on the carpet. "I want to apologize." She looked up to him. "I'm not going to hurt her, I swear. I'm so ashamed of what I did."

The door to the bedroom opened, and Fiona emerged from within. Sarah shifted her gaze. Fiona met it evenly, confident she was safe in her own home with her husband, although she held a hand over her belly to protect her baby. Julian stepped to Fiona and helped her to the couch.

Sarah waited in the background as Fiona settled on the couch, then stepped forward a few feet, still maintaining a polite distance. "I won't be long," she said.

Julian sat down next to Fiona and motioned for Sarah to take a seat opposite them. As Sarah shuffled to the seat, her head still bowed, Fiona and Julian linked hands. They stared at Sarah, waiting for her to break the silence. Finally she lifted her head and said, "I'm sure you know what happened to the…group I was involved with." Fiona and Julian nodded in reply. They squeezed each other's hands until their knuckles went white, each fearing an intolerant diatribe was coming.

"I need to apologize to both of you," Sarah continued. "I understand now that I was confused and searching for something to fill the void in my life. I was drawn to the wrong people and I'm very sorry for that. I'm moving to another city, but I wanted to say I'm sorry, in person, for any pain I've caused either of you."

Fiona and Julian exchanged a surprised glance. Looking back to Sarah, Fiona spoke first. "Thank you, Sarah. We appreciate that."

Sarah glanced down at Fiona's stomach where Fiona's hand still lay. Shame shuddered through her. How could she have ever wanted to hurt an innocent baby? What had she turned into during those terrible months? "And I'm so sorry for rushing at you and the baby that day. I was out of my mind. I hope I didn't hurt it."

Fiona nodded, realizing where her hand was. She made a point of setting it by her side as she spoke. "He's fine. Thank you. I hope you'll find what you're looking for in the next City."

"Me, too," Sarah said. Relieved that they had accepted her apology, Sarah stood and Fiona and Julian stood with her. She started toward the door, then turned back. "You have a good man there, Fiona. I hope you two will be happy. You will never hear from me again."

Fiona and Julian stood arm in arm, watching Sarah walk away from them. "Good luck," Fiona called as Sarah stepped through the inner door. The panel swished closed behind her.

Once he heard the outer door close, Julian turned to Fiona and hugged her, cradling her against his chest. "What a relief. She won't interfere with our lives again."

Fiona looked up, her eyes happy once more. "We're safe." She smiled, then stepped back. She took his hand and tugged him back into the kitchen to resume carving the pumpkin. As Fiona wielded the sharp knife over the pumpkin's face, Julian remembered the binding spell he and Fiona had cast.

"I guess I can release Sarah now," he said.

Fiona looked up from the pumpkin. "Yeah, that's a good idea. Get it out of the freezer."

Julian padded across the kitchen to the freezer and opened the door. He reached deep inside, then removed the black canister. "How do I do this?" he asked as he carried it back to Fiona.

Fiona set the knife down and turned to him. "I don't know. I've never unbound anyone before," she said. She thought for a moment. "Hold it in both hands and say 'Lady, release Sarah from her bonds. May she go in peace.' Then pop the ice out of the container and we'll let it melt in the sink."

Following Fiona's instructions, Julian focused all his energy on the small container and releasing Sarah. When he felt the last of his will to bind her drain from him, he held the canister upside down under a warm stream of water until the ice slipped out. He watched the chunk form a pool in the sink, releasing the binding as it melted. Satisfied that the whole mess was over with, he turned back to Fiona to help her put the finishing touches on the pumpkin's face.

***

On the night of Samhain, Fiona and Julian made their way to the gathering house where Lady Celesta was holding the ritual. Fiona's dark velvet skirt swirled in the brewing late autumn storm. She pulled it tighter around her large belly. Julian carried a pumpkin pie he had baked as his offering to the feast and the humidor of rocks Mariah had bestowed upon him at her death. Black candles flickered in the windows of the darkened structure. Julian's shoulders tensed as they moved closer. Despite the building storm, an unearthly silence surrounded them. He leaned down and whispered in Fiona's ear. "I'm not so sure about this."

"Don't worry. We'll be fine." Fiona stopped at the door. She tapped lightly on the wood.

Lady Celesta whisked open the door. She was draped in a flowing black broom skirt and black velvet tunic. "Merry Meet," she said. As she ushered them inside and took Fiona's cape and Julian's coat, Fiona admired the string of bright amber beads that hung around her neck. Lady Celesta told her they had been a gift from an old Witch who had passed on years earlier. "Have either of you been to a dumb supper before?" Lady Celesta asked as she put away their coats. Fiona and Julian shook their heads no, and Lady Celesta began her practiced explanation. "Once you enter the dining room, please remain silent. There are several empty place settings at the table for our unseen guests. Sit only at those places marked by a white candle. After the meal has begun, listen carefully for any messages your guests might have for you, as this is the one night they can cross over. At midnight, we'll adjourn to the ballroom for the New Year's toast. Any questions?"

Julian proffered the box his aunt had given him. "Where should I put this?"

Lady Celesta led them to the dining room. She pointed toward a large altar draped in black silk crepe at the end of the room. A large white candle burned atop the altar, casting a dim glow on the items below it. Julian set the box down among a collection of photographs and personal mementos, then turned to follow his hostess back to the long banquet table set for forty. Several living participants were already seated at the table, which was covered in the same black crepe as the altar.

A thick black candle burned at each place set aside for the guests from the other side. Lady Celesta showed them to their seats marked by thick white candles. They sat down with an empty space between them, and empty spaces on either side of them for the ghostly visitors. Lady Celesta returned to the head of the table and rang a large bell three times to signal the opening of the ritual. Once all eyes were upon her, she moved to the eastern corner of the room. She began to glide clockwise around the room, sprinkling saltwater on the hardwood floor with a stalk of dried lavender. After completing her first circle, she moved once again to the East and made the sign of the invoking pentagram. She repeated this at each quarter until she had returned to her place in the North.

She stopped and stood silent at the head of the table, her eyes lifted toward the heavens, until her breath became slow and deep. "Lady of darkness, Lady of night, protector of those journeying to the other side, join us in this rite as we call to our friends behind the veil. Protect us from the uninvited and keep us on this side of life." She paused to take another deep breath. "Lord of death, Lord of the dark home, protector of the wandering spirit, join us in this rite as we call to those who have passed. Protect us from the uninvited and keep us on this side of the veil." She paused once more, then turned her attention to her living guests. "You may each now invite those you wish to join you from the Summerlands. Please do so in your head and begin you invitation with 'I invite these and none other.' We will not speak again until the end of the feast."

In silence, Julian called out to Mariah to join him at the dumb supper. A cold flutter moved across his cheek, then a distinct presence slid into the seat between him and Fiona. A voice echoed through his mind, *I'm with you, Julian. Thank you.* He recognized the gentle cadence of his aunt's peaceful voice and words.

Fiona reached a hand across the space between them to stroke his back. She wondered at the chills on her forearm until she heard Mariah's words in her own mind. *Keep care of him for me. And use that book often. I have hidden many secrets in it.* Fiona nodded through the tears welling in her eyes and the lump forming in her throat. She brushed her hand down to her swollen belly, then felt another hand join hers there. *He will be well,* came the voice in her head. *I promise. How I wish I could have met the child in the mortal world. But I met him on this side. He is very sweet and anxious to be with you.*

Julian turned to Fiona, eyes wide with shock, to see if she too was hearing the message his aunt had chosen to share. He spoke once more with his mind. *Thank you, Mariah, for all you taught me. I miss you so much every day, but I know you will be happy in your next life. I love you.*

I love you, came the silken reply. *Now I want to eat. I haven't had a good pumpkin pie since I passed!*

Fiona and Julian exchanged amused smiles, then shrugged. They served Mariah a large slice of the pie along with green beans and mashed potatoes as she requested, then prepared their own plates. As they looked around the table, they saw several of Lady Celesta's covenmates in various states of joy and sorrow. Some laughed and smiled while others sobbed uncontrollably, but not a tinge of regret showed in a single eye. Every person was celebrating the lives of their beloved dead in a way that would allow them to find peace with the loss after this night was over.

The room remained silent except for the clattering of silver against china until the large grandfather clock in the corner of the room chimed twelve times, signaling that the New Year had begun. At the head of the table, Lady Celesta rose. "Spirits who have joined us tonight, we thank you for your presence here and are honored by it. The dumb supper has concluded, but we move now to celebrate the dawning new year. Please stay if you wish and go if you must. Blessed be."

The room repeated the last, and then Lady Celesta raised her arms and eyes skyward. "Lady of darkness, thank you for joining us tonight and protecting our dead as they move between the worlds. Farewell and blessed be." She paused. Again the gathered celebrants repeated the last before she continued.

"Lord of death, thank you for joining us tonight and protecting us from the uninvited spirits. Farewell and blessed be." She paused another moment for the participants to repeat after her once more, then turned and drew a banishing pentagram in the north before continuing around to the other quarters.

When she returned to the north, she picked up the natural wood broom by her place, then moved once more counterclockwise around the room, sweeping away the circle she had cast and any lingering spirits not remaining by invitation or choice. She returned to the head of the table and said, "It is time to move to the ballroom for a champagne toast. Don't be surprised if our invisible guests join us."

The clatter of chairs sliding back and people shuffling to their feet filled the room. *I don't mind if I do,* Mariah said in Fiona and Julian's heads. With a jovial laugh, the three of them moved out to the ballroom. It was adorned with streamers in bright colors and a Happy New Year banner similar to the one hanging from the spiderweb in Fiona and Julian's apartment. Fluted champagne glasses were passed around the room, then Lady Celesta raised her glass. "Happy New Year!" she yelled. Her guests echoed the sentiment. Julian took a sip as Fiona raised the glass to her lips and kissed the outside of it, then sprinkled a few drops on the floor with her fingertip.

The audio terminal in the corner came to life with festive dance music. The floor swirled with happy dancing Pagans and merry spirits who twirled around the room, raising up a bolt of energy that kept their loved ones moving. Ecstatic energy rolled through all of them. When Fiona could dance no more, she stepped to the side of the room to collapse in a chair.

Julian followed her. "Do you want to go home?" he asked.

A jaunty waltz started, and Fiona shook her head. "No,

we can stay. Go dance with Mariah. I think she's itching for a last dance."

Julian felt a tap on his shoulder and turned to see no one there, but he could feel Mariah's spirit standing in front of him, arms extended for the dance. He held out his arms in the proper positions for a waltz, then began to step in the timeless rhythm his aunt had taught him. He felt her hand come into his and a pressure under his other hand. He wasn't dancing alone anymore.

Fiona watched with delighted amazement as several other revelers, living and dead, joined the dance, twirling in the magical rhythm of days long past. A chill came over her. Thinking she was sitting in a draft, she rubbed her hands over her arms to warm them, then realized that several spirits had gathered around her. She placed a hand over her stomach to protect her child, but soon became aware that the spirits were offering her son good wishes and blessings. She relaxed and listened gratefully as each spirit offered a gift worthy of royalty.

From across the room, Julian watched the bright smile spread across her lips. What could be going on over there? As he spoke the question in his mind, Mariah answered him. He was honored by the gracious gesture and amazed once again by how little of the world he had known before he'd met Fiona.

The waltz ended. The clock struck one. *I must be going,* Mariah said.

Julian nodded. *Thank you for coming. It was good to...speak to you one last time.*

I wouldn't have missed this for the world, my dear. Tell your father I miss him.

I will, Julian said. He made his way over to Fiona, who suddenly found herself no longer surrounded by spirits.

"Well, that was something," she said.

"I know. Mariah's leaving now."

Thank you for letting me know my child is healthy, Fiona told her.

You're welcome, my dear. Take good care of that little one. He's going to be a handful. The energy around them vanished with a flash. Mariah was gone.

Julian moved back to the dining room, retrieved the humidor from the altar, then returned to help Fiona off the chair. They went out to the closet. Julian swirled the large cloak around her to protect her from the chill of the late night air outside. They said goodbye to the other participants, then thanked Lady Celesta for once again playing hostess. They stepped outside expecting to be greeted by a stark wind tearing around the building. Instead, a spooky calm had descended. Fiona and Julian were able to move easily to the PRT station.

As they stepped into the waiting car and settled back for the ride, it dawned on Fiona that they hadn't given any thought to baby names yet. "We know it's a boy. We'd better make a list," she said.

"I propose the name Julian."

"Now, now. One of you is plenty," she teased. "I was thinking of something a little more godlike."

"I'll leave the list making to you," he said. "But I retain veto power."

Laughing, Fiona nodded and took his hand. She squeezed it tight in hers, aware that in just six short weeks the little boy inside her would make his first appearance in the world, whether or not they had a name chosen.

Chapter 14

What Child Is This?

The list started with traditional names like James, but as neither Fiona nor Julian had traditional names, she ruled those out quickly. Julian suggested a combination of both their names. His own name was a loose combination of Jensa and Eion, but neither of them could come up with a combination of Julian and Fiona that sounded right.

As the weeks passed and Fiona grew rounder of belly, she turned to ancient myths and legends for name sources. She found many possible names, but nothing struck her as the perfect name. Fiona was on the couch reading yet another myth when she decided to give the process a rest. "Maybe we're not supposed to know until he's born," she said.

Julian nodded without turning from his terminal. "Let's just wait then. He'll let us know what name he wants."

With Yule now only a few weeks away, Fiona changed her focus to decorating the apartment for the winter holidays. She pushed herself onto her feet, then tottered toward the hall closet they used for storage. She cradled her belly to support the weight of it. "You need to go buy a Yule tree," she said to Julian as she walked out of the living room.

"I do?" he asked, spinning in his desk chair to see what had prompted the abrupt declaration.

"Yes. I'm getting out the decorations now. They'll look silly piled on the floor."

At the mention of Fiona doing any sort of bending and lifting, Julian jumped out his seat. He skittered down the hallway to the closet. "You sit down. You can't get the boxes out by yourself," he said. Happy to oblige, Fiona toddled back to the sofa. She sank into its welcoming cushions while Julian carted the boxes out to her. Once he had completed that task, he grabbed his jacket off the peg by the door and headed out. "I'll be back in a few minutes with the tree." Fiona nodded and began unwrapping the ornaments while she awaited Julian's return. She chuckled as she recalled how she had struggled to get the tree home by herself last year. He had no idea what he was in for.

Thirty minutes later, Julian was back, panting and wrestling a six-foot Fraser fir through the door. At his call for guidance, Fiona pointed toward the corner. Julian shoved the tree into the corner, then turned the tree until the bushy side was facing the living room, while Fiona used the remote control to find holiday tunes on the audio terminal. Festive carols filled the room. Fiona got up, disappearing into the kitchen. She returned with a tray holding two glasses of eggnog and a pitcher of water.

"I don't think I'm that thirsty," Julian said.

"No, the water is for the tree," she said, giggling. "The eggnog is for us."

Julian laughed at his assumption, then bent with the pitcher to fill the base. After he had given the tree a good drink, he swapped the pitcher for a glass of eggnog. His gaze fell on the assortment of ornaments spread across the couch cushions. "Don't worry. I'll put up all the ornaments, too."

"I can put some on the lower branches," Fiona said. "But first you have to put the lights on." She motioned toward several disheveled coils of mini tree-lights.

Julian groaned at the prospect of having to untangle the mess again. He would find a better way to store them this year. He set down his glass, then began the long process of wrapping the tiny colored bulbs around the green branches under Fiona's watchful eye. Once all the lights were on the tree, Fiona pushed herself off the couch again. She picked up the first ornament, then hung it on one of the few branches of the tree she could reach without bending or straining.

After a few minutes of Fiona's decorating, the middle of the tree was thick with ornaments. Julian was sitting on the couch enjoying his eggnog. When Fiona came back to get more ornaments, he suggested he finish hanging the decorations under her direction. Fiona agreed. She sat down to supervise Julian. Sometimes he obeyed her orders, sometimes he didn't, but the tree branches were soon heavy with colorful ornaments.

Julian joined Fiona on the couch to finish his eggnog and admire their handiwork. As he put one arm around her, she dropped her head down to his shoulder. "Good job, love," he said, placing a kiss on her forehead.

Fiona inspected the tree from her place beside Julian. "You missed a spot," she said.

"No, I didn't."

"Yes, right in the very middle." She pointed toward the empty spot in the middle of the tree. "There's a big hole."

Julian glanced where she was pointing, then shook his head. "No, there isn't."

"Well, I see it," Fiona said. She peeled herself off the couch, then moved to the tree. She repositioned an ornament and filled in the hole. Julian got up as she returned to her seat. He moved the glass ball back where he had originally hung it. Fiona sighed in exasperation.

Julian sat back down with Fiona and caressed her swollen belly. "You can decide when you get here," he said to the child inside.

Fiona giggled and rolled her eyes. "Put a little pressure on him, why don't you?"

Julian nodded, then silenced her needling with a kiss. They melted into each other's arms to express their love for each other with gentle caresses and sweet kisses.

***

A week and a half later, Julian was hard at work at his terminal while Fiona sat on the couch reading an article on her page-viewer. Julian said something under his breath, then nodded. Fiona looked over at him. "What's that, honey?

"I'll tell you in a minute."

Fiona accepted that and went back to her reading. After a few more minutes had passed, Julian stood and walked over to her. "What would you say if I told you I had written a ritual?"

"Your first!" Fiona said, looking up from the article. "I would say let's do it." She took the page-viewer Julian held out for her. He had downloaded his ritual into it. She read it over, then looked up into his nervous eyes. "Sweetie, that's wonderful. We'll do it now."

Grinning with pride and excitement, Julian dashed away to gather the candles he had decided to use for the ritual. As he precisely arranged the altar, Fiona re-read the ritual, surprised she hadn't thought of it before.

When Julian was ready to begin, he called her over to the altar where he had set up a chair for each of them. It was also his first time performing the majority of a ritual, but he quelled his anxiety about making a mistake. Fiona had told him the Gods weren't overly concerned with perfection from their worshippers. He picked up his athame, then traced a circle in the air around them and the altar to create their sacred space. He rose and walked around the altar, drawing invoking pentagrams in each direction as Fiona had taught him. He glanced at Fiona to see if he was doing okay. The pride reflected in her eyes told him he was.

He took his seat again, then held a lighter over the Goddess candle as he said, "Lady Aphrodite, we call you before us today to witness out rite as we declare our promise to keep our relationship sacred and foremost in our lives. We ask you to bless us with your power of love." Fiona sniffled at the words, then turned to face Julian. He reached out and took her hands in his. "Fiona, darling, I swear to you that I will hold our love sacred. I will never forget all you mean to me, no matter how much our lives change. I promise to devote time to you, and just you, each and every day for the rest of our lives."

Tears flowed freely from Fiona's eyes. Julian slipped his hand out of hers to wipe them away. Fiona smiled. "Julian, sweetie, I promise to keep our love in my heart and renew it daily through my thoughts and actions. I will never let our lives come between us. I will make time for you, and just you, each and every day for the rest of our lives." They both placed their hands on her belly. Fiona continued, directing her intention to the baby inside her. "Sweet child, we made our promises to you at Midsummer, and we will keep them."

She paused, then Julian continued the promise. "Never fear that we don't love you when we desire time without you. That time will strengthen our bond and make our family better." The baby inside Fiona responded with a gentle kick. They knew he had heard and understood.

Julian leaned forward and kissed Fiona. "I love you," he said.

Fiona returned the kiss and whispered, "I love you," into his lips. They let their lips wander over each other, tasting the salt from Fiona's tears as they sealed the bond of their words.

After a moment, Julian leaned back and lifted the candle snuffer. He held it over the Goddess candle as he said, "Lady Aphrodite, we thank you for witnessing our rite and blessing us with your power of love. We will hold our words sacred always. Farewell and blessed be." He rose, drew a banishing pentagram in each direction, then walked widdershins around the circle to release it. The ritual completed, he reached for Fiona. He pulled her onto her feet and into his arms. "Thank you," he said.

"For what?"

"For letting me do my ritual."

"Oh, sweetie, you never need my permission to do a ritual.

It was perfect. I'm very proud of you," she said, placing her lips on his once more.

Julian blushed, but he shared her pride in his accomplishment. His first ritual, written and performed.

"Now let's go start that quality time," Fiona said.

Julian nodded, then they went into the bedroom for a cuddling session.

***

"I think we should have our families over for Yule again," Fiona said during breakfast the week before the holiday was upon them.

Julian nodded over his Cornflakes. "Good idea."

Fiona rose from the table, then waddled over to her terminal. On the way, she stopped to fill in the hole on the tree. She didn't know why she bothered. Julian removed every ornament she put in that spot. She continued to her terminal, then collapsed her heavy swollen body into the chair. She stretched her arms around her ready-to-burst belly and called up her message program. There was a note from Julian's mother in her mailbox. Fiona clicked over to it and called out to Julian. "Your mom already beat us to it. She invited us to her place for dinner."

Julian looked up from his breakfast. "Are you sure that's a good idea?"

Fiona waved away his concern. "I'll be fine. I made a deal with the baby that he won't come until after Yule."

***

On the morning of Yule, Fiona learned that unborn children eager to greet the world don't make deals. Her contractions had started the day before and by the time the sun was beginning to peek over the horizon, they were five minutes apart. She padded into the bedroom after having been awake all night and nearly knocked Julian out of bed with what she thought was a gentle push.

Bleary-eyed, Julian looked up at her. "What?"

"It's time. He's coming. We have to go to the birthing center."

In an instant, Julian was out of bed. He raced around the apartment as if he was the White Rabbit late for his appointment with the Queen of Hearts. He ran first into the closet and got her suitcase, then out to the living room for the midwife's numbers even though he knew the birthing center had them, then back to the bedroom to collect Fiona, who was dressing for the trip. "There's no time!" he cried, hustling her toward the door.

Fiona resisted and moved back into the closet. "My water hasn't even broken yet," she said, pulling a sweater off the shelf. Julian hemmed and hawed while he waited for Fiona to finish getting ready, glancing at his watch repeatedly. He should be timing the contractions or something, but he had no idea when the previous contraction had been, having been awakened by Fiona after it had ended.

Another contraction rolled through Fiona as she was pulling the sweater around her shoulders. She cried out. Julian rushed to her side. He helped her breathe through the contraction until it was over. Fiona stood upright again and finished arranging her sweater, then pronounced herself ready to go. Julian ushered her out the door, supporting her as they shuffled down to the PRT station and then into a PRTV. The car zipped off. As another contraction hit her, Fiona moaned.

She squeezed Julian's hand just a smidgen too tight, and he moaned with her. Now he knew why the birthing class instructor had told him to make a fist before giving her his hand. He would remember that during the next one.

They arrived at the birthing center and went directly to the check-in desk. The nurse took them to a private room and told them the midwife would be called. She normally arrived within ten minutes. As they waited for her, another contraction seized Fiona. Julian watched her experience the pain, feeling helpless. Would he really be able to guide her through this?

The midwife sailed into the room five minutes and one contraction later. After a brief examination, she told Fiona she was at three centimeters. She still had awhile to go, but her water had broken, so it might not be too long.

"But I didn't feel a whoosh."

"Oh, it doesn't have to be a great rush of fluid. It could have just been a slow trickle," the midwife said.

Fiona flushed a deep red. She had felt some moisture a

day ago and thought she had wet herself. Every so often in the last few weeks she'd had little accidents. This one hadn't seemed any different.

The midwife nodded with understanding. Julian told her the contractions were five minutes apart. "Good, good," she said. "Why don't we see if we can hurry things along? It will be easier for you if you move around. Go for walks, sit up, talk, distract yourself when you can. The center has a beautiful indoor garden."

Fiona nodded, then rolled off the bed, pulling Julian along with her. She was anxious to get the birthing process over with and meet their son in person.

"Are you sure that's a good idea?" Julian asked for the umpteenth time during Fiona's pregnancy.

The midwife smiled at his fatherly concern. "Don't worry. The baby won't come out without me," she reassured him.

White holiday lights twinkled between the trees and bright paperwhites and red amaryllis added color to the winter garden. In between her contractions, Fiona and Julian wandered through the pleasant atrium and admired the holiday garlands hung over the balconies. Benches placed along the walkways at six-foot intervals were the perfect height for collapsing into during contractions. Fiona found sitting among the flowers soothing as her pains came closer together. When they were three minutes apart, she asked Julian to take her back upstairs. She was ready to start the painkillers that would ease the pain of childbirth.

They returned to the room, then Julian helped Fiona put on the special sweatsocks she had brought. On the previous full moon, she had charged them to keep her calm during delivery and bring her extra energy during the most difficult part. Leaning back on the raised bed, she asked Julian to call their parents to let them know they wouldn't be coming to dinner.

Julian called Vyviane first. After a brief hello he said, "We won't be at my mom's tonight for dinner. Fiona's in labor." As Vyviane shrieked, Julian had to hold the phone away from his ear. She promised she and Gregory would be right over. He delivered the same message to his own parents, who also said they would not miss the birth of their first grandchild.

As he disconnected the call, another contraction rocked through Fiona's body. It was followed two minutes later by another. He knew from their class that this meant Fiona was getting close to delivering. He tried to help her do the relaxation exercises they had learned and practiced, but nothing seemed to work. He grew more and more frustrated by his inability to help her as her contractions came closer and closer together. The midwife finally suggested that he step out of the room for a few minutes while they started Fiona's epidural.

He emerged from Fiona's room to find both sets of their parents in the waiting room. They leapt to their feet as he walked through the doors. He motioned for them to sit back down. The baby hadn't come yet. Gregory and Eion reassured him he was doing the best he could. They understood how difficult it was for a man to witness his beloved partner in such pain and not be able to do anything to relieve it. A nurse came out to the waiting room. Fiona was transitioning and had asked that Julian return to the birthing room. Elated and panicked, Julian jumped out of his seat, then dashed back down the hall. Their excited parents called out best wishes for a speedy delivery.

When he arrived in the birthing room, Fiona was up on her knees, getting ready to begin pushing. He rushed to her side to offer his support. The midwife reminded Fiona how to breathe the baby out as she had learned in the birthing class. Fiona struggled against her fear. She wanted to stop labor and go home. She called out to the Goddess to help her through this difficult experience as She had helped so many other women before her. A soothing presence joined Fiona. As the warmth of the Mother enveloped her, her fear eased a bit.

After an hour of pushing, the boy's head pressed out of the birth canal. The midwife let Fiona rest a moment, then asked her to breathe again to help birth the child's shoulders. The rest of the baby slid out with the shoulders. He wailed to announce his arrival. Julian helped Fiona settle into a sitting position, then their tiny, squalling son was swaddled in a blanket and placed in Fiona's waiting arms. Tears of joy and love formed in the Fiona's eyes as she held her crinkled son for the first time. After a moment, the nurse took the baby from Fiona to clean him and give him a check-up, then the midwife helped Fiona push out the placenta. The final stage of labor was over.

The nurse and midwife declared the child healthy. The nurse brought the newborn to Fiona and set him back in her arms. Fiona and Julian gazed down into his face. Julian stroked his soft cheek, feeling a rush of love he had never experienced before. Moments later, both sets of grandparents were ushered into the birthing room to see their new grandchild.

"Do you have a name yet?" the midwife asked.

Fiona glanced up at her. "No, we wanted to wait until we saw him."

As they looked down into the face of their child, a name that hadn't been on the list came to them. "Conall," they said, choosing the name of the mighty Celtic warrior and sorcerer.

"Conall," said their parents, nodding in agreement. A worthy name for the young boy.

Julian took his son in his arms. He looked down into his sweet face and gently stroked his skin with one finger. "Conall. My son. I hope you remember all the promises I made to you at Midsummer. I will keep them, I swear."

Fiona watched as her husband cradled their son to his chest. She memorized the image as one she would cherish over the years.

After each grandparent had held the baby, Fiona and Julian were left alone in the room to bond with their son. A nurse would come later to teach them the fine art of breast-feeding and diaper-changing.

***

Two days after Yule, Fiona and Conall were released. Fiona and Julian went back to their apartment to introduce the child to his new home. Julian set Fiona's bag down by the inner door, then watched as Fiona carried Conall over to the tree to show him the bright colors. The baby cracked his eyes slightly. Fiona sat down next to the tree, still looking down at her son. From the door, Julian watched his family. As he stood there imagining the future that lay before them, he recalled the two things he had kept hidden from Fiona until this day. He padded across the room to the closet and dug out the box marked "For the Future." He opened the lid, then removed the envelope he had placed inside it when they were moving and a small package he had added to the box only a few weeks before.

Fiona looked up as Julian approached her with both items. He joined her on the floor, then reached out to take Conall from her so she could open the envelope and package. She turned the thin white envelope over in her hands and glanced into Julian's smiling eyes. She recognized it as the one from the box. She unsealed the flap and slipped out a piece of folded parchment. She unfolded the note. It was a handwritten letter Julian had written after they'd agreed to start trying to conceive. As she read the letter, Fiona wept, touched by the words written to an unconceived child.

> *My dear child,*
>
> *You are still just a thought in my mind and a hope in your mother's heart, but we are preparing a space for your in our lives. You cannot know how much you will change us and how much we will grow as you grow. I love your mother deeply. Because of her, I have realized that you will make our lives complete. I am eager to experience the world through your eyes and learn from you as you learn from me.*
>
> *The idea of fatherhood frightens me. I don't want to let you down, and by the time you are old enough to read this, I already will have many times. But my hope is that you will know how deeply my love for you runs, for I already love you in spirit. I will do my best to raise you to be a good, honest person and teach you all that I know. When I make mistakes, and I will, know that they are out of love.*
>
> *My dear child, you will bless my life in ways I cannot possibly know and I hope to do the same for you. This much, at least, I promise: my love for you will not fade, no matter how you change, how you grow, how you become your own person.*
>
> *Love,*
> *Your father, Julian.*

Fiona had not known how deep Julian's emotions about fatherhood ran. She would treasure the letter and keep it safe until Conall was old enough to understand the words written on the page. She wiped her eyes, then set down the envelope and picked up the package. As Julian watched, she unwrapped the soft tissue to reveal a small ornament nestled inside. It was a small wooden sun and a small wooden moon surrounding a tiny wooden star. The star represented the child created by Fiona, the moon, and Julian, the sun. Underneath the celestial symbols was a tiny scroll bearing the words "First Yule."

"Oh, Julian, it's . . . ." Fiona held the ornament tightly in her hand and leaned forward to hug Julian, being careful not to crush their tiny star. She pulled away, then smiled as she realized why Julian had insisted on leaving a hole in the center of the tree. She reached up and hung the ornament in exactly that spot, then settled back on the floor.

Julian handed their son back to her, then shifted around to sit behind her. He wrapped his legs around hers, then pulled her back against his chest with their son cradled against Fiona's chest, so he could hold them both.

Fiona snuggled into Julian's welcoming embrace. She slid her gaze back down to her son, awestruck that this perfect child had come from them and to them. She said a silent prayer to the Goddess thanking Her for all the gifts She had bestowed upon them.

Conall opened his eyes. He peered into the faces of his mother and his father, both looking down at him, their protective arms shielding him from the world. He closed his eyes once more, secure in the instinctive knowledge of a newborn that he was safe and would be always in the loving home of his parents. He didn't remember now the promises they had made six months before, but in time he would learn them again because his parents would live them out every day for the rest of his life.

For More

Spilled Candy Books,

visit

www.spilledcandy.com

We offer free articles on spirituality, free excerpts of our books, a free ezine, a free ebook of magickal recipes, and books by some of the best spiritual authors on Earth.

We are truly blessed....find out why by visiting our web site or asking your local library or bookstore to order our books for you.

*ATTN religious organizations--if you plan to use our books in teaching circles, please write Spilled Candy for special discounts.

Brightest blessings!

Want more?

Order Form

Check the appropriate block & circle format desired.

Witch Moon Rising, Witch Moon Waning
____Trade Paperback $13.95

Access
____Trade Paperback $14.95

Once Upon a Beltane Eve
____Trade Paperback $15.95

The Temple of the Twelve
____Trade Paperback $17.95

Shipping/Handling FREE using this form

Total: $

Name:

Address:

Email Address:

Mail to: Spilled Candy Books, P O Box 5202, Niceville FL 32578

___Check_____Money Order ____Credit Card (Visa/MC)

Card #

Expiration Date   Card Type: Visa or MC
Name on Card:

Signature: